NOT MıNE TO TAKE

KEIRON COSGRAVE & CHRISTINE HANCOCK

INDIUM

WHAT IF YOUR HOPES AND DREAMS
BECOME YOUR WORST NIGHTMARE?

PRAISE FOR NOT MINE TO TAKE

'Intriguing, strong characters and full of atmosphere. Incredibly evocative…'

ADAM CROFT #1 International Best Selling Author of Her Last Tomorrow & Tell Me I'm Wrong

'Excellent! Intriguing plot with well drawn characters. The pace picks up to a gripping, dramatic finish that kept me guessing to the end - 5 stars!'

The Word Is Out - Alyson's Reviews

<u>AMAZON READERS</u>

'A triumph 5 stars!'

'Incredible!'

'Tense and beautifully written…'

'A great storyline. Great characters. Would definitely recommend.'

COPYRIGHT

www.indiumbooks.com

Facebook: K W Cosgrave Author
Cover design: KWC
Proof reader, Editor, Co-author: CBH
Publisher: Indium Books
Second Edition
May 2021(P)
First edition published in April 2020 under C B Cox

Reader's note: This novel has been written in British English.

CHAPTER ONE

FEBRUARY

My birthday is in September, not February. It's a schoolboy error made by a husband who doesn't care.

Blinded by the sun reflecting from the road ahead, I drag the sun visor down and wipe the tears from the corners of my eyes. Skidding the Range Rover into a parking space, I step out into the raw, frigid air. I pull my coat and scarf tight around my neck, yet the chilly east wind still nips my cheeks. Stepping to the rear, my right foot almost slips from under me and I slide across the ice. Reaching the rear, I fling open the tailgate, lean in and lift out four bin bags and dump them on the pavement. The bags bulge with men's high-end designer gear. If I had to replace the contents, I'd struggle to get change from ten grand. Lifting the cover, I heave out a petrol can and settle it on the pavement beside the bags.

The tailgate closes with a dull thud and I turn towards the ten-storey brick and glass edifice in which my husband, Christian, works. It's a citadel of capitalism, one of hundreds in The City of London. Christian works in futures. I've often wondered: *is buying*

and selling futures actual work? Who knows? Who cares? I don't.
It isn't important anymore.

I draw breath and exhale. Condensing, my breath billows away on the breeze. Captured in the building's shadow, I shiver and drag my collar up.

Rounding the car, I drag the nearside passenger door open, lean inside and snatch a bouquet of pure-white gardenias from the rear seat. The handwritten note tied to the bouquet reads:

Happy Birthday Darling. Love always, Chris x.

Ten kisses form an inverted triangle below the message. *Is it meant to represent a heart, or something a little more feminine?*

It doesn't matter, since they're not for me. I'm sure of that. A good friend of mine sent me an image attachment: him, kissing a statuesque brunette in Hyde Park. All I'll say is, it wasn't a kiss you'd give your grandma! I hadn't wanted to believe it until now.

I pitch the bouquet onto the bags, retrieve the petrol can, unscrew the cap and recoil from the heady fumes. The urge to retch consumes me. I hold the can at arm's length and douse the bags liberally with petrol.

The pounding in my ears increases to a crescendo. My breathing quickens.

I remove a cigarette lighter from my coat pocket and spin the tiny serrated wheel. The lighter sparks but refuses to spit flame.

Why won't the damn thing light?

Consumed by rage, I grit my teeth, ball my fists, and stamp my feet in frustration. The lighter refuses to do its job. My thumb becomes raw. I'm about to lob it onto the bags, when an inch long flame shoots out. I stare at the flame in utter disbelief. Coming to my senses, I toss the lighter onto the bags crowned with the bouquet of gardenias.

Trembling and mesmerised, I watch the fire take hold. Wide-eyed, I stand on the pavement spellbound by the flames. A loud crack breaks me from my reverie.

Retrieving my phone, I stab the screen and open recent calls. Christian's perfect smile fills the small screen. His wide smile threatens to steal my resolve and the conversation I've rehearsed in my head a hundred times since accepting delivery of the misdirected gift this morning. Tabbing to recent calls, I select Christian from the list and press the phone tight against my ear.

He collects on the second ring. 'Hey, beautiful, what's up?'

Hearing his smooth baritone, my throat contracts and I struggle to breathe. Given the enormity of what I'm about to say, the words won't form.

Anger wins out. 'Look out of the frigging window.'

'Erin?'

I imagine him striding across the office, halting at the window with the phone pressed against his ear. On cue, he appears in the precise spot I expected.

'What the hell, Erin?' Stuttering panic displaces smooth informality.

'Sack your incompetent secretary, dickhead,' I say. 'Today is not my birthday.'

'Fuck.'

'Whose birthday is it Christian?'

I hear him draw breath. He's gathering his thoughts, getting his story straight, working a plausible angle, *fabricating*. After a long pause, he says, 'Darling, you've got this all wrong. Stay right where you are. I'm coming down.'

'Ugh, I don't think so. We're finished.'

'Darling, please, let's talk. We can't let it end like this.'

Afraid we can. 'I'm seeing my solicitor. I suggest you do the same. Fuck you, Christian. Find a corner. Curl up. And die.'

Killing the call, I swing into the Range Rover, start the engine and drive off. Ice ricochets against the floor pan. In my mind's eye, I see Christian gazing down in stunned silence as the rear lights fade into the distance, mumbling, 'Come back, Erin… Come back…'

With my fingers turning white on the steering wheel, I step on the accelerator.

I have to get away.

CHAPTER TWO

The journey to our West Sussex home passes in a blur.

I step inside, slam the door and put the key in the lock. If Christian shows his sorry adulterous arse, then so be it, he'll be locked out. Tough titty. I lay my handbag on the floor, spin, and settle my back against the door. The firm hand of anxiety tightens around my throat and I struggle to breathe.

How could he do this? To me? To us?

The leaden feeling in my gut releases, rises into my throat, and I race through to the kitchen. At the sink, I retch until my ribs are sore. When I'm done, I collapse into a blubbering heap on the floor. Bereft and broken, tears cascade down my cheeks.

Bella – my ten-year-old golden retriever – appears in the opening, head cranked on one side, ears laid flat, tail pushed up between her legs. She seems confused. 'C'mon girl.' Ears lifting, she rushes at me and nuzzles her beautiful golden face into mine. 'What am I going to do? It's just me and you, now.'

Bella's placid bottomless brown eyes meet mine and she licks my face. We lay on the kitchen floor cuddling and before I know it, an hour has passed. Christian has stayed away. I can't bear the thought of seeing him, let alone speaking to him. Relief courses through my veins like morphine.

When the voices inside my head finally fall silent, I hear the pings of arriving text messages. Dragging myself up on the worktop I down two glasses of water. With my thirst satiated, I pull a chair from under the table, sit and stare across the idyllic suburban garden beyond the window. As my focus shifts, I catch my reflection returned on the inside face of the glass. It isn't a pretty sight. I see eyes underscored by dark circles, a mess of hair and puffy, lobster-red cheeks. A bead of snot rolls towards my top lip from my left nostril and I swipe it away with the back of my sleeve.

I call the only person who can help me out of this emotional hell: my agent, Olivia. She collects on the second ring of the third attempt.

'Erin, I'm busy. Is it urgent?' Olivia says, timbre businesslike and dismissive.

'Sorry. I had to call. Only...'

'What's wrong?'

'Christian,' I say. 'He's having an affair.'

'Stay there. I'm coming to get you.'

CHAPTER THREE

MAY

Olivia approaches the table clutching a three-inch thick manuscript. She arrives, glowers, and releases it. It lands on the table with a dull thud and I flinch. She's got my full attention.

'Archie rejected it.' Dispensing with the sugar coating, she's gone straight for the jugular.

Emerald green eyes burn behind chic, black-rimmed glasses. Olivia doesn't need them. They're purely cosmetic – a fashion statement – yet they complement her jet-black, pixie-cut hair and expensive French couture, perfectly.

I love her. Olivia Pope is my agent and best friend. I know where I stand with her. She broadcasts her feelings like Katie Price on a psychiatrist's couch. She prides herself on letting a person know exactly what she's thinking. Yeah, she makes enemies, but who doesn't in business?

She lowers into the chair opposite. Uncomfortable under her glare and scathing frown, I look away. *Is there a friendly face amongst the mahogany, copper and tinted glass of the trendy*

Sloane Square coffee shop? No. I'm invisible to my fellow Londoners. All around me people are either deep in conversation, transfixed by smartphones, or satiating caffeine addictions. Alone in my misery, I inhale the heady coffee aromas to get my caffeine fix by osmosis.

The hubbub in the coffee shop hovers a needle width below maximum. My head throbs. The angry whir of the coffee grinder and the steam train hiss of the milk frothing machine, make me wince. Leaning forward, I study the smooth edge of the table, press my hands between my knees and close my eyes. Olivia's talking, but I'm not listening. Dull thuds arrive through the ambient noise. I look up to see Olivia rapping her knuckles on the table. I give her doe eyes. I need caffeine and I need it bad.

'What the hell were you thinking?' Olivia barks. 'You're a romantic novelist and a pretty successful one at that. But this...' Pausing, she stabs an immaculate French manicured nail on the manuscript. She's venting. There's no point in trying to stop the inevitable. I sit back, fold my arms across my chest and wait for her tirade to gather momentum. In time, her angst will burn itself out. '...is dog shit.'

'Nice,' I say. 'Descriptive.'

'And accurate. Though it pains me to say it, Erin, even the writing isn't up to your usual standard. As for the storyline... For crying out loud, it's got more venom than your snake in the grass, soon-to-be, ex-husband.'

I roll my shoulders, exhale a silent sigh and click my neck. Olivia's tirade is nowhere near as barbed as I feared. I can't blame her. Fielding an unpleasant call from Archie – my publisher – can't have been easy. He's the type that, when given the chance, likes to show his macho side.

Olivia's right, of course. *What the hell was I thinking?* I've been in denial ever since I submitted the manuscript. It was, *is,* a crock of shit. I ought to have missed the deadline by the proverbial country mile and used my marriage break up as an excuse. I ought to have delayed, but no, not me, because I'm pig-headed. And if I'm being completely honest with myself, I break out in sweats whenever I think about my publisher, Archie.

Archie is a tour de force in the publishing world. Disappoint *A.J.* and you do so at your peril. Instead, I'd made my fingers bleed, bashing out words that reflected my dark state of mind and a second rate storyline. The book I spat out was a lifetime away from the light-hearted romances my fans have come to love and expect.

When I wrote the novel, my heart was a facsimile copy cast in lead. My faith in humanity, shattered.

Sitting here now, I don't think I'll be able to write meaningful words ever again. I visualise the headlines:

BEST-SELLING AUTHOR DITCHED. FAIRYTALE OVER.

'Well?' Olivia asks, her glare searing into my hopelessness.

We've been in the coffee shop for ten minutes and I've said three words. Tears balloon in the corners of my eyes.

Seeing my hurt, Olivia's resolve softens. 'I could murder him for what he's put you through,' she says, lips pursing with indignation. 'Married to the sweetest, prettiest, most up-and-coming novelist in London, yet still the dirty bastard feels compelled to screw around.' Olivia looks to the counter and waves a waitress over.

'Olivia, please don't,' I say, dabbing my tears, hoping she won't notice. 'I don't want to talk about him.'

Someone make it stop.

I don't want to cry in public, not in front of Olivia, my hard-ass confidante and closest friend. But here she is, mentioning his name, bringing it all back, making it real. My fragile composure crumbles. Tears courses down my cheeks and I wipe them with my sleeve.

'I see, so now you're choosing the right to silence. Not only have you lost your talent, but you've lost your voice too.' Olivia's scowl is so deep, she has to adjust her glasses.

Afraid of 'pissed off, Olivia', I brace for the sermon. It doesn't arrive. Instead, her expression subtly alters, indignation dissolves, tenderness appears, and she cups my hands across the table.

'Ignore me. I, *we*, will get through this, together. How can I be mad at you?'

I make to reply, but Olivia places two fingers across my lips.

'Don't say a word. You're even more gorgeous when you're vulnerable,' she says running the back of her hand over my cheek, wiping away my tears. 'Look at you with your corkscrew blonde locks, baby-blues, and the sweetest, most kissable lips this side of eternity. Why don't you do yourself a favour, darling, and come over to the other side? Trust me, there will be plenty of interest.'

Olivia's coming on to me. She swings every conceivable way depending on her mood.

The waitress arrives with our caffeine free, skinny chai lattes. The tension evaporates with the steaming mugs. I loathe chai latte: much prefer a black, caffeine-packed java. Given my current predicament, who am I to argue with Olivia's health kick? Blowing over the cup, I take a sip. The sweet, cinnamon taste catches at the back of my throat and my stomach turns cartwheels. I swallow the lump in my throat and draw a long invigorating breath. I meet Olivia's sombre expression with a doleful look of my own.

'I'm sorry,' I say.

I'm being pathetic. Olivia is being cruel to be kind. I know she's got my best interests at heart, but it does nothing to dispel the resigned inadequacy swarming inside of me. I want to cry.

I clear my throat. 'How can I write sickly sweet love stories, when all I feel is hate?'

I know she understands, but I'm under contract to write a novel a year for three years. If I lose my publishing deal, I'm contractually obligated to return a sizeable chunk of my advance and I'll struggle to pay the rent on the Fulham flat I've moved into since my marriage fell apart. Christian won't help. A mutual friend informed me that his new mistress is bleeding him dry. He has zero empathy for me, or my financial fortunes. Olivia would lose not only her commission, but worse still, her reputation. It would be the deepest cut for both of us.

'Look. Forget about Christian. Relegate him to history. Put him out of your mind.'

Olivia exudes pragmatic concern. 'Kind Olivia', the Olivia I love, appears in the chair opposite.

'You do know this three book deal is just the beginning?'

'Really?'

'Yes, really. You, darling, are on an upward trajectory. Everyone...' She leans in, whispers, 'Pardon my French. Everyone's allowed one big fuck up. It's how you bounce back that's important and what defines you as a person.' Olivia places slender fingers on the manuscript. 'I want you to get your head together, rewrite this rubbish, live long and prosper.' Raising her cup, Olivia proposes a toast. I'm in no position to disagree. We chink cups.

Painting on my best game face, I tell myself I'm going to write my best novel within three months. It's going to be tough. Three months is tight. But I'm more than capable, once I get my act together.

'Three months is all I need. Three months, and Archie will be holding his next bestseller in fat, hairy mitts,' I say with conviction.

'Wow! That's more like it,' Olivia says, fixing me with those killer green eyes. 'What's the plan?'

The plan?

'Scalaig Lodge,' I blurt.

It came from nowhere; was the first thing that entered my head. Irrespective, it's said.

'I'm all ears.' Olivia sits back, pushes her glasses along her nose and crosses her arms over her chest. 'Tell me more.'

'The flat is claustrophobic and soulless. Truth be told, I'm lonely. It's doing sweet Fanny Adams for my creativity. And I haven't had a holiday since the Maldives two years ago.' I see images of sandy beaches, azure lagoons and champagne-filled nights. I shake my head to break the spell. 'I need space to breathe and fresh air in my lungs. A different view will help me get my mojo back. Exorcise *him* from my mind, heart and soul.'

Olivia smiles with her eyes, exhales. 'That's more like it, good for you. A writing sabbatical on Scalaig is a fabulous idea. It's such a beautiful place.' Shoulders visibly relaxing, she lifts a lipstick and vanity mirror from her handbag and touches up her lips. Clipping the lid on the lipstick, she says, 'When it isn't pissing it down, Scotland in summer is out of this world. You can say all you like about Christian, for a while at least, he spoiled you rotten. I mean, not everyone is lucky enough to *own* a bloody island. You absolutely must go,' Olivia says, checking her watch. 'Sorry, babe, but I'm going to have to dash,' she says, lifting and gesturing the waitress over with a waved hand. 'I've got an important meeting with A.J. at half eleven. Sommers Moore has introduced a new royalties calculation tool. Damn thing's driving me insane. A.J. is giving me a one-on-one training session. It's a pain in the bum, but needs must. Payments are getting held up.' Olivia places a twenty pound note on the table. 'Pay the bill, darling. And keep the change. I expect the staff are having a fag and a chinwag around the back. Promise to let me know your movements. OK?'

I nod. 'OK.'

Olivia stands, slides the manuscript over, shoulders her handbag, leans in and air-kisses my cheeks. 'Important Olivia', exits stage left.

CHAPTER FOUR

Processing our meeting, I reflect upon the commitments I've made.

Has Olivia abandoned me to wallow alone on a remote island bereft of ideas? Will the ruthless black dog of depression take me down? Or has she thrown me a lifeline? Injected hope? Forced me to face up to reality?

I'm sure of one thing: I need coffee. A caffeine hit will help clear my head. I've already paid and pocketed the change, so I dig deep into my handbag for my purse. It eludes my searching fingers. Annoyed, I spill the contents of my handbag across the table and rejected manuscript. There's a tortoiseshell hairgrip, a moleskin notebook, a Montblanc pen, a bunch of keys, bulging leather purse, lip gloss, and a mobile phone. Collecting the purse, I step over to the counter and order a double espresso. A chocolate chip muffin yells my name from under the glass. Since a sugar rush will do me good, I add it to my order.

Five minutes later, a twenty-something waitress in a green apron sidles up to the table with my caffeine and sugar fixes. Trying hard not to gawp at her nose ring and distended earlobes, we begin a farcical game of 'where to put the contents of the tray'.

Finding enough space amongst the paraphernalia strewn across the table, proves difficult. The waitress maintains a, 'the customer is always right,' smile, until, tiring of the game, huffing, she dumps the mug on the manuscript and the muffin on the table. It appears her training has yet to cover, 'dealing with blondes whose life is on spin-cycle.'

Collecting the muffin, I mumble an apology. The waitress shrugs, spins on a heel, and flounces off. I click my tongue against my front teeth.

The customer is always right... *Right?*

Exhaling, I push my unruly fringe behind my ears and cross my legs. In doing so, my knee crashes against the underside of the table. Horrified, I reach out, but already it's too late. It happens in slow motion. The mug wobbles, tilts and falls on its side, spilling steaming hot coffee over the manuscript, and I slide away from the table. My much needed caffeine fix pools and absorbs into the paper. Reaching for a serviette, I beg the ground to open up and swallow me whole. But no one has noticed. No one cares enough.

Am I invisible? Am I in denial?

Christian's infidelity has affected me more than I dare admit. I've let him destroy not only my self esteem, but my joie de vivre, too. I've become a victim. Accepted the lion's share of the guilt for our marriage breakdown, while Christian shrugged it off. Despite being the guilty party, he's come out on top.

'I won't let you win,' I mumble under my breath.

Refilling my handbag, I shuffle the sodden manuscript to the bottom. Rising, the chair legs screech on the polished concrete. The suited man on the next table shifts his attention from the laptop screen to identify the miscreant who would dare disturb his inner sanctum. Our eyes meet. I challenge him to say something with a glower.

Go on... Dare you...

Bolting for the door, a newfound feeling of determination anchors in my gut. I've made Olivia happy. Promised her a manuscript – my best novel ever – within three months. I have a goal to deliver against and purpose to my sad and lonely existence. The prospect of time alone on Scalaig fills me with trepidation. I'm a city girl at heart. How will I cope alone in the sticks? *Relax. The change will do you good.* I tell myself.

Christian bought the tidal island of Scalaig – cut off from the Isle of Skye twice a day by the Atlantic Ocean, and linked by a causeway – as a wedding gift, almost ten years ago. I should get over myself and use it, since it's devastatingly beautiful. It's criminal of me keeping Bella cooped up in a poky flat when I own an island. Bella loves gardens, vast skies, walks on the beach and fresh, salty sea air.

Name a dog that doesn't?

CHAPTER FIVE

JUNE 4TH

I've been putting off making this phone call for days. So much so that I'm wearing a hole in the carpet. To make matters worse, I have the mother and father of all headaches. Tom Thumb – high on an energy drink – smashes a timber mallet against the inside of my skull. I stand at the window staring out across London's undulating skyline. As my anxiety calms, I select his number. My hands tremble like it's minus forty.

At first, Christian is unreceptive, agitated. He snaps as I explain my plans.

Why does he do this to me? Why do I let him? Grow a pair, woman!

He must sense my anxiety. Down the line, I hear a chair being pushed back, air forced from a cushion and the rustle of papers being moved. Though it's early, he'll have been in the office hours. I imagine him sinking into the plush, tan leather recliner.

Inside my head, Tom Thumb goes into overdrive. I press the index finger of my free left hand against my temple and wait for the lecture to begin. A sigh wends its way to my ear along the line. What he says next takes me by surprise. Christian negotiates a hundred and eighty degree turn and concedes that I ought to take some time out on Scalaig.

'Erin, it's not doing your state of mind any good stuck in that poky flat, like some kind of recluse.' His words, not mine.

Well, thanks a million, nice of you to say so, CHRIS!

I never call him, Chris. I always call him, Christian. His mistress abbreviates his name to Chris.

Whose fault is it anyway, that I live in a poky flat? Electing silence, I say nothing.

Instead, growing a pair, I say, 'I've a deadline to deliver against, so please don't call, e-mail or text. If you need to contact me for anything, go via my solicitor. Two weeks and the divorce papers ought to be ready to sign. Once the decree absolute comes through, we'll be able to get on with our lives.'

He won't like any of that. The line falls silent. I imagine him dragging the phone from his mouth, mumbling expletives. He says, 'We all have deadlines, Erin, *dear.* Deadlines aren't just the sole preserve of writers, you know?' The contempt in his voice is palpable. 'Not even *has been* writers.'

Ouch!

Not wanting to say anything I'll later regret – to voice the ultimate put down – the words die in my throat, and I kill the call. Rage swarms and hisses through my ears. The room sways and my vision blurs. Aware I've stopped breathing, drawing breath, I cast a steadying hand onto the windowsill. I breathe away the fury and a surge of oxygen reaches my brain and the red mist clears. A movie plays inside my head.

Christian stands behind me nibbling my ear, hands firm on my shoulders, bulging groin brazen in the cleft of my back. Shrugging off his embrace, I spin to face him. 'I hope she bleeds your balls and bank balance dry, you two-faced, duplicitous bastard,' I yell. 'Get your hands off me!'

Christian's apparition dissolves into the ether. I need to calm down.

Massaging the tension in my neck, I take deep breaths. Following my yoga instructor's advice, I inhale through my nostrils and exhale through my mouth. My heart rate steadies to a rhythm that calms the pounding in my head. I'm not accustomed to such feelings. This isn't *who* I am. I like to think I behave with maturity; that I don't rush in. I've had my fill of high drama and maxed out emotions, since I separated from Christian.

I take a moment to remind myself how far I've come and tick off my achievements. I've given Olivia and A.J. a firm commitment to deliver within three months the first of three novels. Also, I've told Christian about my plans to take a sabbatical on Scalaig. Having given notice to my landlord, soon, this place will be history.

There's no going back, and nobody to hold me back.

I stare at the blur of grey opposite. The blur finds focus. An apartment block appears and my eyes are drawn to a man and woman. The man steps behind the woman and kisses the nape of her neck.

My phone vibrates in my hand. I blink, turn to face the room and stab the green call accept button. 'Hello?'

'Ms Moran?'

'Speaking.'

'Ms Moran, it's Sonia, the administrator from the removals company. I'm calling about your move.' Sonia explains in infinite detail the arrangements for the packing, collection and delivery of my things to a temporary storage unit in Luton with automaton-like, corporate efficiency. I'm only taking clothing and essentials to Scalaig, since the lodge is furnished and equipped.

Life moves on. The Earth keeps spinning, and I'm determined to move with it.

* * *

Half an hour later, I'm downstairs in the foyer waiting beside packing cases containing my things from our former marital home in West Sussex. They await collection by the removal company. Rhoda – our Spanish housekeeper – sent them over when I first moved into the flat, but I never found time to unpack them. Rhoda has taped a note to the top of the crate – I recognise her handwriting. It informs me of her sadness at our sudden departure. That she's going to work for Christian in his townhouse in West Hampstead. That, out of respect for me, she thought I ought to know. She says she needs the money.

Yeah, whatever… Rather you than me, babe. It takes all sorts…

I look to the suitcase and Louis Vuitton holdall on the floor at my feet.

Even though I have a wardrobe of clothes at the lodge, I've crammed a suitcase with jeans, lambswool sweaters, t-shirts, shorts, swimsuits, and summer dresses. The West Coast of Scotland can be surprisingly sultry during the summer months. To the holdall, I've added my MacBook, cables, a phone charger, lined A4 paper and the manuscript requiring major reconstructive surgery. From the room that passes as my office, I've collected a silver photo frame. Stalling, I caress the image of my parents. In the picture, they're sat on a bench surrounded by chrysanthemums, in the garden of their New Forest home. I took it in the week before my mother died. It's a copy of the photograph I placed in my father's coffin when he left me to join his soulmate, less than a year later.

Staring at the luggage, a knife of melancholy punctures my heart and I pull my dough coloured lambswool cardigan around me. I give myself a hug and press the photograph against my chest.

Bella barks – more of a throaty huff – and breaks the spell. She stands by the entrance, lead hanging from her jowls. I bend down, collect and stroke her ears, chuckling.

'Sorry, darling, you're going to have to be patient. We need to pack the car. We'll have plenty of walks on Scalaig, promise.'

With the word 'walk' echoing in her ears, all is well in Bella's world. And, for the moment at least, all is well in mine.

* * *

I see the caretaker, Alan, amble over to my building and let himself in. Handing him the flat key, I say my goodbyes. He says he'll miss us both. I inform him the removal company have promised to collect my crates within forty-eight hours. Asking him to make a note, I stress the importance.

Stepping out of the nondescript block, I make my way to the basement car park, vowing never to return.

I consign Christian and London to history.

CHAPTER SIX

I program the sat-nav to display the quickest route to Skye and Scalaig. At six hundred miles, the journey is long and tedious. I reach over my shoulder and drag on Bella's harness. Since she means so much to me, I check the harness not once, but twice. Checking my make-up in the vanity mirror, I decide I'll have to do. Next, I adjust the rearview mirror, once, twice, three times. I'm spinning everything out, and I'm not sure why.

I've never driven to Scalaig on my own, before. Control was Christian's thing, and as a result, he insisted on driving. I suppose it's a metaphor for our relationship. Christian drove with one hand resting on the steering wheel, or perched on my knee. On long motorway stretches, he'd drape his arm over my shoulder and stroke my arm. My role was to keep us alert with chitchat, feed him and Bella snacks, and point out landmarks en route.

Sometimes – having put Bella in kennels – we'd fly to Glasgow, hire a car and drive to our 'love nest' on Scalaig. Other times, we'd fly, taxi to the marina at Inverkip and hop aboard Christian's luxurious sailing yacht.

It sounds romantic and it was. It would be insincere of me to say it wasn't.

As the dashboard clock clicks past nine, I spin the key, take the ramp and exit the car park into blinding sunshine. Repositioning gold-mirrored Ray-Bans from the top of my head to the bridge of my nose, I feather the accelerator and join the traffic heading north towards the M25, out of London.

An hour later, joining the motorway, I allow myself a smile. I imagine warm sunny days, walks on the beach, swimming in the bay and peaceful evenings sitting on the veranda reading and sipping wine. I plan to rekindle my love affair with writing and develop friendships with the gentle, neighbourly folk of Scaloon, who will soothe my broken heart and restore my faith in people.

At least, that's what I hope.

Behind me, satisfied our adventure is finally underway, Bella settles into the blanket and trumpets a long, doggy sigh. Experience tells me she'll be asleep in a mile or two.

Passing Uxbridge, I take the exit for the M40. The sky has darkened. Drizzle mists the windscreen and kisses the tarmac. The wipers deposit long, greasy streaks across the windscreen and the view ahead blurs. Dragging on the stalk, I douse the windscreen liberally with screen wash. The windscreen clears, and the motorway comes into sharp relief.

Three hours later, part shrouded in drizzle, the mountains of the Lake District glow ethereally in the low sun. The motorway curves left and rises towards high ground. Pine-clad hillsides enclose the motorway on both sides. Bella's snores echo around the cabin.

I feel jittery; my mouth is dry. I'm overcome by an intense feeling of homesickness for the bright lights, glistening towers and hustle and bustle of London.

When the radio news turns to Boris Johnson's latest spat with Corbyn, I select Bluetooth. Half a minute later, Sheryl Crow reminds me that a change will do me good; a smile sneaks up on me and slackens my lips. I rattle my fingers on the steering wheel in time with the beat. I'm not ready to give up my Sheryl Crow obsession, just yet.

The A74 is easy going. Passing Moffat, the reflected sun glistens and dances from the rippling surface of a lake set in the grounds of the motorway services. The sat-nav confirms there's a little over two hundred and fifty miles to run before I reach Scalaig. On this journey, there are no high-fives or 'four down, two to go, Mrs M.' countdowns from Christian, as we cross county lines.

Bella grumbles. Her face fills the rearview mirror. 'The traffic Gods have blessed us, Bella,' I say, our eyes meeting in the small rectangle of glass.

We're making good time and the traffic is light. So far, we've sailed north without getting caught in traffic. *Don't jinx it, Erin.* I tell myself.

The thrum of rubber across tarmac is hypnotic. My mind drifts back through time…

CHAPTER SEVEN

I first met Christian at a black-tie charity event at the height of the global economic crash in 2009. Black Friday flashbacks haunted London's Financial District. Millions of people were losing their livelihoods. Distraught office workers were being led from desks carrying boxes by over zealous HR managers.

As fortune would have it, my second novel – an uplifting story of love in the depths of financial adversity – was fresh to the market. Olivia's career was taking off, too. Somehow, my debut novel had sold half-a-million copies in the first month alone. It was a major achievement for a small, independent publishing house. I was Olivia's first 'major' signing. Olivia understood the value of networking. Insisting I, 'break my book-signing virginity,' she arranged a signing at a charity fundraiser in aid of the homeless.

I was twenty-five, naïve, an incurable romantic, and as nervous as hell.

Olivia insisted the signing would be a walk in the park. She suggested I could hide in the toilets if my nerves got the better of me. She told me to, 'Smile, sign your name, and charge them twenty quid for the privilege. It's such a worth-while cause. You're quite literally feeding the homeless. They need all the help they can get,' she said, slipping away to mingle with the good and the gracious of London's literary elite.

I was doing just that when George Clooney came over and halted at the table. He collected a book, beamed, and flicked it open at the dedications page.

'Would you mind signing it to Christian with all my love?'

No doubt you've guessed, it wasn't George Clooney.

'Err… Yes,' I stuttered, accepting the book.

'I'm Christian,' he said, with a rakish grin and a wink. 'The book is for me.'

I signed and returned the book to him with a thin smile.

'Thank you. Appreciated,' he said, studying my signature. 'Erin Davis. What a lovely name.'

'I like it,' I said. 'And so does my book cover designer.'

'Yes, I'm sure he must, what with it being so short.'

Even now, eleven years on, I remember the way he said my name. Anyone would have thought I'd written my name in melted chocolate. My heart hammered so hard inside my chest, I imagined hearing it above the din of the string quartet.

'Since you're doing this for such a good cause, I'll buy them all.'

'You really don't have to.'

'No, I insist. I like to do my bit whenever I can.'

Christian took a roll of bank notes from an inside jacket pocket and stuffed it into the collection box. Straightening, he thrust out a hand, and we shook hands.

'Would you like me to sign them?'

'If you wouldn't mind?'

'Not at all, it's no trouble. It's the least I can do. You're very generous.'

Ten minutes later, wrist swelling, Christian waiting still beside the table, I'd signed a hundred copies. 'All done. I can have them delivered to an address of your choosing, if you like?'

'That won't be necessary. I'll have someone pick them in the morning from reception.'

'OK. Consider it done. And thanks again.'

After an awkward half minute of silence, Christian moved in for the kill.

'Would you care to join me for dinner, Ms Davis? A mausoleum has more life than this place. And truth be told, I'm famished.'

With the book signing concluded early – with no more books to sign – how could I refuse?

And that's how it, *we*, started. How Christian swept me off my feet. Ours was a whirlwind romance and my first grown up affair. In hindsight, I fell in love with Christian in haste. My parents adored him, and thought him perfection personified.

At 33, Christian was eight years my senior, and like me, an only child. That's where the similarities ended. My parents had retired from academia in their late fifties with little interest in money and power. They preferred to potter about in their half acre plot all day, gardening, doing odd jobs. In contrast, Christian was born into a wealthy, influential family and became a successful entrepreneur in his own right.

A talented yachtsman, Christian crewed with the ill-fated 2003 Jaguar team. His yacht sank during the America's Cup selection challenge. The US Coastguard plucked him from the sea. It had devastated him. After much soul searching, he'd vowed never to compete again and relegated sailing to a hobby.

For our honeymoon, we sailed around Scotland on Christian's fifty-footer, a gorgeous Jeanneau he'd christened, *The Storm Petrel*. As luck would have it, the weather was unusually clement. We had drifted around picturesque islands and explored idyllic coves. I spent the entire trip imagining myself as Grace Kelly in Capri pants, twin-sets and espadrilles, swanning about on deck to Bing Crosby's True Love.

It was heavenly.

One evening, just before sunset, we anchored in the cove of an uninhabited island and hopped into the motorised launch. Coming ashore, we dragged the launch out of the sea and collapsed into an exhausted heap on the sand. Collecting driftwood, we made a fire, ate a simple picnic of bread and cheese and shared an expensive bottle of Veuve Clicquot while watching the sun sink below the horizon.

Under a star-flecked sky, we set off to explore our 'secret little island.' With blankets draped over our shoulders, we scrambled through crisp bracken and followed overgrown paths meandering through tall pines. At an opening in the pines, we came across a derelict log cabin. Though the handle moved and the latch clicked, the door refused to budge. Determined to see what delights lay within, Christian stepped back and blasted the door open with his shoulder. Collecting my hand, he led me inside. Stepping over the threshold, into the dank and dark interior, the sour stench of animal scat ran to my nostrils, and I reeled back.

'Scared?' Christian asked.

'Not when I'm with you, no,' I said, hanging on to his elbow.

Once we'd grown accustomed to the darkness, the interior of the cabin revealed itself. Only ten feet square, someone had furnished it with a metal framed single bed, a small table and a solitary chair. Someone, I've no idea who, had gone to the trouble of wrapping the mattress in polythene and sealing it with gaffer tape. A child's wicker fishing basket lay on its side in one corner, with its open lid hanging by a straw thread. A china mug – half full of twigs – hung from a hook under the small window, above the table.

Christian dusted off the mattress. Ancient springs complained under his weight as he settled on the bed. With desire burning in his eyes, he patted the mattress.

You have got to be joking?

'Sit down. It's surprisingly comfy. Let's sleep here tonight. It'll be fun.' Sensing my reluctance, he paused, added, 'At least someone had the good sense to protect the mattress.'

'But someone might come?'

'Chill. You worry too much. Anyone can see it's abandoned.'

'But it stinks to high heaven. There'll be the bats, spiders, and Christ knows what else,' I said, stepping back, dragging the blanket around my shoulders.

Through the gloom, I made out Christian shaking his head, biting his lip. 'Don't be a wuss. Nothing can hurt you here. I'll look after you. C'mon, live a little,' he said, ripping the gaffer tape from the mattress.

'Ugh! Live a little. Is that your idea of a joke?' I said, wide-eyed.

'Don't be like that. Where's your sense of adventure? I'll be your, Romeo...'

'And I'll be your, Juliet,' I interjected. 'A little corny, don't you think?'

'Not at all. Spending the night here will be fun.'

Christian stood, swept me off my feet and dumped me onto the mattress.

'There, not so bad is it?'

'I'm not sure,' I said, flicking gossamer from my face. 'This place is *minging.*'

'It's not so bad,' he said, settling his hand on my thigh, fingers creeping towards my waist. 'I'll make sure you're appropriately compensated...'

Despite my protestations, that night we made love on the dirty mattress in the filthy cabin. Afterwards, exhausted, Christian slept like a baby. I spent the night clutching the blanket to my neck, hanging onto every sound.

As dawn broke, the full horror of where we'd slept became clear. Cobwebs the size of backyard hammocks spanned from the bedhead to the ceiling. Intricate lace patterns shimmered and danced in the low sun. Flies fluttered to horrific deaths in webs the size of my fist. Shiny black beetles scurried across the floor like bumping cars at the fair.

Stabbing Christian in the ribs with my elbow, I put my mouth against his ear. 'Christian, wake up. This place is alive!' I said, dragging my knees under my chin.

Stirring, he raised up on an elbow and wiped sleep from his eyes. 'Sleep well?'

'No, I did not! I was awake half the bloody night.'

'Aww, I'm sorry, darling. You're not a country girl are you, Mrs Moran?'

'I'm a city girl and proud of it. I like sanitation, clean sheets and running water,' I said, jabbing him in the ribs. 'Let's get out of here. Please.'

'Ugh, if we must,' he mumbled, tucking his shirt into his shorts, preening sun-licked hair.

Dragging the door closed behind us, we left the cabin to the spiders and beetles. Outside, fresh dew and pine replaced the fetid air of the cabin. Sucking deep, invigorating breaths, I replenished my lungs. My relief was short-lived as a lightning bolt of pain flashed through my right foot.

'Ouch,' I cried, hopping around, reaching for Christian.

'For crying out loud, woman, what the hell's a matter with you now?'

'I caught my toe on something. It hurts like hell.'

Looking down, I saw a timber post projecting from the undergrowth. Christian lifted it out and revealed a foot square timber sign.

FOR SALE
SCALAIG
(ISLAND)
ENQUIRE SCALAIG CASTLE

'It's a sign,' Christian quipped.

'No shit, Sherlock.'

'No, Erin, it really *is*,' he said, wiping away earth and debris, holding the sign aloft.

'It's decided. I'm buying it. Scalaig. I love it,' he said, turning to me. 'Almost as much as I love you.'

My jaw almost hit the ground. 'You're not serious?'

'I'm deadly serious. Can't you feel it? This place is special. It's got a certain, *feel*. I'm going to do the deal, today. You see that I don't.'

Later that day, much to my bewilderment, my chagrin, Christian shook hands on a knockdown price with the island's owners, Hamish and Isla Cleland, and set the wheels in motion with his solicitor to buy Scalaig. Sunning myself on the stern of *The Storm Petrel*, I overheard Christian instruct his solicitor to register the title deeds in my name.

Racing to the bow, as Christian dragged the phone from his mouth, I asked, 'Have you lost your mind?'

'It's done. Scalaig is yours. *Ours*. Now and forever. My wedding gift to you.'

'But it's too much,' I protested. 'It's a bloody island!'

'Nothing is too much for you, darling. I'm going to build a lodge. It will be out of this world. Imagine the holidays? The long weekends? Imagine coming here to write? It'll be a sanctuary. A little piece of heaven on earth.'

And that was that; the deed, done. What point arguing? Christian acquired Scalaig just like he had acquired me.

True to his word, within months, he used a local builder to build an idyllic, stone lodge complete with veranda and writing den overlooking the bay.

We named it Scalaig Lodge.

Thereafter, we spent many romantic holidays, long weekends and Christmases on Scalaig, but I'd never stayed there alone, or wrote a single word in the den, until now.

Later, I learned Scalaig had been in the Cleland family for

centuries. The financial crash had wiped out Hamish Cleland's investment portfolio and forced the Clelands to sell Scalaig, so they could continue to live in the castle and pay private school fees for his fifteen-year-old son. It must have been an enormous wrench to sell Scalaig. With his usual magnanimous arrogance, Christian convinced himself he'd done the Clelands a favour.

I was never so sure.

CHAPTER EIGHT

According to the sat-nav, Scalaig is a little over three miles ahead.

'Not far now, Bella,' I say, glancing in the rearview mirror.

With Sheryl Crow and my daydreams on loop, the Range Rover has gobbled up the miles. Rounding a corner, I catch my first glimpse of Scalaig at the southern end of the narrow causeway. I swing the Range Rover onto the gravel area across from the castle overlooking Scalaig and kill the engine. Scalaig Castle dominates the mirrors. The dashboard clock reads 10:05 p.m. In two hours, the moon will disappear, and darkness will envelop Scalaig. The tide is already turning.

Unbuckling Bella, I spring the rear door. Bella leaps out onto the gravel, yawns and performs a near perfect upward dog stretch. Stepping out of the car, I yawn and stretch. Suddenly, my vision swims and I cast a steadying hand on the door. A moment later, the fluid in my ear canal settles, and the ground under my feet, firms.

I can't help but feel disappointed that there's no welcoming committee. I'm being ridiculous, since no one knew I was coming. For a second, I mull over visiting the Clelands to inform them of my arrival and plans. Given the hour and impending darkness, I decide against it.

Turning, I hear the gentle slap of the ocean meeting the fore-shore and drink in the cool invigorating air laced with salt, seaweed and pine.

Bella seems taken with the castle. 'Not now, darling, we'll catch up with the Clelands tomorrow.'

I'd better go and check the tide times on the community notice-board. As far as I know, high tide is in two hours, just after midnight. The schedule confirms this. There's just enough time to unload and carry essentials across the causeway to the lodge.

I've already decided the Range Rover will stay right here, parked on the gravel by the castle, during my stay. I'll walk, jog or cycle everywhere. Exercise will become part of my healing ritual.

Scalaig is a tidal island connected at low tide to Skye by a raised area of seabed hewn into a narrow, flat-topped causeway, centuries ago, by persons unknown. Four wheeled vehicular access is impossible. Twice a day at high tide, the Atlantic swallows the causeway cutting off Scalaig from Skye.

If it's solitude I seek, then I'll find it in spades on Scalaig, of that I'm sure.

Grinning, I turn to Bella. 'C'mon you, time and tide won't wait.'

Aware of the tide and the onset of the night, I sling my handbag over my shoulder, tuck Bella's bed and blanket under my arm, and check to see if there's anything else I regard as 'essential.'

Nope.

I'll return in the morning.

Swinging the tailgate closed, in my peripheral vision I glimpse a fleeting orange glow in one of the castle's many second-floor windows. I turn to the light, but it's already gone.

Are the Clelands at home? Did they witness my arrival? Hear the car pull up?

Hesitating, I ponder if I ought to introduce myself. A quick scan of the impressive render and stone facade, and I've convinced myself the castle is unoccupied. I must have been mistaken.

Stepping around to the driver's side, I close the door with a flick of the hip, blip the locks and hitch Bella's bed against my chest. With Bella following behind, we take the twenty weather-ravaged timber steps down to the causeway. I take the steps one careful step at a time and set off across the barnacled, pockmarked rock. Inside, I buzz with anticipation. Since we'd given Christmas a miss, it's been almost a year since I last visited Scalaig. In my naivety, I'd assumed Christian had become bored with routine. I ought to have known better.

Whoever said hindsight is a wonderful thing, was on to something.

Bella shadows me across the causeway. Stepping off rock onto soft earth, I adjust my load, bolt up the short flight of steps and set off along the granite sett path linking the lodge to the causeway.

Rounding tall pines, I see Scalaig Lodge. Constructed from red tinged stone under a blue slate roof, from the outside, the lodge appears to be single storey, yet inside there are two floors. Two south facing apex windows project through the roof above the main elevation. A decked veranda spans the elevation below the apex windows. Climbing two steps, I arrive on the veranda. Bella scrabbles up the steps and slips to a halt beside me.

Releasing Bella's bed and blanket, I turn and scan the vicinity. Satisfied no one's watching, I reach up and unclip the key from its secret cubby hole in the veranda soffit. Jangling the key, I beam like a child on Christmas morning. Bella studies me with sullen indifference.

Standing on the welcome mat, I face a hand-painted seagull soaring against a luminous orange, purple and pink sunset, painted on the top half of the door. Gaelic calligraphy above the image reads, 'Scalaig Lodge.' I spin the key and push on the door. Against the gloom, I reach inside and fumble for the light switch. I've never felt so vulnerable, or alone. Squinting against the darkness, I flick the switch and the interior floods with stark white light. As I step inside, Bella bounces past me and rushes about reacquainting herself with the lodge. I kick the door closed with a heel.

The lodge is cold, damp and imbued with the earthy tang of cigars and the sharp carbon of burnt wood. Dust tickles inside my nostrils and I fight the urge to sneeze. Releasing my handbag to the floor, I slump into my favourite armchair, close my eyes and let the stillness of Scalaig Lodge wash through me. The low thrum of rubber passing over tarmac and drone of internal combustion, fades.

Feeling myself drifting off, I wake with a jolt. I go through to the kitchen and pour myself a glass of water. As the pressure in the pipes increases, they complain and shake. Water splutters, spits and becomes a steady stream. I let the tap run, half fill the glass and take a long drag of the cool liquid. I stand, massaging my eyes at the sink. Downing the last of the water, I think about making coffee.

But I'm dead on my feet. I haven't got the energy.

At my ankles, Bella addresses me with puppy dog eyes and nuzzles her wet nose against my leg. I fill her bowls with fresh water and dry kibbles. She gobbles at the food, eyelids batting. When she's had her fill, we creep upstairs. A sleigh bed dominates the main bedroom. Bella leaps up, circles twice, flops onto the mattress and settles her jowls along her paws.

The sheets are cold and damp. The familiar notes of Christian's cologne run to my nostrils. His ghost haunts this place. In the coming weeks and months, I'll do everything I can, to exorcise it.

Tomorrow is a new chapter.

This is *my* house, on *my* island, and I'm going to enjoy it.

Irrespective of the sheets, I enter the delicious embrace of sleep with a contented smile.

CHAPTER NINE

Day 1

A fist-sized bat dive bombs my face in the darkness of the sultry bedroom. At the last moment, I crank my neck right and cotton-soft fur brushes my left cheek. The bat disappears into the shadows of the raftered ceiling.

A minute passes and I feel a pair of tiny needles prick my neck. I look down and see a bat suckling. My quizzical expression reflects in beady black pupils.

Jolting awake, I break the spell.

The heat is unbearable. My skin glistens with a sheen of sweat. I stretch, yawn, drag the sheets aside and swing out of bed. Padding into the en-suite, I lift the lid and settle on the toilet. Bella enters. I feel her wet nose brush my calf. She sits, cocks her head on one side and watches me pee.

'Yes?' I ask. 'How may I help you?'

Bella can twist me around her paw. The look in her eyes suggests food, and a walk.

'Let me shower. Have coffee. Then we'll go for a walk. OK?'

Moments later, beads of icy water hammer my body. The water is so cold that the soap won't lather. I reach for the towel, but my scrabbling fingers find an empty rail. I could scream.

Shivering, I step onto the landing, reclaim a towel from the airing cupboard and wrap it around my middle. While I'm there, I switch on the hot water. Returning to the en-suite, I release a smidgeon of ice-blue toothpaste onto my toothbrush and depress the button. Nothing happens. It's dead. The nightmare becomes actual. Much to my annoyance, I use a manual brush.

'Don't tell my hygienist,' I tell Bella's reflection.

From the walk-in wardrobe, I select a pair of cropped blue jeans, a grey t-shirt and a baby-pink sweatshirt with a silver-star motif. For the moment, I ignore the neat rows of Christian's slacks, shirts and blazers, telling myself I'll deal with them later.

I stand at the window, gazing across the vista. Half way down, the meeting of silver-blue ocean and sky at the horizon, is indistinct. In the foreground, above the pines, the ocean meets the shore in a long sweep of green and grey. This place is beautiful. Christian's infatuation was entirely understandable.

In my mind's eye, I see a yacht – *The Storm Petrel* – gliding serenely across the ocean. Its gleaming white sails billow forward of the bow under the hand of the wind. A lengthy sigh escapes my lips.

'Oh, Christian,' I say aloud. 'What have you done?'

Sensing my misery, Bella nudges her wet nose against my calf.

'I know, girl, I know… What was I supposed to do?'

Stalling at the bottom of the stairs, I scan the lounge and remember how proud Christian was with his interior design choices. I'd given him free rein with decoration and the choice of furniture, but had drawn the line at antlers and stuffed fox heads. Two, three-seater brown leather sofas with tartan cushions sit opposite one another across an oak coffee table. A tartan rug sits on the polished wooden floor beneath the coffee table. A squishy, brown corduroy armchair flanks a stone fireplace. Charred logs and a layer of grey ash teeter on the grate. It's Scottish baronial in miniature. A terrible pastiche not to my taste. I add a makeover to the expanding list of things to do.

A photograph of two lovers in a carved oak frame hangs above the mantlepiece. The woman is wearing a flapper style dress in champagne coloured rough silk. She clutches a heart-shaped bouquet against her tummy. A ring of white flowers pins golden curls. The man towers over her. His arms loop her waist. The woman's demure gaze is stationary on the ground. He stares down the lens, lips curling at the edges. The flowers are white gardenias.

Need I say more?

It's a wedding photograph.

'I'll deal with that later,' I tell Bella, turning away.

CHAPTER TEN

I yearn for a caffeine fix.

Leaning against the worktop, I stare into space and wait for the kettle to boil. The ding of an incoming text message interrupts my torpor.

Olivia! 'Damn it, Bella. I forget to let Olivia know we arrived.'

An icon tells me I have one new message from Christian. I bristle.

Morning... how was the journey? Don't forget to switch on the water heater and fetch logs... this time of year... nights can be... cooooollldddd...

C xxx

What the hell is he playing at?

I've told him in words of one syllable not to contact me. Insisted all communication should be via my solicitor. I don't want Christian holding my hand through every domestic chore.

Why can't he leave me alone?

I slam the phone down and it skids across the worktop, ricochets from the tiles and comes to rest perched over the sink. Stomping about the kitchen, I ball my fists. I won't encourage him with a reply; won't give him the satisfaction.

With the kettle boiled, I make a steaming mug of black coffee and lift onto a tall stool. Minutes later, the burned caramel elixir has steadied my frazzled nerves, and I sit trying to fathom the unfathomable.

Two cups of coffee and the best part of an hour later, I'm revived.

It's half-past nine. In three hours the high tide will cut me, and Scalaig, off from Skye.

I ruffle Bella's ears. 'C'mon, lovely, let's go fetch the rest of our things. Then we'll explore.'

I stuff the phone into a back pocket and head outside. Stalling on the veranda, I hide the key under the pot of withered geraniums by the rocking chair and make a mental note to buy a replacement plant. Stepping down from the veranda, I halt and pat a jeans pocket.

Car keys. Doh.

As I let myself back in, I swear I hear Bella tut.

'I know, I'm sorry,' I say, stroking behind her ears. 'What am I like, eh? Don't worry, old girl, I promise to get my act together.'

After the false start, we trot off along the path together and pass through the picket gate. Passing the bird table and empty feeders, I add birdseed to my ever expanding shopping list.

'C'mon, you, keep up. Follow the Yellow Brick Road…'

Arriving at the car, I open the door with the fob, lean in, retrieve a pair of Ray-Bans from the centre console and stab the tailgate release. The tailgate rises with a pneumatic hiss. Rounding the tailgate, I see the expensive Louis Vuitton luggage set. There's a suitcase, matching vanity bag and gym holdall. They're the trappings of a failed marriage to a wealthy man.

A storage box sits against the wheel arch containing the tools of my trade: notebooks; reference books; dictionary; post-its;

pencils; erasers; ballpoint pens; highlighters, and assorted coloured pens. It's a stationery fetishist's wet dream. Another box contains assorted cooking ingredients. I enjoy cooking and wasn't sure that the shop in the nearby village of Scaloon would stock my favourite brands of mayonnaise, stockpots and Himalayan pink salt – ingredients which I consider essential.

My mind turns to Olivia. Remembering I've yet to call her, I sigh. 'It's too early to call her anyway, Bella.' Disinterested, Bella stands on the clifftop watching a seagull pecking at the remains of a dead fish washed up on the beach. 'Anyhow, there's no point calling her now, she'll be with her personal trainer, *training*.'

Olivia has been having a lesbian affair with her personal trainer for over a year now.

Laughing at my own joke, I return my attention to the task at hand. It will take two, perhaps three, return trips to empty the car. Since I'm alone, I'd better make a start before the tide turns.

Heaving the suitcase and vanity bag out, I steer my gaze towards the castle in the hope someone might see me and offer to help. There's still no sign of life. Even if Hamish Cleland is at home, likely as not, he's retired. I imagine him snoozing by the fire, or with his nose buried in a copy of The Telegraph, checking out share prices. I can't imagine him being my knight in shining armour.

Huffing, I set the case down on its wheels, balance the gym and vanity bags on top and steel myself.

By the time I return to the car, my sweatshirt is living up to its handle. I roll up my sleeves, push my sunglasses along my nose, and mop beads of sweat from my brow.

'Bella, I'm out of shape. It's time I got fit.'

I've spent the last three months hiding away on the pretence of a demanding schedule. Told myself I needed solitude to write. Fact is, I spewed out a second-rate novel, and hid away from everyone. Consequently, my mental and physical health suffered. I snort out my frustration by hefting the box of stationery from the boot and place it on the gravel. It's heavy and will need a trip all of its own.

I arrive at the lodge, dump the box on the veranda and steel myself for the final trip – only foodstuffs remain. Bella hunkers down and refuses to join me. She doesn't care if we have Himalayan pink salt or not. I'll make the last trip, alone.

Approaching the car, I notice it's sitting much higher on its suspension now that I've relieved it of its burdens. The sun sits high overhead. It's getting hotter. Insects hum and buzz. A clacking blackbird chastises an unseen interloper. Hefting the box out, I lock the doors with the fob and set off towards the causeway.

Negotiating the steps, I feel the hairs on the back of my neck prickle. I sense I'm being watched. I glance over my shoulder towards the castle and scan the windows for signs of life. Nothing stirs. Harrumphing, I shrug, turn and set off along the causeway.

Halfway across and already my feet are drenched; the speed of the rising tide has taken me by surprise. Giggling a nervous giggle, I quicken my step.

Reaching Scalaig, I climb the steps, reach the path, settle the box on the ground and turn to face Skye.

The Atlantic Ocean has swallowed the causeway, whole.

Above me, a seagull screeches on the updraft and billowy white clouds momentarily blot out the sun. Sunshine becomes shade. Alone and marooned, I'd forgotten just how isolated Scalaig can feel at high tide.

Collecting the box, I set off for the lodge.

CHAPTER ELEVEN

I change out of sodden trainers into walking boots and reward Bella with a hike around the island. She doesn't need a guide. Bella knows every path, nook and cranny on Scalaig. Or so I like to think. She could find her way to the cove blindfolded. Her instinct tells her to stay away from the sheer cliffs beyond the woods south of the lodge.

We spend the afternoon exploring. Scalaig is three acres of amazing scenery, flora and fauna.

At the cove, I launch sticks and Bella cavorts in the surf. A dozen throws later, my arm aches. A yapping Bella drops the stick and shakes the salty ocean from her matted, yellow fur, drenching me. Her yaps become imploring barks.

'Bella! Stop,' I squeal. 'What the hell's a matter with you?' Yapping, she rushes towards me. It's all part of the game. She's the happiest I've seen her in a long time. Hiding the stick behind my back, I lower onto the sand. It's the signal the game is over.

Bella bounds past, peppering my face with sand.

'I'll get you for that.'

She turns and barks.

Smiling, I lay back and gaze at the sky. A minute passes. The world quietens. In my peripheral vision, I glimpse Bella rolling in the grass where the cliff meets the beach. My chest inflates with pride. She's a beautiful creature.

Returning my gaze to the sky, I can't help but smile. I'm surfing on a blissful wave of optimism. It's an unfamiliar feeling. I *can* live and enjoy a single life.

Just when I'm thinking about taking forty winks, the distant, though distinctive, bellow of an outboard motor punctuates my serenity. The realisation that you're never very far from someone makes my heart flutter. Raising on an elbow, the horizon spins. Lightheaded, I sit up and drag my legs under my chin. A minute passes. The spinning subsides. Half a minute, and it ceases altogether. Bella nuzzles against my forearm. Feeling Bella's wet nose, I look down. 'C'mon, girl, it's time we had a bite to eat.'

We bound up the steps two treads at a time. Arriving at the lodge, I throw myself into the rocking chair, drag off my boots and socks, and rub the sand off of my feet.

Twenty minutes later, I've rustled up a meal of pancakes and berries drizzled with organic honey. I eat the sweet, doughy delight, sitting at the table gazing out through the kitchen window. It's my first meal in over twenty-four hours and it's delicious.

With my hunger satiated, I haul the case upstairs and lift it onto the bed. Crossing to the window, I open the blinds and throw open the casement. Golden sunlight, birdsong, the sound of the ocean and pine scent, floods in.

I realise I can't put it off any longer. Crossing to the wardrobe, I drag the doors open and face a line of Christian's clothes. They take up half the wardrobe. I take a sheet from the ottoman and cover them.

Out of sight, out of mind.

I won't have to look at them ever again. In time, I'll pluck up the courage and have myself a bonfire. I might even make a Guy Fawkes effigy of my cheating husband, and throw it on the fire for good measure.

I fill the wardrobe, shoe racks and drawers with my things. Finishing up, I push the empty case under the bed and tell myself I won't need it for months. Next, I turn my attention to the vanity bag. I remove and arrange perfume, cosmetics and skincare on the dresser and on the vanity mirror shelf in the bathroom. Next, I plug in my toothbrush. Opening the wall cupboard, I shovel Christian's toiletries into a bin bag and dump it into the coir bin beneath the dresser.

Out of sight, out of mind.

Feeling satisfied with myself, I curtsy to Bella. She studies me, turns and pads away. I stick my tongue out and throw myself onto the bed.

Go girl, go...

'How about a Scooby snack?' I call after Bella.

Springing up, I skip downstairs to the kitchen. There, I drink coffee while Bella worries on a chew stick.

I swallow the last dregs of coffee. 'OK, darling, much as I'd like to, I can't spin this out any longer. It's time I got some writing done.'

Bella cranks her head on one side, saunters past me and flops onto her bed.

'Please yourself. Laying down on the job won't get it done, will it?'

I collect the stationery box and my handbag from the armchair and heft them upstairs to the second bedroom.

An oak desk sits under the window with a long vista across the garden, pines, cove and ocean. Arranging my writing paraphernalia on the desk, I place the laptop centre stage and the photograph of my parents within touching distance. I lean forward and kiss the photograph.

Love you. Miss ya.

In one corner, a battered easel supports a puncture-free cork pin board. On the narrow shelf at its base, I balance post-it notes, marker pens and a box of pins, in assorted colours. That done, I arrange reference books, a dictionary and a thesaurus on the book-shelf by the easel. Smiling, I run a finger along the spines of ten hardcover books. They're my books. My life's work beautifully wrapped in designer dust covers. Each cover features a bestseller rosette. I take a long look. Satisfied my workplace feels *right*, I close my eyes and sigh.

Olivia. I must call, Olivia.

Returning downstairs to the lounge, Christian's steel-blue eyes follow my every move. It's a cringeworthy photograph. I curse the man behind the lens who took it. Curse too, the man holding my hand, who became a love rat.

Collecting my phone from the arm of the sofa, I select Olivia from contacts.

She answers on the second ring. 'So nice of you to call. You're not dead, then?'

Cutting. 'Passive aggressive. Does your therapist know how you greet people?' I reply. Erin Moran is back in the room.

'Impressive. If only I could afford a therapist, darling. Truth is, my cash cow of an author has lost her mojo and dropped me in the brown stuff.'

Barbed. 'Ouch!'

'You know I don't mean it,' Olivia says. 'What have you been up to? Anything interesting?'

'Settling in. This and that. Getting organised. New broom,' I say. 'Clean sweep.' If I sound chirpy, it's because I am.

'Good for you. And work?'

'Perfect. I'm all set.'

'I'm delighted to hear it. Carpe diem. Go upstairs and get your tight little ass working on that manuscript,' Olivia says. I imagine her smile.

'I'm all set for tomorrow. Promise.'

'A.J. is demanding regular updates until he's got his next best-seller, *your* next bestseller, in his sweaty mitts,' Olivia says. Elvis style, her smile will have left the building. Olivia is putting me on notice.

Though she can't see me, I nod. 'End of August. Promise. I won't let you down.'

I owe Olivia big time. She's put her reputation on the line for me.

'Call at least once a week. Text, every day. No excuses. OK?'

'OK.'

The line falls silent. 'Olivia?' No reply. Olivia has ended the call. Dragging the phone from my ear, I stare at it in shock. Never has she been so blunt. So cold. The flashing battery icon catches my eye. I step over and plug the phone into the socket by the front door.

Outside, daylight is fading fast and my tummy is rumbling like distant thunder. Bella appears at my leg, licking her lips.

'Time for supper, gorgeous. Let's see what Rhoda's left.'

Lowering onto my haunches, I slide out the cavernous drawer at the base of the fridge freezer and reveal a plastic-wrapped pepperoni pizza, a serving of tuna pasta in a Tupperware container and a half-eaten tub of chocolate chip ice cream. Though it isn't much of a selection, beggars can't be choosers. Grumbling, I drag out the ice cream, rock the drawer and swing the door closed.

I take a bottle of chardonnay from the chiller and step outside. Bella joins me on the veranda. Settling into the rocking chair, I balance the ice cream on my lap, pour a glass of wine, sit and inhale the rich oak and vanilla notes. I take a sip and exhale a contented sigh. Over my shoulder, I hear the ocean lapping against the causeway as it prepares to cut Scalaig off from Skye, again.

Bella is curled up at my feet. The look she gives me suggests she's unimpressed with my nutritional choices. 'Don't worry, darling, we'll pop over and see old Mr Barr tomorrow.'

Sitting back, my mind stills. It's a couple of minutes past nine, the sun has set and the air has cooled. My eyelids droop and my chin slumps onto my chest. I feel myself drifting off to sleep. The caw of a seagull jolts me awake, and I run a hand over my face.

'Bedtime, Bella.'

I make my way upstairs, undress, wash and roll into bed. Bella leaps up and settles along the bottom of the bed.

As I fall asleep, a newfound sense of renewal courses through my veins.

CHAPTER TWELVE

Day 3

I wake early, shower and dress. I choose blue jeans, a grey t-shirt and a favourite navy cardigan. Racing downstairs, I make a simple breakfast of tea and toast, and promise myself something more substantial later. Once fed, Bella slips outside and I smirk. She's doing what we all need to do most mornings.

I write best in the morning. By 6:00 a.m., I'm ready to tackle the re-write. I collect a tortoiseshell hairgrip, scrape my fringe behind my ears, and select the file shortcut. Waiting for the file to open, I rattle my fingers on the desk. Five seconds and the word, 'BETRAYAL,' appears in the middle of the screen in bold caps. I scan the opening line: *In the dead of winter, I'm betrayed.* Despondency taunts my optimism. Olivia was right. It's woeful. I flick my notebook open to the plot outline and spend ten minutes reacquainting myself with the characters, plot, heroine's peril, love interest and the inevitable, headlong rush towards the happy ending. Taking stock, I remind myself that one person ruined this book and my life: Christian.

With the original story refreshed in my mind, I open a new document and write a new working title, 'SCALAIG.'

With my fingers hovering over the keys, words elude me. Too afraid of making mistakes, I'm overthinking. A million thoughts rampage through my head like invading Vikings across a beach, and none of them make sense. I'm experiencing writer's block – the curse of every writer.

With my thoughts refusing to coalesce into coherent sentences, I drag my eyes from the screen, sit and gaze out of the window, chewing on a pencil. In the middle distance, the breeze ruffles the ocean into whitecaps. Twenty metres offshore, a gannet dives headlong into the surf and reappears with a long silvery object wedged between its beak. The instant I crank the window open, the room resonates with the rasp of the surf and a symphony of birdsong.

I sit and listen. Close my eyes. My mind calms. When I do eventually open my eyes, fifteen minutes have elapsed and the Vikings have moved inland. Once more, the therapeutic effect of nature has triumphed.

I type. At first, the words stutter onto the screen. Then, as my imagination ebbs and flows, the words gather momentum. Sentences and paragraphs flood onto the screen. I enter 'the zone.' Become my heroine; feel what she feels; sense what she senses.

Writing is a muscle. And, like all muscles, you either use it, or you lose it.

Time evaporates. I write until I can no longer ignore the nagging throb in my groin. It's 10:00 a.m. and I haven't moved from my desk for four hours. The word count at the bottom of the screen reads 3,025. Maintaining this momentum, the first draft would be ready within a month. I disregard the notion as dangerous, since rushing presents its own dangers.

Pressing 'SAVE,' I sit back and stretch for the ceiling. The change of position threatens to release the contents of my bladder. I stand, turn, and make a dash for the bathroom. I pee for what seems like an eternity. When I'm done, I slosh cold water over my face, apply tinted moisturiser, lip gloss and anti-frizz oil to my curls. Smiling a satisfied smile to my reflection returned in the mirror above the sink, I realise how thirsty I am.

As I pass through the lounge into the kitchen, I'm conscious of the cynical blue eyes following my every move from the photograph above the mantelpiece. I grit my teeth and drag a footstool over to the hearth. Clambering up, I spin the frame over to face the wall. A small gold sticker in the bottom left corner catches my eye. It names and shames the man behind the lens. Even then, the image was dated in style and politics. I remind myself that Christian chose the photographer. Consigning his mocking stare to the wall, my lips quiver with mischievous delight. Stepping down from the footstool, my gut cramps. I need to eat, but the cupboards are bare. It's time I ventured into Scaloon for a grocery shop at Barr's. Some human contact will do me good.

Sensing an imminent outing, Bella rises, stretches and pads to the door. 'C'mon you, let's go and see the neighbours.'

CHAPTER THIRTEEN

We keep hybrid bikes in the shed at the side of the lodge: they're mountain bikes equipped with racks, panniers, mudguards and road tyres. Mine has a basket attached to the handlebars and is perfect for transporting groceries. Though it's a tad village vicar, I don't care. The shed key hangs on a hook under the veranda roof, protected from the ruthless Atlantic storms which batter Scalaig irrespective of the season.

Collecting the key, I make my way to the shed. A thin layer of rust covers the key. I jiggle it into the lock. After several failed attempts, the lock finally releases. As the rickety door opens, a fat, furry moth flies out brushing against my cheek. Moths freak me out. Captured by sunlight, a fine cloud of pixie dust hangs in the air in the opening. Brushing it aside, I step into the dank interior. The fetid sharpness of decaying timber envelops me. Gossamer fingers lick my face. Something tiny with multiple legs scurries along my arm. Feeling grubby, I shake my cardigan, wipe my hair and face.

The bikes lean against the wall on my left. I grasp the nearest by the handlebars. To my relief, it's mine. Backing out into the sanctuary of daylight, I flick the door closed with my hip and corral my phobias inside the shed. Dusting the saddle, deciding that it's good to go, I place my purse in the basket. With Bella trotting ahead, we set off on a mini adventure to Scaloon, two miles distant.

Approaching the causeway, unease eddies in my gut. I halt overlooking it. The worn-to-smooth rock glistens in the sunlight. Rock pools pockmark the surface. I push the bike down the steep incline beside the steps and reach level ground at the causeway. Easing onto the saddle, I push off. It's a race to beat the tide, and I haven't ridden for a while. I pedal with a slow cadence and grip the handlebars tightly.

Reaching the other end of the causeway, I halt at the bottom of the wooden steps. I'd forgotten all about them. I dismount and push the bike up the muddy incline beside the steps. Supporting the bike, I climb the incline one tortuous step at a time until I reach the gravel area and the car. At the top, I stop to gather my breath and waft my t-shirt at the neck.

Stop making excuses! You need to get fit. This isn't good enough. I chastise myself.

Settling the bike on its side, I step to the car and check the doors. Satisfied they're locked, I turn to face the castle. Turrets, subtle pink render and narrow Georgian windows dominate my field of vision. Scalaig Castle is pure gothic baronial in style. A haphazard selection of windows positioned at irregular intervals covers the six storeys. A formidable studded black painted front door sits central in the ground floor elevation. Though it looks capable of resisting a siege, the paint is grey and flaking along the vertical joints. Weeds grow in the gutters. Green stains streak the facade. The castle possesses an unloved, 'seen better days,' appearance. A low stone wall – half covered in ivy – separates the castle from the lane. A path leads from a picket gate to the front door. Christian mentioned once it had twenty bedrooms and a huge basement with a vaulted brick ceiling. Nothing moves in or around the castle.

With my curiosity getting the better of me, I cross the lane, pass through the gate and stride to the front door. There, I feel compelled to wipe my feet on the threadbare welcome mat. Why, I'm not sure? Remembering Bella, I glance over my shoulder. She's stayed by the gate and appears reluctant to come any further.

I reach up, collect the ornate lion head knocker and rap twice. Deep thuds echo inside. I imagine a vast hall with antlers, enormous portraits, parquet flooring, dark oak panelling and an exquisite plaster ceiling.

I listen hard, but hear only silence.

After a long minute, I hunker down and lift the letter box. The inside flap is down. I try to push it open, but it won't budge. Straightening, I settle my right eye against the keyhole.

'Hello?'

Inside, nothing stirs. My call goes unanswered. I'm about to leave, when I hear what I think are footsteps. I place my ear against the letter box.

The silence is absolute.

I knock again. Stand and wait.

I must have been mistaken.

Did I hear a rat in the basement? Are the Clelands away on holiday?

I always associate them with skiing, but it's early summer and there won't be any skiing. Then, I recall how Isla Cleland was ill the previous September. Resigned that the house is unoccupied, I pray all is well with my nearest neighbours.

Collecting the bike from the gravel, I cycle off towards Scaloon and Barr's.

CHAPTER FOURTEEN

I pedal with a slow cadence so Bella can keep up. A tyre catching in a rut would be bad news. As far as I know, the nearest hospital is fifteen miles away in Portree. Truth is, I'm a wuss on two wheels.

I cycle for ten minutes along a stone path, dipping in and out of woodland and skirting the ocean until we reach Scaloon. Dismounting, I realise it would've been quicker to walk.

In the weeks after he'd bought Scalaig from the Clelands, Christian went to great lengths to research the island's history. Keen to impress, he wanted to hold his own in any barroom discussion with the locals. Becoming well-versed in local tradition and folklore, he schooled me on his findings. Christian hated being thought of as the rich Sassenach interloper, throwing his weight and money around with zero emotional investment in the area.

With a population of less than a hundred, Scaloon is a sleepy hamlet relying on fishing and tourism. Several trawlers and lobster cobbles operate from the small harbour. The waters off Scaloon teem with Atlantic cod, haddock, and lobster. Village life centres on the community centre, Church of Scotland chapel, post office, The King's Head Inn, old school house and Barr's.

The Barrs have run the shop in Scaloon for over a hundred years. Its latest proprietor, Alasdair, has built a fine reputation. Though he sells most things, Alasdair specialises in sustainable local produce: chicken; eggs; fresh fish; lobster; homegrown vegetables, and salad sourced from local growers. Barr's hardware section is second to none. If Alasdair doesn't stock something, then he'll source and deliver it from his network of suppliers within days. With Alasdair in charge, no one need ever leave Scaloon.

Arriving at Barr's, I dismount and prop the bike against the wall. Standing there, I'm surrounded by flickering red neon and a buzzing sound reverberates in my ears. The neon sign above the door announces Barr's, 'OPEN,' in quarter second bursts. Bella pads up, tongue lolling from the side of her mouth. I instruct her to sit. Collecting my purse from the basket, I push through the door and a cheerful bell announces my arrival. I glance up and locate the source of the problem. The neon sign flickers and buzzes like an annoyed wasp caught behind glass in a heatwave. Within seconds, a grey haired man in a functional brown smock appears through a strip curtain.

I greet him with a warm smile. 'Good morning. It's Alasdair, isn't it?'

The man settles his hands on his hips and appraises me with circumspection. His brow furrows between caterpillar-like eyebrows. 'Do I know you, Miss?'

I repress a shrug. 'I'm Erin Moran from Scalaig. Don't you remember me?'

I imagine cogs whirling inside his head. His brow stays furrowed. Eventually, his frown relaxes. 'Of course. Sorry. Yes. I've got you now... Mrs Moran from Scalaig. It's nice to see you,' he says, with a broad smile, wiping his palms down the front of his smock, thrusting his right hand at me. We shake hands. 'Would I be correct in saying it's been a wee while since I last laid eyes on your pretty wee face? Are you planning on staying long?'

Not wanting to give too much away, I shrug. 'To be honest, I haven't decided, yet,' I say, checking myself, unwilling to burden a relative stranger with my troubles. 'I'll see how my writing goes.'

'Aye, that's right, you're an author, aren't you? I was forgetting. Did you bring a list?'

I'm with a great salesman. He doesn't appreciate small talk.

'Sorry, no,' I say, shrugging. 'I forgot.' It's a white lie.

Alasdair sighs. 'Not to worry. I'm sure we can work it out together,' he says, wringing his hands. I imagine pound signs racking up inside his head. 'It's often the best way.'

We pen a list of coffee, tea, milk, eggs, chicken, steak, fruit and vegetables. It represents my usual dietary choices. Alasdair suggests I add fresh fish, bread and treats.

Feeling relaxed in his company, I say, 'You're going to be seeing me a lot over the coming months, Mr Barr. Is there any chance I can arrange a regular delivery? It'll save me the hassle of coming in. As you know, the weather can be volatile.'

Alasdair smiles. His brow – above cloudy grey eyes – smooths. He wrings his hands.

I ask him if he stocks Bella's favourite dog food. Alasdair says he doesn't, but promises to order it in.

'I'm going to need wild bird seed, too,' I remember. 'Poor things keep pecking at an empty table. It's heartbreaking, watching them.'

Alasdair, licking a pencil, adds bird seed. We finalise the list. Mentioning I'm cycling, I ask him not to overdo it. He disappears through the strip curtain dividing the shop from the rest of the building, leaving me alone to twiddle my thumbs. Five minutes later, he returns clutching a torso-sized brown paper bag against his chest. He places it on the counter. Inside, I chuckle. The greatest salesman has ignored my request. There are enough provisions to keep me going for weeks.

'How about I add this wee lot to your account? You can settle up at the end of the month? Mr Moran came in and wiped the slate clean, months back,' Alasdair says, sealing the bag with clear tape.

What did he just say?

'Sorry?'

'I said... Would you like me to add this wee lot to your account? Your husband has wiped the slate clean.'

'My husband was here?' I bark, instantly wishing I hadn't; the blood in my veins turning to ice. 'When?'

Alasdair takes his chin between his thumb and forefinger. 'Now, let me think...'

His silence is interminable.

'It must've been about mid-February, or thereabouts. Aye, that would be about right. I remember it now because there was snow on the ground. He ordered half-a-ton of firewood, but never collected it. It was very remiss of him.'

'Are you certain it was Christian?'

Seemingly concerned he's dropped Christian in the brown stuff, he backtracks. 'I think so... Of course, there's every chance I'm mistaken. My memory isn't what it used to be.'

I feel for him. 'That's right, silly me, I remember now,' I lie.

Inside, I'm screaming. *I know what you were up to... Cheating bastard...*

Alasdair smiles an understanding smile. My cheeks redden. Angry and embarrassed, I bite my lip and divert my gaze to the shelving past Alasdair's right shoulder.

The moment passes.

'Shall I have Rory deliver your order direct to Scalaig? It'll take two, maximum three days, to pull together. Is that alright?'

'Perfect.'

'Good. Is there anything else I can do for you this fine morning, Mrs Moran?'

'Please, call me Erin... *Alasdair.*'

'Erin, it is,' he says, winking.

I feel myself relaxing. A thought pops into my head.

'Actually, now you come to mention it, there is something, yes. The Cleland's place. Scalaig Castle. Is it empty? I've been past several times already and there doesn't appear to be anyone at home. Are they on holiday?'

Alasdair frowns, makes to say something, then seems to decide against it. He takes a firm grip on the edge of the glass counter with both hands and leans forward. His forearms are Popeye wide. He pauses, says, 'You haven't heard, have you?'

I shake my head. 'Heard what?'

I pray my dark thoughts of earlier were the product of an over-active imagination.

'Hamish and Isla Cleland died in a skiing accident last December,' he says. 'Tragic it was.'

'What happened?'

'Freak accident. A snow making machine ran out of control and drove right over them.'

I imagine him reliving reading newspaper articles, studying grainy photographs taken at the scene. I shudder.

'Oh my God, that's awful,' I say, wondering how I'm going to extricate myself from the hole I've dug for myself. Then I remember. 'Didn't they have a son at boarding school? How is he?' I can't for the life of me remember the name of the awkward teenager I'd met ten years before. 'His name has slipped my mind.'

'Aye, they do. *Did.* Son's name is Callum. Of course, he's all grown up now. He was living in Aberdeen when the accident happened. There was a daughter, too, a couple of years older. She left home on the day of her eighteenth birthday. As far as I know, she's not been seen since. I cannae remember her name,' Alasdair says, scratching the side of his nose. I follow his gaze past my right shoulder towards the door. There's nobody there.

I clear my throat. 'When I last saw Callum he was just a boy. Being orphaned is horrid. I know from personal experience,' I say, adding, 'The castle looks a little, not wanting to be unkind, *unloved.* Does anyone live there anymore?'

Alasdair shrugs. 'I'm not sure. I haven't been past that way for a wee while. That place, it doesn't interest me in the slightest.'

We seem to spend a lot of time shrugging. Alasdair releases his grip on the counter and places his hand on the grocery bag, wide eyes burning into mine.

'I'll carry this out to your bicycle, if you like?'

Suddenly, Alasdair seems to be in a hurry to get rid of me. He stares through me, like I don't exist.

'It's OK,' I say, scooping up the bag. 'I can manage.' I turn to leave.

How strange?

A sense of unease roils through me. When I mentioned the Cleland's son, Callum, Alasdair seemed to clam up.

Is he trying to hide something from me?

Alasdair rounds the counter, strides over to the door and holds it open. His warm smile has returned. The heat in his eyes has dissipated. 'Rory will deliver the rest of your groceries. I'll see to it, myself. Rest assured, there won't be any mistakes. Take care of yourself, Mrs Moran,' Alasdair says, thrusting his right hand at me. I juggle the grocery bag into the nook of my left elbow and accept his outstretched hand. His handshake is limp and sweaty.

'Thank you, Alasdair. That's very kind of you,' I say, swallowing my unease.

'It's been nice talking to you. Be sure to pop in anytime you're passing, if only for a chat. I know how lonely it can get.' The return of Alasdair's friendly, easy going manner, eases my anxiety.

'I will.'

'And watch the tide times.' He taps his forehead with a forefinger and waves me off. 'Anyone can get caught out. We wouldn't want the ocean taking you, now would we?'

The uneasy feeling returns.

'I will. Thanks for reminding me.'

At the bike, I place the groceries in the basket, swing onto the saddle and click my cheek at Bella. My mind races.

I never mentioned I'm alone. I suppose he just assumed I am? Am I becoming paranoid?

I mustn't let my imagination run away with itself. It's a common problem for writers, romantics and worriers like me.

With a shrug and a sharp intake of breath, I push off for Scalaig, the lodge, and home.

CHAPTER FIFTEEN

Passing through Scaloon's deserted streets, I try hard to quieten the incoherent ramblings jangling around my brain. I turn right on to the path running parallel with the shore. Nature seems intent on reclaiming the stone setts. Verdant moss and grass shoots fill the joints. Gnarled tree roots – the thickness of my wrist – thrust from the mossy banking and seem intent on bringing me down.

My mind drifts to the tragic deaths of Hamish and Isla Cleland. Mr Cleland loved to talk about skiing. It was his passion. He was an expert skier.

Cycling along the path, a movie plays inside my head.

Hamish and Isla glide down a snowy hillside in matching blue ski suits. Stunning alpine vistas reflect in oversized, reflective lenses. Hamish spins to a halt across the slope. Fifteen feet above him, Isla digs her ski poles into the snow and draws up. Behind the lenses, their smiles are radiant. Sparkling diamonds of sunlight reflect from the snow. Ten seconds pass. Hamish turns and studies the route down the mountain. Returning his gawp to Isla, his eyes flare with terror. A huge orange tracked vehicle glides silently down the slope towards her. A man waves frantically from the cab perched high above the snow. Isla, oblivious to the impending danger, waves at Hamish. He bellows under a cupped hand.

'Isla!'

Already, it's too late.

Isla disappears beneath the distended belly of the giant snow monster. The last thing Hamish Cleland sees is a huge radiator grille before he, too, becomes one with it.

Reaching the castle, my guts perform somersaults and my heart races. Setting my feet on the ground, I bring the bike to a halt and suck air. Sitting there, I eject the snowy video nasty playing inside my head.

Oblivious to my state of mind, Bella trots ahead. She knows the way home from here. Within seconds, she's disappeared from view.

'Are you alright?' A male voice enquires behind me, in an even tone.

My hand flies to my chest. The bike wobbles. I turn to the voice. A man steps out from the treeline. He's dark-haired, bearded, in hiking boots, blue jeans and a maroon fleece. I age him in his mid-twenties. He stands hands on his hips and studies with suspicion.

'Shit. You made me jump,' I say, in a voice an octave higher than normal.

His expression softens. 'I'm sorry. I didn't mean to startle you,' he says, stroking his close-trimmed, ginger-flecked beard. He moves closer, stalls. Only two feet separate us.

Rolling the bike back a quarter of a wheel, I recover some personal space.

'I didn't notice you as I rode past,' I say.

He nods over his shoulder. 'I live in the castle.'

'You're Callum?'

'Yes.'

'I'm sorry to hear about your parents,' I blurt, without thinking, beg the ground to open up and swallow me.

'Thank you. Kind words. I loved my parents, dearly,' he says, in a smooth monotone.

A half-minute of awkward silence fills the space between us.

'Sorry. I ought not to have said anything. It was very insensitive of me. The accident, it was tragic.' I need to move the conversation on. 'I'm Erin. Erin Moran. I own Scalaig. I knew your parents. Not well or anything, but I respected them. They were lovely people,' I say, recovering my composure.

Breathe. I tell myself. *This guy is a hunk. I never knew.*

'I know *who* you are,' he says, pausing. 'What you own.'

I wait for him to elaborate, but his expression is inscrutable. He seems to look straight through me. It's a strange expression, part way between sorrow and resignation. Once again, I feel uncomfortable.

What is it with the locals? They seem to favour pregnant pauses and blank, enigmatic stares.

I clear my throat, glance left to Scalaig. 'I must get back. The tide...'

'I know all about the tides.'

More silence you could cut with a knife.

'Yes... Well... It's been nice meeting you, Callum,' I say, in a weird rasp.

His expression warms and his hazel eyes glisten. He nods towards the basket. 'I can help with your groceries, if you like? The causeway can be treacherous. The tide's turning. It can be dangerous.'

'That's alright. I'll be fine. I'll go slow.'

I hope he doesn't think I'm being rude?

I soften my intonation. 'Another time, perhaps?'

He shrugs. 'Goodbye, Mrs Moran.' He nods and turns on a heel.

'Goodbye, Callum,' I shout after him.

I catch myself staring at him as he walks away and try hard not to fixate on the rise and fall of his butt cheeks. At the gate, he halts, turns, beams a smile and waves. Him, standing there at the gate, reminds me of my father at the school gates, waiting for me to go inside, when I was a child.

Blinking away his stare, I roll the pedal up and push off.

CHAPTER SIXTEEN

Hot and bothered, I arrive at the lodge to find Bella watching from the veranda. Panting, I place my hands on my knees and imagine Bella asking, 'What took you so long?'

Lowering onto my haunches, I tickle behind her ears.

'Well, wasn't that an interesting afternoon? Thanks for sticking around to offer moral support. Appreciated.' I say, sniggering. 'I'll tell you what... Why don't we grab a bite to eat and take a walk along the beach? What do you say?' Bella's ears prick up at the mention of the word, 'walk.' Tail wagging, she yaps. 'I'll take that as a yes.' I say, stepping to the door.

Transferring the groceries from the bike to the kitchen, I fill the fridge and cupboards. Finishing up, I put the kettle on. Since the weather's set fair, I decide on a picnic.

I go upstairs and change into shorts and t-shirt and shuffle on flip-flops. Returning downstairs, I collect the backpack and fill it with a ham sandwich, crisps, bottles of water and a bag of kibbles for Bella. I rinse, dry, and pack her bowl.

Five minutes later, arriving on the bottom tread – where the steps meet the cove – I slip out of flip-flops and launch onto the golden sand. Bella rushes into the surf chasing driftwood.

Spooked, protesting sandpipers, chatter and launch into the air. Smiling at her playful antics, I set off across the sweeping arc of golden sand towards the timber jetty at the far western end of the beach.

At the half way point, I inch barefoot into the surf. The oscillating ocean laps at my ankles and fizzes between my toes. It's biting cold. Standing there, I feel the tension in my feet release. When I can't bear it any longer, I step out onto warm sand. The sun is hot on my face, neck and arms. A warm breeze envelops me. I hear the distant slap of the ocean against the rocky headland.

Arriving at the jetty, I turn to face the sun, settle my back against the barnacle-encrusted timbers and slide onto the sand. I close my eyes, drink in the salty air, the hypnotic rasp of the surf, and enjoy the scorching sun.

Waves of contentment surge through my veins in time with my heartbeat.

Opening my eyes, I sit gazing across the ocean.

The stroll has been therapeutic. Not a trace of tension remains in my neck. Lost in a warm, fuzzy feeling, I exhale a deep sigh, shuffle forward, push my sunglasses along my nose and lay back on my elbows. Tiring from the surf and the sandpipers, Bella ambles over and slumps down next to me.

She's my ever faithful companion. I adore the very bones of her.

Closing my eyes, I see a delta of black rivers against a crimson background. As my mind replays the day, my consciousness ebbs and flows until the hand of sleep takes me.

Minutes later, my mind spirals into the abstract chaos of a new dream.

Alasdair Barr stands behind a counter, clutching a roll of banknotes against his chest. Seeing me, he smiles a manic joker smile. Alasdair's image fades to grey, and Callum Cleland's face comes into focus. He sits on the parapet of Scalaig Castle, feet dangling over the edge. A telescope hangs from his right hand.

Meanwhile, back at the lodge, naked at an apex window, I fling open the curtains. Callum rotates the telescope towards me. Uncomfortable under its all-seeing eye, I shout for him to stop and drag the curtains closed. Fifteen seconds pass and I force myself to peek out through the gap. Callum laughs and directs the telescope towards my unsuspecting heroine – my female protagonist – cycling towards the castle. I see Callum's face in close up. Hungry eyes. Flaring nostrils. Saliva pooling on his chin. My heroine's scream reverberates around the lodge…

It breaks the spell.

Waking, I bolt upright and reach out for Bella. For an instant, I've no recollection of where I am. Coming to, my vision clears and I see the beach, the jetty, and Bella. I must have slept for hours. The sun has lost its heat, and the tide is just inches from my feet.

'Home time,' I tell Bella, rising, collecting my things.

Arriving at the lodge, I remember that I ought to give Olivia a progress update.

I send her a text.

Productive day… first two chapters complete… happy bunny! E xxx.

Within seconds, a kissing lips emoji pings back. I reply with a Kermit the Frog GIFF bashing away at a typewriter. Olivia pings a thumbs up. I stall, hovering my thumb over the screen. The moment passes. Deciding against a five set text tennis match, I settle the phone on the worktop.

With my dream still rattling around my head, I settle at my desk and add five hundred words to my novel. It's an acceptable word count for the day. Pressing, 'SAVE', I close the laptop down and decide on a shower.

Within two minutes, hot water cascades over me. Steam fills the room. I stand under its warming embrace.

After showering, relaxed and contented, I curl up in bed and fall into a dreamless sleep.

It's still dark when my eyelids finally flicker open. In the twilight zone halfway between sleep and consciousness, I lay gazing at the ceiling. Deep within the lodge, I hear a floorboard creak. Captured by its spell, I freeze, hold my breath and wait.

It's nothing. Relax.

Unseen, from the floor at the bottom of the bed, Bella whimpers. I imagine she's chasing imaginary seabirds across imaginary beaches. Flipping onto my right side, I press my head into the pillow.

Under the wind, the lodge creaks and groans. Sleep takes me once more.

CHAPTER SEVENTEEN

Day 8

There's a gentle rhythm to life now. I write in the mornings and evenings and take inspiration and solace from the long view towards the Atlantic beyond the desk. The light from the vast skies is luminescent. Seabirds arc and swoop on the currents. Sitting in the first floor apex, I'm surrounded by the sound of the ocean caressing the shore. There's an invigorating freshness to the air which fuels my imagination. It's at the opposite end of the spectrum to the omnipresent toxicity of London.

I no longer wear a watch. I'm trying hard not to look at my phone. Every other day, I send Olivia brief updates, but she never replies. I'm grateful that she doesn't. I'm measuring time by the sun, moon and tides.

Most afternoons, I take Bella for a walk on the beach or in the woods south of the lodge. Sometimes, I hike to the west side of the island where I sit dangling my feet over the clifftop, enjoying the magnificent sunsets.

My writing is flowing and progress is good. This latest novel is shaping up well. The characters live and breathe. I've slept more in the last week than I did in the previous five months. I feel like I'm hooked up to oxygen. Even my visit to Barr's in Scaloon feels like an eternity ago.

Bella rises and pads to the door. She whimpers to be let outside to pee. We go downstairs past the wedding photograph turned against the wall. Christian's steely-eyed glare no longer witnesses our passage, and I allow myself a smirk.

Swinging the door open, Bella bounces across the lawn towards her favourite peeing spot in the long grass at the edge of the lawn.

Suddenly, everything darkens and a youth steps out from the shadows blocking the opening. My heart leaps and steals my breath. 'Holy shit!' I exclaim without thinking.

Bella, hunkering down in the long grass, continues to pee.

Some guard dog you are...

I study the youth. Estimate him to be in his mid twenties, but it's difficult to be exact. Man-boy would better describe him.

The man-boy stands stock still, saying nothing, addressing the timber deck. Thick forearms support a cardboard box. His build is pure human pit bull. A mop of brown hair extends past his eyes. His red and black checked shirt is a minimum of two sizes too big for him. His loose fitting washed-to-white jeans have seen better days. In places, the soles of his shoes are detached from the tops. His right foot turns in at an awkward angle. Imagine Rain Man, but twenty years younger and built like Mike Tyson.

Though we face one another across the threshold, his gaze remains fixed on the deck. After a long minute, he thrusts the box towards me.

Was that a grunt? Is he mute?

'Are you Rory?'

'Aye,' he says, voice deeper and older than his probable years might suggest.

Again, he thrusts the box forward.

'I'm sorry. Only… Only, you took me by surprise,' I say.

'Aye.'

'Would you mind bringing the delivery inside?' I say, settling my back against the open door. I don't know what I expected the delivery boy to be like, but it certainly wasn't someone like Rory.

He ambles forward and strides over an invisible step at the threshold. Once inside, he stalls on the welcome mat, wiping his feet. The feet wiping continues for a full minute. As he wipes, his head rocks.

Is he counting each wipe?

I try not to stare, but it's hard not to.

Convinced his shoes are clean, he announces, 'Ten.'

He seems a little, well, it pains me to say it, *slow.*

I step past him. 'The kitchen. Follow me.'

I halt at the table. Rory, carrying the box, enters, and stands beside me.

'Thank you, Rory. Just there.' I point at a cleared area of worktop next to the microwave.

Furtive eyes study me from beneath a mop of hair. Rory steps past, sets the box down and takes half a step back. Scrutinising it, he huffs, places huge calloused hands on the sides and adjusts it so it aligns with the edge of the worktop.

He repeats the ritual three times. It must not have been perfect.

Feeling awkward, I smile a thin smile and massage the back of my neck. He is exhausting.

Rory fixates on the box. He's checking again! Pausing, squeezing his fists together, he steps away.

'I'll fetch my handbag,' I say, moving away from the huge man-boy taking up half of the kitchen.

'Aye,' Rory says, arms limp by his sides.

Returning to the kitchen, I thrust a ten pound note into his huge hands, turn and head for the front door. I wait for him to leave with my back pressed against the door, staring blankly at the wall opposite.

Rory remains in the kitchen.

Angling my face towards the kitchen, I call, 'Thank you, Rory. That will be all for now. You can go.'

A gear must engage inside his head. He lumbers through the lounge, strides over the invisible step, and much to my relief, departs.

'Bye, Rory. I'll see you soon.'

'Aye,' he says, head down, striding along the path towards the causeway, clubfoot dragging a quarter of a pace behind him.

Passing through the gate, he spins right and marches away. Two minutes later, he disappears into the pines. His departure leaves me pondering the encounter. It's obvious he has learning difficulties, or maybe he suffered some kind of head injury? Anyway, despite his awkwardness and strange manner, he seems harmless enough.

'He's a strange one, isn't he, Bella? I thought he was a mad axeman. How about you?'

Not understanding, Bella continues to sniff at the soil under the fence.

Putting the groceries away, I earmark a fillet steak for dinner. Moving outside, I stroll over to the bird table and spill birdseed across it. Thanks to the greatest salesman, Alasdair, and his son, Rory, Bella and I, the birds, won't go hungry.

I drag the door closed on the latch and inform Bella that we're going for a walk. Bella takes off towards the cove. I call her to heel. She slides to a halt, spins and scampers back.

'Not this time. Let's walk in the woods.'

CHAPTER EIGHTEEN

Scalaig's woods are as old as Scotland. Tall pines create a near impenetrable canopy through which little sunlight can pass. Transitioning through the treeline, it's as though someone has turned off the sun. At ground level, the darkness is almost complete. Strolling along the footpath, the scents of wet soil and pungent pine enter my nostrils. Shuffling through a thick layer of needles, dark ferns claw at my calves. Bella nuzzles her nose deep into the mulch, hunting out rabbit scent. Dust tickles the back of her throat, and she sneezes. I can't help but laugh.

I'm stood in an amphitheatre of birdsong. Finches chirp. Pheasants clack. Wood pigeons coo: an aural opiate if ever there was one. Close by, yet unseen, a woodpecker pecks industriously at a tree trunk. The telltale rattle seems to come from every direction.

Ahead, with the pines thinning, the canopy gives way to open sky. Passing through the treeline within four paces, we arrive at the clifftop. Coconut-sized rocks litter the ground. Foot-high scrub replaces pine needles underfoot.

Bella creeps to cliff edge. She's been here before. Knowing our walk has reached its outer limit, she sits. Joining her, I sit, fold my legs under my bottom and take in the view. It's an impressive panorama of inlets, islands, ocean and sky. In the middle distance, two sailboats float serenely past. A small motorised cobble – skippered by a solitary figure – motors past. Its heading suggests its destination as the cove. *Our* cove.

It gets me wondering. *Who? And why?*

Leaning forward, I scan the kelp-strewn, rocky foreshore below. Huge boulders, worn smooth over millennia, pepper the foreshore. They form a natural barrier and a series of deep ravines. Sparkling quartz peppers the bedrock.

Below me, the cliffs are almost vertical. Only the most intrepid of climbers would attempt to scale them. Twenty metres along, the cliffs are not so precipitous. Narrowing my eyes, settling a flattened palm over my brow, I identify a route down. Since I'm no adventurer, I cast aside the notion of scaling the cliff as too dangerous.

Gazing across the vast ocean, I toy with Bella's ears and her tail swishes. Scenes from my novel play out in my mind's eye. Connections clarify. Plot twists solidify. Opportunities present themselves. I'm in my happy place.

Rising up, stretching, I say, 'C'mon you, time's up. We'd better be getting back. It'll be dark soon.'

CHAPTER NINETEEN

Returning to the lodge, I prepare a steak meal and sit on the veranda. The steak is tender and delicious. Settling the tray on the deck, I snuggle into my cardigan against the chill.

It's been a long evening and my eyes feel gritty from staring at the laptop screen. I massage my eyeballs. With my hearing in a heightened state of awareness, I hear the trickle of water across a hard surface.

How? Where?

I rack my brain, but an answer eludes me. An expedition beckons, though not today.

I open my eyes in time to see a song thrush strut across the lawn towards the bird feeder. A robin – guarding its territory – launches itself at the intruder with its claws bared. The thrush gives ground and scuttles away to pastures new.

Since it's too late for coffee, I decide it's wine o'clock. Lifting the bottle from the fridge, I pour a half glass of cool, crisp Chardonnay. I take a sip. It's sublime. It will help ease me into the evening and sleep.

Returning to the veranda – I've done enough work for one day

– I lower into the rocking chair. Getting comfy, my mobile vibrates in a cardigan pocket and breaks me from my torpor.

A text... Who from?

I ought to have know. Christian.

hello gorgeous. missing me yet? can I come over… tonight? I'll keep you company… C xxx

Has he got shit for brains? More importantly ... where is he?

My blood runs cold.

Furious, I shove the phone into my pocket, too quickly. The phone misses its target, falls, crashes against the deck and breaks apart. The body skittles across the veranda and pitches over the steps onto the footpath. Plastic pieces fly everywhere. The screen fades and dies. Underneath me, the battery balances over a gap between the boards. The battery cover has disappeared. It must have fallen through a gap.

'No!' I yell, collecting the battery with pinched fingers.

I'm such an idiot.

Bringing the body and battery together, I fumble to re-attach them. The battery won't attach. Studying the phone, I notice several of the plastic tabs have broken off. The battery cover is nowhere to be seen.

I'm screwed.

Slumping into the rocking chair, an invisible hand grips my throat, squeezes and flushes out hot, angry tears. My hands shake. There's a braying behind my right temple.

You monster!

If Christian is hoping for a reconciliation, he's out of his tiny mind. When his shadow falls across me, either literally or metaphorically, however good a mood I'm in, I go to pieces.

You've no right to occupy my thoughts! Who the hell do you think you are?

I lift from the rocking chair and go inside to calm down.

Raging, I stomp around the lodge. I pick things up, put them down, clench and unclench my hands. My strop lasts half an hour. When my angst finally abates, my peace of mind, much like my phone, is shattered.

'I could kill you!' I roar at the picture turned against the wall above the mantelpiece. 'Leave me alone, slimy *bastard*!'

A quarter of an hour later, shattered and emotional, I crawl into bed. Not having the energy to undress, I curl into the foetal position and cry myself to sleep.

Dream demons haunt my fitful sleep.

I'm chained to a bed in an ink black room, enveloped by absolute silence. A door opens and stark white light floods in. The silhouette of a man stands in the opening. A bunch of flowers hang from his right hand. He raises his hand. The flowers fly and land on my face. The putrid stench of death fills my nostrils, my mouth and lungs. Suffocating, I scrabble at the flowers. Hidden amongst the blooms is a slab of maggoty meat. I cast the blooms away. My lungs scream for oxygen...

Choking, I bolt upright, sit and sway. On the floor beside the bed, Bella stirs. I reach down and stroke the top of her head.

The nightmare passes.

Laying back, I suck long breaths. After a minute, my breathing normalises, my pounding heart slows and I feel myself drifting off.

CHAPTER TWENTY

Day 9

I'm burning up. I grab the duvet and pitch it onto the floor. I'm blinded by diagonal shafts of golden sunlight blasting in through the open window. I cover my eyes and the remnants of my dreams float off and join the dust motes. Dull thuds echo around the bedroom. The walls vibrate. Coming to, I decide it must be the window shutters flapping against the reveals in the breeze. Removing my hand, I direct a vacant stare at the ceiling. The ceiling fan is static.

I've no energy. My dehydrated brain throbs in time with the shutters and I breathe deep, raspy breaths. The motivation to go downstairs for a drink eludes me. Laying there, I feel the metronome tick of the shutters in my chest. Recovering the duvet, I pull it over my head. Within minutes, the heavy hand of sleep drags my eyelids down.

The day passes in a blur of fitful semi-consciousness. I sleep. Wake. Sleep.

Coming to, I realise it's dark outside.

What time is it?

The smatter of rain against the glass displaces the shutters dull thuds. The air is cooler, fresher. I run my fingers over parched lips.

I promised myself something to drink, hours ago. Didn't I?

Beyond the window, an owl screeches.

It must be night. Where did the day go? How long have I been asleep?

Untangling my legs from the duvet, I crawl out of bed and make my way to the bathroom. There, I run the tap until it's cold and hook my mouth around it. Shooting pains rocket through my temples and I press the heel of my hand against my forehead. My father used to call it brain freeze. It always happened when I wolfed down ice cream. Haunted eyes stare back at me from the mirror. Black mascara smudges my cheeks. A manic pterodactyl has battled with my hair. I'm naked. A mess. I can't remember undressing.

What happened?

The door into my memory palace screeches open, and the memory of Christian's text message walks in beaming like an arrogant prince.

I mustn't let the bastard drag me down.

Removing the mascara with a wetted tissue, I wash my face. The cold makes me shiver, brings me around. I slip on a bathrobe, pad over and close the shutters. Rain puddles on the floor under the window.

Damn it!

Grabbing towels from the airing cupboard, I mop the floor and dump the soaking mass into the shower cubicle. Returning to the bedroom, I step over to the window and close the shutter. As I do so, I glimpse a faint orange light hovering above the end of the causeway. It's enough to stop me in my tracks. Leaning across the windowsill, I press my nose against the glass and see the dark outlines of the causeway, foreshore and castle.

Is my mind playing tricks on me?

Exhaling a sigh, I pull the shutters closed.

In the kitchen, I flick the switch on the kettle and settle my weight against the worktop. Images of my phone smashing against the veranda deck and Christian's text message bounce around my head.

I've let him get the better of me. Allowed him in.

I need a decent coffee. I drag the coffeepot from the cupboard, add coffee and water, settle it on the hob and light the gas. Huffing, I make my way upstairs to my writing den and switch on my laptop.

The laptop confirms the time as 10:42 p.m. I've been out of it for over twenty-four hours.

I'm annoyed and angry. I've let myself down.

'This is mad,' I say aloud.

Don't they say talking to oneself is the first sign of madness?

I shake my head in disbelief.

The sharp pungency of coffee breaks the spell and I return downstairs.

Settling my shoulder against the kitchen door jamb, I take a first tentative sip of coffee. Five minutes later, the caffeine hit has permeated every nerve ending and I feel human again. I also feel annoyed with myself and not a little stupid.

Why did I allow one text message to provoke such an extreme reaction?

Life is challenging enough, without getting hysterical. I've lost an entire day because of him. I'm losing it.

Never again, Christian Moran. Never again!

Rolling my shoulders, I feel the tension in my muscles dissolve. Cranking my neck, my spine creaks and cracks and a surge of oxygen reaches my befuddled brain.

Where's Bella? I wonder.

I call without reply. The front door is slightly ajar.

I'm sure I closed it on the latch last night?

Dashing to the door, I fling it open and step outside.

'Bella! Bella!' I call into the darkness.

Where the hell is she?

I cup my hands into the shape of a megaphone. 'Bella!'

Where is she? Idiot. I reprimand myself. *You left the door open. She's your responsibility. This is your fault.*

Glancing right towards the causeway, I see the top of Bella's head bobbing above tall grass. She pushes through the gate, tail swishing on the ground, floppy tongue lolling from her mouth. She bounds along the path. I bend down to greet her, and she nuzzles her rain-soaked face into my lap.

'I'm sorry little one. Silly me, left the door open. You must be starving? Supper time?'

Closing the door, I dry her off with a towel, replenish her bowls with fresh kibbles and water. She turns her nose up at supper and pads upstairs.

'I know. It's been a funny day. I'm not hungry either,' I say after her.

Since I've slept all day, and I'm wired on caffeine, I'm not ready to turn in just yet. My imagination continues to fire on all cylinders, so I might as well get some writing done.

Once upstairs, I settle into the chair, awaken my laptop, pull the hair from my face and reach for the hairgrip. I scan the desk. It's not there. Pushing back in the chair, I scan the floor at my feet. Nothing.

Where the hell did I put it?

I tell myself I've misplaced it and not to dwell on it. Shrugging, I tuck my hair behind my ears, crack my fingers and start typing.

To my relief, the words flow. The word count rises. After two hours, I've written two thousand words and I've shaken off the torpor of the last twenty-four hours. I'm doing what I do best; I'm in the 'zone.'

At 03:00 a.m. I press, 'SAVE.' Rising, I turn off the light and make my way to the bathroom. There, I brush my teeth, wash and undress. Dragging the bathroom door closed behind me, I make my way to the bedroom and crawl into bed. Snuggling beneath the duvet, I hear rain pelting against the slates.

I drift off to sleep.

CHAPTER TWENTY-ONE

Day 10

I wake, slip out of bed and lurch to the window. The rain has moved on and imbued the air with a newfound crispness. White clouds dapple an astral-blue sky. Jet contrails divide the stratosphere into neat triangles. It's a beautiful morning and I fully intend to make the most of it.

With plenty of time before high tide, I rustle up a cooked breakfast of scrambled eggs, bacon and toast. It satisfies the pangs of hunger ripping at my guts. I can't remember my last proper meal.

After breakfast, I give myself permission to relax before the drive into Portree to get my phone repaired. Though it's an inconvenience of my own making, it's also an excuse to get away. It's ten days since I arrived on Scalaig, in the middle of the night, tired but with a sense of freedom and adventure coursing through my veins. Scalaig is starting to feel claustrophobic. I'm going stir crazy. My imagination is running wild.

Take a chill pill, Erin. I tell myself.

Throwing the bedroom window open, I lean outside and inhale. In my head, Sheryl Crow reminds me that a change will do me good. It's decided. I won't delay a moment longer. A couple of hours R & R in Portree is exactly the distraction I need. I might even grab a pub lunch. Do some shopping. Treat myself.

Spinning from the window, I set off for the kitchen.

After loading the dishwasher, I collect the components of my shattered phone and seal them in a food bag. Collecting my car keys and handbag, I tell Bella that I'll be home in time for dinner and drag the door closed on the latch. Having checked nobody is watching, I place the key under the plant pot and make a mental note to add a new plant to my shopping list.

Given I've plenty of time, I stroll across the causeway. Half way across, studying every square inch of the rock, I notice chisel marks where my pioneering predecessors worked the surface. It fires my imagination.

Christian researched Scalaig's history to the far end of a fart. One snowy winter evening, snuggled up in front of a towering log fire, he regaled me with rumours of a labyrinth of tunnels under the island used by smugglers and as a lookout against the English. Another time, he described how three women had disappeared within a five-mile radius of Scalaig, a decade ago. The latest – a teenage backpacker from Yorkshire – had disappeared in the early noughties after becoming separated from her boyfriend. She was last seen crossing the causeway towards Scalaig. It was the stuff of folklore. Christian appeared to get a kick out of scaring me.

'You scumbag, Christian Moran.' I growl, remembering his macabre expression.

At the top of the wooden steps, I see the Range Rover. Leaning right, I look to the castle. Nothing stirs. There's still zero evidence of occupation. I feel a sense of relief. A second later, I feel a frisson of annoyance at my indifference.

What's wrong with you, woman? Don't you like social interaction?

Blipping the locks, I swing into the driver's seat, ditch my handbag on the passenger seat and pull on the seatbelt. I spin the key and hear staccato clicks. I turn the key again. The starter clicks, grinds and expires to silence. I turn the key. Nothing.

I don't need this. What the hell is wrong with it? Why won't it start?

'Don't panic. The engine will be cold. Battery low,' I say, to my reflection returned in the rearview mirror.

Give it a minute. Try again.

A minute passes. I spin the key, again. Still nothing. I bash the steering wheel with my palms. Gripped by frustration and despair, the steering wheel bashing lasts a long minute.

Now, what am I supposed to do?

A bearded face appears at the door. The face twists and the crease between his eyes deepens. Startled, I shrink back and cover my face with my hands. My heart performs somersaults. Through the gaps between my fingers, I realise I'm looking at Callum Cleland.

A twirled hand suggests he wants me to drop the window. Dragging on the switch, the motor whirls, the glass falls two inches and judders to a halt as the power fails.

'Stop doing that!'

'Doing what?'

He doesn't know.

'Sneaking up on me. It's unnerving.'

'I'm sorry, Mrs Moran. Are you having trouble?'

He doesn't seem to comprehend how disconcerting creeping up on people, is.

'Yes,' I snap, biting my bottom lip to prevent it sticking out like a petulant child. 'Damn thing won't start.'

'I can take a look if you like?' he says, with a thin smile. 'I like to tinker.'

I'm being a bitch. It's not his fault.

'I really don't mind,' he adds, smile widening.

'Thank you. I'd appreciate it,' I say. I need help and there's nobody else.

Cut the guy some slack. I tell myself.

'Pop the bonnet,' he says. 'Don't touch the ignition until I say so.'

He rounds the bonnet and rests his hands on his hips. It endows him with an air of authority. I release the bonnet pull. He lifts and props the bonnet open on the stay. Appearing at the edge of the bonnet, he makes a spinning gesture with his left hand. The starter motor whirls and clicks, but the engine refuses to start. Callum disappears from view under the bonnet. Two minutes pass. He reappears, drops the bonnet and returns to the driver's side door, all the while running a hand over his chin. His close-trimmed beard scratches against his palm. He takes a sharp intake of breath, exhales through his nose. It's what men do when they're about to deliver unwelcome news to women about something mechanical.

'Is it terminal?' I ask, playing my part in the gender stereotype game.

'I reckon the starter motor's bust.'

It does nothing to stem my anxiety. I slip out of the car beside him. Realise he towers over me. He must be six-three if he's an inch. Maybe more?

'Damn it. I needed to go into Portree, today. I've errands to run. Any idea where I can get it repaired?'

His shoulders rise and fall. 'No garage in Scaloon, I'm afraid. Last place closed down a year back. There's too much competition from cheaper places in Portree, and on the mainland.'

'What about a recovery truck?' I need solutions, not obstacles.

'I'm afraid not. There'll be one in Portree, though. They've most things there.'

Breathe, Erin... Breathe...

'I don't mind having a go at fixing it. Two days and I'll have a new motor. I've had a good look, access isn't a problem. There's plenty of space,' he says. 'It's more or less a straightforward swap out.'

At last, he's giving me solutions, not problems. Anxiety steps aside and relief enters.

'Could you?' I must sound desperate and vulnerable. Taking half a step back, I stand tall. I'm trying to make myself bigger beside this skyscraper of a man; hoping to recover a semblance of dignity.

Christian is tall, but this guy...

'I can. It's no bother.'

'That would be great. Thank you. Of course, I'll pay you for your trouble, time and parts.'

'Parts, yes. Time and trouble, not necessary. Leave it with me. When the parts arrive, I'll drop by the lodge,' he says, earnestly. He holds his hand out. I drop the keys into his upturned palm, collect my handbag from the passenger seat and slam the door. Callum blips the locks.

He's handsome and possesses an air of mysterious intensity.

Turn down the romance author, Erin. I tell myself.

'Can I use your phone? Like a moron, I dropped mine. I was going to drive into Portree to get it fixed. I need to text someone. Let them know I'm going to be out of contact for a while,' I say.

'I don't have one,' he says, shrugging. 'I don't like, or use, modern technology.'

'That's a joke. Right?'

Who doesn't have a phone?

'No. I've absolutely no need for one. I'll get the starter fixed as soon as I can,' he says, steering his gaze past my left shoulder towards Scalaig.

I can't decide whether he's preoccupied or bored?

'That's very kind of you, thank you. I'll wait to hear from you,' I say, hoisting my handbag onto my shoulder. 'I'd better be getting back. The tide's turning.'

'It is. I'll bid you a good day and hope to see you around, Mrs Moran.'

'It's Erin. My name is Erin.'

'See you later … *Erin*,' he says with emphasis, turning to leave.

Damn it.

Resigned to defeat, my shoulders droop. I can't do anything about the car or phone, today. I have to get a grip, get over it, and accept I'm going to be out of touch with everyone a little longer. On the plus side, it'll keep me focused on writing and provide a brief respite from Christian and his annoying texts. Olivia won't be unduly concerned. She's used to me and my writing habits. She understands that once I'm in the zone, days turn to weeks and weeks to months. She appreciates my life enters a repeat cycle of writing, drinking coffee, sleeping, eating and walking Bella. Everything else becomes secondary to my core goal of finishing a novel. Christian never understood. Olivia *gets* me.

Arriving at the lodge, I find Bella sitting behind the door polishing the wooden floor with her bushy tail.

'We're marooned,' I say tickling her ears. Expecting a walk, she stands by the door. 'I'll work for a couple of hours, then we'll go for a walk on the beach, promise.' Bella, cocking her head on one side, makes sad eyes at me.

I've convinced myself she understands my every utterance. I resolve to write for a couple of hours before going for a walk. It's a goal of sorts.

Sensing she isn't going anywhere soon, Bella woofs, ambles past, slumps onto the veranda and settles her jaw along her paws. I imagine she's sulking.

She's funny.

I stand in the door opening, wiping sweat from my forehead. Humidity claws at my skin. The midday sun has evaporated puddles from the cobbles and dew from the foliage. Heat haze shimmers in the air. Sweat trickles down my back and tickles the base of my spine. I'm dressed for a trip to the city in tight blue jeans, chambray shirt and black ballet slippers.

This won't do. I need to change out of these clothes, they're too restrictive.

Satiating a raging thirst, I sink half a pint of water in a single gulp. After a shower, I change into shorts and t-shirt. I feel fresh and my body refuses to be still. My limbs fizz with nervous energy. I shake and loosen my hands, crack my neck, stretch my spine. Five minutes later, I stop fidgeting. I've worked myself into a lather for a trip to Portree and now I've a surplus of pent up energy clambering to escape. It dawns upon me how untidy the lodge is.

Rushing around, throwing open windows, I make the bed and fill the laundry basket with the dirty clothes discarded on the bedroom floor. 'Tidy house, tidy mind,' my mother used to say. Bundling up wet towels, I dump them into the laundry basket.

With disarray brought to order, I grab a chilled bottle of Evian from the fridge, race upstairs, settle behind the desk and fire up the laptop.

The words race from my fingers. I live my protagonist's life and put aside my own. Writing is invigorating. It elevates me from reality. The old manuscript is history. My writing is alive. I don't feel the need to refer to the story plan. I've become the female protagonist. I feel what she feels. The words dance onto the page in vivid Technicolor. The problems of the past few days fade.

Onwards and upwards...

Losing track of time – stiff from sitting – I yawn, stretch and shut down the laptop. I need fresh air. It's time to take a walk – the walk I promised Bella hours ago. I grab an apple from the bowl and water from the fridge. Sensing the walk is imminent, Bell yaps. Her claws scrabble against the floorboards as she stretches.

Stepping outside, the humidity has returned to bearable levels. Bella scuttles off towards the cove and I set off after her. We assume our designated roles of thrower and retriever. It's great fun. Haphazard clumps of wiry grass punctuate the sand. The ocean shimmers blue and silver. Just below the horizon, white sails punctuate the heat haze. Lost in the tranquility of nature, my tummy rumbles. I decide it's time to head back.

At the lodge, I feed Bella and throw a Caesar salad together for myself. We spend the evening on the veranda. I treat myself to a cool glass of chardonnay. Bella chews her latest toy. Pouring a second glass, I collect the latest *Jack Reacher* thriller from the shelving unit behind the rocking chair. I may write romance, but I like to read an eclectic mix of genres.

I read for the simple pleasure of reading.

CHAPTER TWENTY-TWO

Day 14

Refreshed after a long and undisturbed sleep, I wake before sunrise, shower, go downstairs and enjoy an espresso and scrambled eggs on toast. I plan to work all morning, enjoy a late lunch, and take a mid-afternoon walk.

Bounding upstairs, I settle behind the desk and stab the laptop to life. Having read over and edited the words I wrote yesterday, I sit and stare at a blank screen ensnared by nagging self-doubt.

Two long hours later, a blank tableau of virgin white pixels taunt me from the screen and a sense of unease fizzes in my gut.

Take a walk. Clear your head. Give yourself permission. It'll do you good. I tell myself.

I have to do *something*, or I'll sit here torturing myself over the scourge of authors everywhere: writer's block.

Stepping outside, I pause on the veranda and click my tongue against my front teeth. Needing no encouragement, Bella appears and races over, tail wagging. Passing through the gate, I turn towards the cove. Already, Bella is ten yards ahead.

Quickening my step, I massage my forehead in the hope it might provide some respite from the bass drum braying behind my forehead. The acid fizz in my gut morphs into a tangible knot of anxiety.

In time, these physiological reactions to my mental anguish will pass. They always do. I've been here before. My creative muscle needs to rest. A break from the screen is all I often need. Even though logic tells me it's true, and no matter how many times I remind myself, it scares the living daylights out of me.

Have I lost my writing mojo forever?

Whispering demons hunker on my shoulder, sowing seeds of self doubt.

Are they a portent of failure? The end of my career?

The thought pops into my head uninvited. Pursing my lips, I try hard to silence the crippling voices of self doubt.

Exiting the pines, I see the clifftop, the steps and the ocean. Bella scuttles down the steps and disappears from view. She'll be fine.

Arriving at the cliff, I draw up, close my eyes and breathe deep. A warm breeze caresses my face. Salt stings my lips. The air is redolent with drying seaweed. Bella splashes through the surf.

Reaching for the heavens, I crank my neck left and right and feel the springs of tension releasing from my shoulders. I open my eyes.

A slobbering Bella sits by the shore, drool spilling onto the sand.

My gaze fixes on a yacht anchored in the cove. Captured by the sun, it gleams.

My eyes don't lie.

Do they ever?

It's him alright.

The Storm Petrel, Christian's pride and joy dances on the swell. Hunkered down over the stern, Christian unties the launch.

What the…

In shock, I stall on the bottom step for several seconds, before launching onto the sand and marching over to the ocean. Bella, thinking it's a game, drags up and races across the sand to meet me.

Noticing my arrival, Christian waves. He reminds me of a mannequin in a Ralph Lauren shop window. His dress sense is laughable. Even from fifty yards away, his gleaming, toothy white smile, dominates his face.

'Erin, darling, ahoy,' he calls.

He thinks he's welcome. Stop press: he isn't.

'What the hell do you think you're doing?' I yell, settling joined hands on the crown of my skull. Recognising Christian's voice, Bella bounces on her hind legs. 'Sit. Girl. Sit!' I bark. The 'T' ricochets off of the rocks. Ignoring me, a yapping Bella races into the surf. Cricket ball sized clumps of foam drift into the air and land at my feet.

'I'm coming ashore. Wait there,' Christian calls.

What the f... 'No!'

'Stay there,' Christian bellows, voice dissipating on the breeze.

'Don't you dare. This is *my* island. I don't want you here.'

This can't be happening. He wouldn't dare come ashore. Would he?

Having none of it, he slips over the side and gingerly lowers himself into the launch. With a sharp pull on the outboard, he's underway. Bella is beside herself. She bounces into the surf and swims out to greet him. I stand on the shore, heart turning somersaults. The launch enters the shallows. Christian, ignoring me, drops anchor. He's wound up the bottom of his shorts, shirt sleeves turned up to the elbows. Hopping out of the launch, he wades ashore. Five steps later, he's reached Bella. He bends down, grabs her collar and strokes the top of her head. Celebrating her master's return, she yaps and licks his cheek. Releasing her, standing tall, his eyes meet mine. Just a metre separate us. The fluidity of his movement, his vacant expression and the hunch of his shoulders, tells me he's been drinking. Throwing his arms wide, he pushes through the surf towards me.

No, you don't...

'I've missed you.'

Stepping back, I say, 'You're trespassing.' I pray my glower spits sufficient venom that he gets the message, turns and leaves, without creating a scene.

He stalls in the shallows. 'You've ignored my texts. Why?'

'Woman's prerogative. I don't answer to you.'

The breakers smash around his ankles. He sways. 'While true, it doesn't mean I'm not worried about you. Scalaig is no place for a woman, alone. It's too isolated. You're – not to put too fine a point on it – vulnerable.'

'I'm fine. Turn around. Go away.'

He lunges forward with grasping hands. I stagger away, almost keel over. Notes of cigars and whisky arrive in my nostrils.

'Don't you dare touch me,' I growl, hoping to conceal the dizzying fear gripping my insides. Glimpsing a rock projecting from the sand, I commit its position to memory.

'I want to talk. There's things to discuss. Surely, you can give me two minutes?'

'There's nothing to talk about. Turn around. Get back in the launch. And go away!' I can't cope. Anger displaces fear. 'Go! Now!'

'Hear me out. You can't stay here on your own. Anything could happen. You're being ridiculous.'

The timbre of his voice suggests he's trying hard to moderate his language. His hands have settled on his hips.

'What part of go away don't you understand? I don't want you here.' I'm yelling now.

He lurches at me. I dodge his hands. 'You're not thinking straight. Look at you ... you're a mess. I'm taking you home.'

Grabbing the rock, I raise it up and feign a throw. It's enough to halt his advances; to throw him off balance. His feet slip from under him and he struggles to stay upright.

'I'm a mess because you won't leave me the fuck alone. I *am* home!' I scream.

Stepping back, he raises placatory palms.

'Eh, calm down. I won't hurt you. You're the last person I want to hurt.'

'I'm not taking that chance,' I snarl, feigning to throw the rock, again. He ducks aside. 'Get out of my sight.'

'Darling, stop! I only want to help.'

'I don't need yours, or anyone's, help. If it's all the same with you, I'll take care of myself.'

Malign acceptance settles on his face. The change in him is obvious. His expression twists into a sneer. 'Stupid bitch, you can't cope on your own. You never could, and you never will be able to. You *need* me.'

The *real* Christian surfaces.

'Need you? I need you like I need a hole in the fucking head.' Spittle courses over my chin. My heart rattles against my ribs. I raise the rock. 'Piss off!'

His shoulders raise into a shrug. 'Look at you. You've let yourself go.'

There's no love. *Was there ever?* Balling and releasing my fists, I explode. 'You total bastard. You've brought other women here to our special place.' There, it's said. I've uncaged and given the accusation wings. I didn't want him to know that I knew, but, eh, it's done. 'You abused my trust. The trust *I* placed in *you*.'

'What? Are you out of your mind?' He tries for innocence, eyelids batting. In hindsight, he's always been a terrible liar.

'Alasdair Barr told me.' I have to calm down. I've involved someone else in our argument, without good reason.

Damn.

'Oh my God, now I get it. You actually believe him!' Laughing, his head rocks back and forth like a Jolly Jack in a glass case at a Victorian amusement arcade. A piggy snort sneaks out. His cheeks flush red with anger. 'Barr is a weirdo.'

'What are you talking about?'

'Ask him about his collection of VHS tapes – the ones he keeps in the back room. A year ago, I went to the shop, and he wasn't there. No one heard me enter. I saw him through a gap in the curtain. His face was almost touching the screen. It was obvious he was watching porn. I cleared my throat to get his attention. He wasn't best pleased when he knew I'd seen him. He's been strange with me ever since.'

'You're lying.'

'Nope. I'm telling you the truth for your own good. You've never been a good judge of character. You need me to protect you from sickos like Barr, and his simpleton son, Rory.'

I hear his words, but won't allow them to register. The master manipulator plies his trade. 'Shut up. I don't need you. I've never needed you. Stop stalking me.' Bella cowers at my heel.

'I'm *not* stalking you. You're out of your tiny mind. You're psychotic.'

'Go! Now!' I yell, feigning to launch the rock again. 'I mean it. This is your last chance,' I say, surprised when my words come out several octaves higher than intended.

He comes at me right arm swinging, but stalls it at the last moment. He's never struck me before. A resigned frown settles between rheumy eyes. 'Don't worry, I'm leaving. What do I want with a psycho like you, anyway? You're a fucking liability.' Turning, he stomps through the waves to the launch, spins it around on the swell and climbs aboard. Four angry tugs, and the outboard motor roars to life.

Hunkering down, I console Bella by tickling her behind the ears and stare at my departing husband.

Arriving at *The Storm Petrel,* he clambers aboard, ties the launch off and stomps to the stern. With the anchor secured, he steps over to the helm. Seconds later, the engine stutters to life and black smoke belches from the exhaust.

Slumping onto the sand by the boulder, I sit with my back against the cool stone.

That was scary.

I sit, trying hard to quiet my broken heart. Tears bubble in the corners of my eyes. I've always known Christian had an edge, an acute sense of entitlement and legendary arrogance, but what he did just then, the way he spoke to me, was unsettling. His ego has served him well in business. He's a ruthless negotiator, a respected entrepreneur and a success in the truest sense of the word. Today, I witnessed another side of his character. Today, I saw pure evil.

I check myself. *Am I overreacting?* The rational explanation is, he's a boy trapped inside the body of a man. A toddler who throws his teddy out of the pram, when things don't go his way. He's having a tantrum. I don't care. His tantrums can last several lifetimes.

I'm doing what I always do, I'm making excuses for him.

I find it astonishing that he has the arrogance to travel to Scalaig and expect me to swoon over him, swallow his crap and fall into his arms.

Does he have an iota of respect for me? Did he ever? Why was I so gullible?

I recall finding a lipstick-stained wine glass on *The Storm Petrel.* He explained it away by suggesting the lipstick belonged to the wife of a business associate.

Yeah, right…

Or the time he rejected an incoming phone call from 'SHURN'. He lied through his back teeth about that one. Insisted it was a Sean Hurn, a business associate from Ireland. He forgot his lie when, a week later, we bumped into a beautiful brunette in a coffee shop. He introduced her as Susan Hurn, a client. She couldn't take her eyes off of him; looked down her plasticised nose at me. Christian ogled her voluminous faux tits the whole time.

The scumbag never once apologised for his behaviour. Come to think of it, I can't remember a single occasion when the word, 'sorry,' has ever passed his lips...

'Get used to the idea that I'm not one of your chattels, Christian Moran,' I shout at the distant white dot ploughing across the ocean towards the horizon.

Rising from the sand, I wipe snot and tears from my face and yearn for the sanctuary of Scalaig Lodge.

CHAPTER TWENTY-THREE

Bella selects her favourite spot by the rocking chair. I hope the events of the last hour have evaporated from her memory. Christian's display of arrogance and acute sense of entitlement preys heavily on my mind.

Somehow, I have to stop him from coming anywhere near me and Scalaig.

Is stalking too strong a word?

I'll call my solicitor. Insist, he meets with Christian for an informal discussion. If Christian tells him to do one, then I'll have no option but to instruct him to seek a restraining order. I need a phone that works. And for that, I need transport. I need the Range Rover operational.

This is ridiculous.

I check the time. There's only two hours until high tide.

By now, Callum ought to have completed the repair?

'Back soon, Bella,' I say, taking her inside, whispering in her ear. 'It's high time I asserted some authority around here.'

***

From the causeway, I see the reflected sun glinting from the roof of the Range Rover. It hasn't moved an inch since I arrived.

Inside my head, a steam of anger dissolves any hope of rational thought.

I quicken my step.

Finding the driver's door unlocked, I slip inside and flick the bonnet release. Raising the bonnet, I don't have a clue what I'm looking at. To my untrained eye, everything appears untouched. An unbroken layer of dust covers the engine and ancillary components. Finger and palm prints are notably absent.

Straightening, I drop the bonnet.

'Callum?' I call without reply.

Where the hell is he?

Turning for the castle, I stomp up the path and rap on the door. It's enough to wake the dead. A minute later, frustrated, I plant my hands on my hips and take a moment to compose myself.

What next? The keyhole.

Shielding my eyes with my right hand, I peer through the keyhole and see the stone slabbed floor, an ornate vaulted ceiling and plastered walls of a dark and narrow hallway. Antlered heads sit between faux candlelight fittings. Through the gloom, I recognise a Queen Anne table. A shiny pair of black men's leather brogues sit beneath the table. A mahogany grandfather clock stands opposite. I could be staring at a set from a sixties Hammer gothic horror movie.

'Callum,' I call through the keyhole. 'You there?'

Nothing stirs. The only sound is the metronomic ticking of the grandfather clock.

Rising, I step left to a window. Burgundy dralon curtains meet my enquiring eyes.

It's conceivable he's in the back garden, reading or sunbathing?

Rounding the corner, I see a mess of overgrown shrubs, brambles and knee-high weeds where once there had been a lawn.

Along the left side of the garden, a vegetable patch has gone to seed. Rusty tools sit inside an abandoned wheelbarrow in the centre of an overgrown path. I imagine Isla Cleland spinning in her grave.

No sign at all of Callum.

I stall, racking my brain.

What next? Will Alasdair Barr have any idea where I might find the elusive Callum Cleland?

CHAPTER TWENTY-FOUR

I find Alasdair sweeping the pavement outside the shop. Above him, red neon flickers and an electronic wasp buzzes. It's time Alasdair did something about it, but he seems oblivious to it. I couldn't cope. It would send me insane listening and watching it every day.

Sensing movement, Alasdair glances in my direction, turns, props the broom against the wall beside the door and folds his arms across his chest. A wide smile suggests he's pleased to see me – a potential customer. I'm sure I see pound signs flash behind his glasses.

'Mrs Moran, so nice to see you. Did you bring a list?' Beaming, he goes straight for the jugular. I'm drawn to the gap between his front teeth. It grabs my attention like a brick missing from a wall. Alasdair wipes both hands down the front of his smock.

'Alasdair, it's Erin. My christian name is Erin.'

'That's right,' he says. 'Erin…'

I'm going to give up. It's obvious he doesn't *do* informal.

'You haven't by any chance seen Callum Cleland, have you?'

'Callum?' he says, brow creasing. 'I can't say that I have. It must be the best part of a year since I've laid eyes on him. I can't be sure. He doesn't come into town very often.'

'Any idea where I might find him?'

Alasdair shrugs noncommittally. 'I suppose he might have gone fishing. Callum prefers solitary pursuits.'

Pulling teeth would be easier.

'The thing is, Callum promised to repair my car. Sod's law being what it is, damn thing's just out of warranty,' I say.

Folding my arms across my chest, I roll my eyes to the heavens and exhale a sigh a teenager would be proud of.

'Are you alright, Mrs Moran? You seem fed up.'

'Is it that obvious?' I've let my guard down. I might as well confide in him. 'My phone has died on me. The Range Rover's starter motor is bust. Callum offered to repair it, so I could get to Portree to sort out my phone.' Realising I'm babbling, I slow down. 'I can't for the life of me, find him.'

'I expect he's gone over to the mainland to source a new starter motor. There's no motor factor on Skye. There's no mystery to it,' he says, seemingly pleased with his explanation.

'Of course… I'm sorry, Alasdair. I'm overreacting. It's only a phone.' A chuckle escapes my lips.

'If I were you, I'd wean yourself off of technology. I expect getting away from technology is the reason city folk come here in the first place.' It's a statement, not a question.

Alasdair is right. I ought to uncouple myself from my reliance on social media, electronic gizmos and phones. 'You're right,' I say.

Alasdair smiles a lizard smile. 'Sermon over. Shall we get down to business? What can I do for you? I've got new-laid eggs and fresh baked bread. It fair melts in the mouth, it does.'

And that's, that. The conversation moves on. The greatest salesman is back on point.

'I don't need anything, Alasdair.'

His expression would suggest I've kneed him in the groin.

'I'd better get back before the tide turns. Any chance Callum will pop in?' I blurt.

'No. None. You won't ever find him here.'

My nerves jangle. 'What do you mean?'

'Don't mean nothing. Callum Cleland takes his business elsewhere, which is fine with me. I'm saying no more on the subject.'

'I see. Sorry. I didn't mean to pry,' I say, cheeks flushing.

'Look. Mrs Moran. Truth is…' Alasdair's words skid to a halt in his throat. When he speaks again, his voice is lower, calmer, more measured. 'Callum Cleland's not welcome here. In the past, he's had run-ins with Rory. It's easier all round if he stays away. Don't think I'm talking out of school, because I'm not. I've told him to his face.'

Alasdair steers his gaze past me. I turn and see Rory Barr approaching. The carcass of a bloodied, white-tailed deer hangs over his right shoulder. The deer's lifeless coal-black eyes address the tarmac. Rory, head down, strides past heading in the direction of the stone barn behind the shop. Passing, he waves with a free hand. I can't be sure whether he's acknowledging Alasdair or me. Arriving at the barn, he disappears inside.

'He's been hunting. There'll be venison available once it's hung,' Alasdair says.

'I'll remember that.' I won't allow him to deter me. 'Hope you don't mind me asking, only, what kind of run-in with Callum did Rory have?' I ask, curiosity getting the better of me. Alasdair's lips tighten, then flatten. Whenever I mention Callum Cleland, he seems circumspect. I've entrusted Callum with the repair of my car. I need to understand what kind of person I'm dealing with.

'It concerned hunting rights,' Alasdair says, flatly. 'Not that there are any around these parts, mind. Callum seems to think there are, but there aren't.' His crabby inflection suggests he's keen on closing down my line of questioning. 'Since you've not brought a list, then why don't I put together a box of fresh produce? I'll pop in one of Dorothy's homemade cakes. There's no charge for that. I'll send it over later.' It's another statement.

'Thank you, Alasdair. That would be lovely. I'd better be getting back.' There's no point arguing. Once again, the greatest salesman is victorious.

I can't deny his superlative business acumen. He inspects me over thin-rimmed glasses. The edges of his mouth lift into a reassuring smile and he settles a hand on my shoulder.

'Don't worry about Callum and Rory. I think of the acrimony between them as young bucks tangling antlers. In any small town, there's bound to be a pecking order. My Rory, he doesn't have much in the way of emotional intelligence. There's no harm in him, though. He can be a little slow on the uptake, sometimes.'

The compassion in his voice stirs something in me. I swallow embryonic tears. Christian, too, in my opinion, scores low in terms of emotional intelligence. I shouldn't burden Alasdair with my problems.

'I'm sorry. Like I say, I'm probably overreacting. It's been quite a morning.'

'Don't you let that Cleland boy upset you, young lady. He isn't worth it.'

'Believe me, it's not Callum's fault. This morning, I sent my husband packing. There was a scene. I'll be fine. I promise.'

Why did I mention it? Damn! Sometimes I have a gob on me like The Mersey Tunnel.

'You're well shot of him. You're too good for him. Mark my words, he's not worthy,' Alasdair says, with conviction. Mindful he may have crossed a line, he adds, 'I won't say another word on the subject. It's not my place. Now off you go.' His benevolent smile exposes the gap in his teeth. His candour is disturbing. I can't bring myself to press him any further. It's all too much.

Alasdair waves me off from the door.

* * *

I arrive at the causeway as the rising tide slips over the rocks. Rushing across with my head down, I take extra care not to slip. If I were to trip and fall headlong onto the pockmarked rocks, it could prove fatal.

Alighting onto Scalaig, I turn and watch the causeway disappear under the ocean. Seawater fills the rock pools at my feet. The sun is at its zenith. Entering the woods, sun and shade dapples the footpath. I step out of the pines and see the lodge. The sun is hot against my face. Already, it's too hot to work. Besides, a dull throb sits where my brain ought to be.

I need to lie down.

It's been one hell of a day. I've been tetchy. Anxious. Guilty of blowing things out of proportion.

Bella follows me inside and I fill her dishes. Slurping water, she turns her nose up at the dry dog food. Thirst quenched, she pads over and flops onto the dog bed, curls up and exhales a doggy sigh. She isn't eating. *Is it too hot?* I don't want to cajole her; she'll eat when she's good and ready. Dehydrated, I slug water from the tap. The moment the cool water enters my stomach, the throbbing behind my temples subsides.

Flopping onto the sofa in the den, I start yoga breathing. I draw deep breaths in through my nose and out through my mouth and try hard to banish the incident with Christian from my mind. I don't want to think about it, *or him*, anymore.

My body and mind demand sleep. An hour in bed should be enough to shake off my torpor. Refreshed, I'll endeavour to get some writing done.

CHAPTER TWENTY-FIVE

Waking, I glance at the alarm clock. It's 10:30 p.m. and I've slept for eight hours. I keep doing this: either sleeping at the wrong time, not getting enough sleep, or sleeping for far too long. Settling against the high stack of pillows, I yawn, stretch and swing my legs out of bed. Rubbing the sleep from my eyes, I stagger into the ensuite, slip out of my clothes and step into the shower. I spin the dial to maximum cold, drag out the lever and step forward. Spears of icy liquid sting my skin. Shivering, I plunge the lever forward and the deluge ceases. Deciding that a cold shower was too ambitious, I spin the dial into the red section and wait for the water to warm up.

An hour later, I'm at my writing desk picking muesli from my teeth.

* * *

Three hours later, I pause with my fingers levitating over the keyboard and check the word count. Two thousand meaningful words has put a smile on my face. It's enough. I can't go on. Pressing SAVE, I sit back and massage my eyeballs.

I've reached Chapter Ten – less than a quarter of the way through the novel – and I'm happy with progress. I've put Christian's antics to the back of my mind. I've not let him destroy my creativity. It's a major coup. I'm rallying, feeling stronger.

Tomorrow, I'll swim from the beach. I've missed the buzz of endorphins releasing. They power my imagination and improve my writing. Shutting myself away is toxic. Seclusion doesn't help when you're trying to breathe life into characters and stories. I shouldn't generalise, but that's how it is for me. Writing is best done on park benches, library booths and coffee shops, or after exercise. The hustle and bustle of people going about daily routines corrals my thoughts. I love the din. Voices feed dialogue and become the catalyst for new ideas, twists and turns. I'm starting to realise it's too quiet around here, and, as such, it's bad for my mental health, and does nothing for my writing.

Something has got to change. 'I need to change things up,' I say to my reflection returned in the dresser mirror as I roll into bed and switch off the bedside lamp.

CHAPTER TWENTY-SIX

Day 17

I stand on the veranda and the shimmering blue ocean calls my name.

Who am I to resist?

Reaching inside, I collect a pair of swim goggles from the hook and drag the door closed on the latch.

Arriving at the cove, I slip out of shorts, t-shirt and flip-flops and race over to the water's edge. I stand gazing out across the ocean. Soft fur brushes my left calf, dark excited eyes meet mine.

'I'm going in. You?' I ask Bella.

Bella throws herself into the surf. Watching her frolic in the shallows, I laugh out loud. Turning, she paddles towards the open ocean. A minute later, sensing she's in too deep, she turns back to shore.

'Wait for me,' I call, adjusting the goggles, diving headlong into the surf.

Five long strokes, struggling to get my breath, surprised how cold the water is, I turn to join Bella in the shallows. The water is invigorating, numbing. Bella paddles hard against the current. Some dogs are swimmers. Bella is a paddler.

Skipping through the surf, I squeal like an excited toddler. With sand replacing ocean under the soles of my feet, I swing onto the beach, lay back and let the heat of the sun warm me.

Memories seep into my consciousness.

Three years ago, I swam most days from this cove with Christian. We'd fool around in the shallows. Joining in the fun, Bella chased sticks and balls. We'd run races to the timber jetty at the far western end of the cove. A cackling Christian rugby tackled me to the ground if ever it looked like I was going to be victorious. His superior height and strength advantage would always win out. He could beat me on the track, but I'm a powerful swimmer and competitive. I always gave him a good race. He's the epitome of a poor loser.

I'm doing it again, romancing my failed marriage. I must cleanse Christian from my mind and soul.

Dragging up from the sand, I enter the shallows on tiptoes. Jagged shells rag at my feet. Smooth pebbles slide from under me. I shuffle forward until the water reaches my hips. Low breakers take my breath. Foam licks my stomach. Shuffling forward, I skim the surface with flattened palms and slip delicately into the ocean. At first, with tentative breaststrokes, I swim in a slow controlled rhythm taking shallow breaths and add speed with each stroke. The swell sweeps me along. The water is ice-cold, yet the air is charged with the heat of the sun. Every second stroke I tilt my face out of the ocean and suck air. Salt water washes over my face, tickles my nostrils and stings my skin. Hot pulses of adrenalin course through my veins.

I've never felt so alive.

In my path, sea vegetables shimmer and refract sunlight. As if racing an unseen opponent, I quicken my pace. The briny ocean supports and injects me with strength. Halfway towards the jetty, catching a lungful of air, I'm blinded by sparkling diamonds of sunlight refracted from the undulating surface. Emeralds and rubies scintillate against a blood red baize on the back of my eyelids.

Closing on the jetty, I reach out and touch the barnacle-encrusted timbers with my fingertips. Reaching my goal, I punch the air with a clenched fist. My chest heaves frantically from the exertion, but I don't care. It's a personal victory. The first of many, or so I like to think.

I stall, treading water, enjoying the burning sensation deep in my lungs.

Two minutes later, feeling calmer, I'm recovered enough to swim back to the cove and the beach. Bella lounges in the shade under the boulder at the centre of the cove. Pushing off on the timber pylon, I take long easy strokes. I'm lost in the joy of swimming. Salt tingles my lips. Currents eddy and fizz between my toes and thighs.

Twenty feet from the beach, clammy fingers grab my right ankle and drag me under. In seconds, ice-cold ocean fills my nose and mouth. Coughing and spluttering, trying to keep my head above water, I thrash wildly. My left big toe grazes the seabed and a bomb of pain detonates in my head. I feel the seabed under the soles of my feet. I've made it to the shallows. At last, able to stand, I shake off the hand. Its grip loosens, though doesn't fully release. Losing my balance, I fall headlong into the ocean with a splash. Greasy fingers envelope my ankle, pulling me back. I kick out, and the hand releases.

Glancing over my shoulder, I see a sinewy arm of kelp float to the surface and realise I'd caught my foot on it.

Bella – joining the splashing game – snatches the kelp in her jaws and, as the salty mess assails her taste buds, she spits it out. Relieved and embarrassed, I launch from the ocean onto the sand, laughing manically at my stupidity.

What did Christian call me? A scaredy cat?

Soaking wet, Bella nuzzles against me. I sit up, stroking her wet head. 'Aren't I the dumb blonde,' I say, rolling her over, holding her down, play fighting in the warm sand. Bella, tiring of the game, bounds away. I laugh so hard that my ribs ache.

Cold and wet, Bella flops onto the sand beside the rock. I lay back soaking up the mid-morning sun. Several more mornings like this, and I'll catch myself a tan.

I spend the next hour sunbathing. It's adios to peaky, unhealthy looking me, and hello to healthy, sun-kissed, me.

Lifting from the sand, brushing myself down, I pull on shorts and a t-shirt. Shuffling on flip-flops, I'm about to turn and leave, when I glimpse what looks like a cobble in the centre of the rocky inlet beyond the jetty. Narrowing my eyes against the shimmer of the heat haze, I decide it's a fishing cobble. A person hovers in the stern. Above him, a dark object rises through the air and splashes into the ocean. The fisherman – if that's what he is – disappears into the wheelhouse. I think I'm watching a lobsterman laying pots, but it's impossible to be sure through the haze.

Calling for Bella to 'come,' I set off for the steps.

Arriving on the top step, I halt and turn to check on the cobble. It's gone, yet only a couple of minutes have elapsed. I check again. Nothing. The inlet is empty.

Did I imagine it? The person in the boat? The cobble? Were they a figment of my imagination? Am I going mad?

Shrugging, with hunger ripping at my guts, I set off for the lodge.

CHAPTER TWENTY-SEVEN

Swimming has improved my mood and sharpened my appetite. I make a late breakfast of bacon and scrambled eggs, add heat with dashes of tabasco.

Afterwards, I sit on the veranda enjoying the sun cooled by the delicate breeze, taste buds enlivened by the bitter tang of hot coffee and chilli. The blueness of the sky is sublime. It's a perfect day. Much too nice to work indoors.

But how? I have no desk. Since I'm a smidgeon over five feet, I struggle to work off my lap.

Then I remember the antique foldaway card table Christian brought to Scalaig one Christmas. Playing cards to while away the long, dark winter evenings represented Christian's idea of fun. So he could massage his competitive ego, more like.

He'd tried to teach me how to play poker. Texas Hold'em, he'd called it. I was a slow learner. In time, I came to understand the different hands: Royal flush, straight flush, straight and all the others in between. My 'poker face' was an epic fail. When he dealt me three of a kind – from my first five cards – I squealed, jumped around the room, and clapped like a wind-up tin monkey.

His poker face was a window to his disgust. Christian never suggested we play poker, again.

I find the table and picnic chairs tucked away behind buckets and brooms in the cupboard under the stairs. Dragging them out, I dust them down and set up a writing station on the veranda. I fetch my laptop, notebook and pencil – the one with the heart-shaped emoji eraser – from upstairs. Olivia bought the pencil from a toyshop on a whim. It makes me smile. Happy with my new workstation, I stand back and admire the fruits of my labour. As far as ad hoc writing stations go, it's perfect. Collecting water from the fridge, I sit down to write.

I've been mulling over a change of direction for my heroine for days. Somehow, I've backed her into a cul-de-sac. I have to figure out how to keep the story moving forward without ruining the plot. It mustn't feel contrived. Settling flattened palms on my lap, I stare out across the garden towards the serried ranks of pines. Thoughts ricochet around my head. Scenarios come. Scenarios go. I rule ideas in, I rule them out. The pines become a singular amorphous blur of green under my vacant stare. Closing my eyes, I breathe deep and my mind enters 'the zone.' I've lost hours, days and weeks, in 'the zone.'

Did Christian ever even notice?

My reverie is fractured by gravel crunching underfoot. I open my eyes and see Rory Barr clutching a cardboard box against his chest. His right foot is perched on the step; unblinking eyes fixed on the ground. He steps back, kicks at the ground at the edge of the path. Dust covers the bottom of his trousers.

'Rory. Hi. Nice to see you.'

'Aye,' he grunts. This three letter word appears to be his entire vocabulary.

'I see you've brought my groceries. Thank you,' I say, with a nod towards the box.

Rory moves forward and thrusts the box at me. 'Aye.'

Rising, stepping past the card table, I say, 'Would you mind carrying it into the kitchen, please?'

Eyes down, Rory steps onto the veranda. Slinking back, I open the door, settle against it and watch Rory wipe his feet on the mat. He counts as he wipes. As he counts, his mop of greasy brown hair bounces. At the count of ten, he stops wiping and counting. Ritual complete, he strides over the non-existent step at the door and follows me into the kitchen. There, he places the box on the worktop and aligns it with the edge. This time, he nails it first time. Stepping back, he dips his head and wipes his sweated brow with the back of a huge hand. For a nanosecond we make eye contact, before his gaze returns to the floor.

Conscious of the heat, I ask, 'Would you like something to drink?'

Rory peers at me through a gap in his vertical mop of hair, face twisted into a confused frown.

Does he understand the question?

'A glass of water, soft drink? Tea? What can I get for you?'

'Aye,' he says.

Taking his reply to mean he'd like a soft drink, I lift a can of lemonade from the fridge and hand it to him. He drags on the pull and drains the contents in a single gulp. Wiping his mouth with a sleeve, he smacks his lips, burps, and concludes the drama with an, 'Argh.'

An awkward quarter minute of silence passes.

'Good,' he says, returning the can.

He can speak words other than 'aye'!

Without further ado, he turns for the door. I follow him outside. There, he stalls besides the card table, causing me to pull up behind him. Hesitating, he takes an exaggerated step right, as if the table is blocking his path. It isn't. Craning his neck like a bird, he cracks his fingers, tightens and relaxes his fists. His attention remains fixed on the table.

Nonplussed, I say, 'I'm an author, Rory.' I'm not sure why, but I feel the need to explain the table and writing paraphernalia.

'Aye,' he growls, stepping off the veranda, loping off along the path, right foot lagging half a step behind him. Reaching the tree-line, he disappears into the shadows. I catch myself shaking my head in disbelief. Rory is strange. Dark possibilities rampage through my mind. Casting them aside, preferring not to dwell on them, I decide he's harmless enough.

Returning to the kitchen, I investigate the goodies Alasdair has sent. The box contains fresh eggs, cured ham, salmon fillets, salad, vegetables and the pièce de résistance, a lemon drizzle cake: baked – I can only assume – by Alasdair's long-suffering wife, Dorothy.

'This'll up the calorie count,' I inform Bella, placing the cake in the fridge. I promise myself coffee and cake later, as a reward for a good day's writing. If I don't achieve my target word count, then there'll be no cake.

It's a bargain I make with myself, that I mustn't break.

CHAPTER TWENTY-EIGHT

Moving outside, there's no sign of Bella in her bed, or on the veranda. I'm just about to call her when she trots up the path. With her tongue lolling from her mouth, she seems to smile.

'Where have you...' Surprised to see Callum following in Bella's paw prints, I fall silent. He halts, one foot on the veranda.

'I hope you don't mind, only, I gave her a doggy treat. Was that alright?' he says, fixing with intense glare.

'I suppose so...'

Ascending the steps, he stalls in front of me, with Bella at his heel.

'I saw Rory Barr. You OK?'

'Fine. Why wouldn't I be? Rory was delivering my groceries. Nothing unusual in that, is there?' I say, scowling.

'I see. Does he often do that?'

This feels like an interrogation, yet he's grinning.

'Once a week,' I say, 'or thereabouts.'

What's it got to do with you, mister?

'Rory's a poacher,' he says, grin morphing into a sneer, demeanour stiffening. 'Rory has a nasty habit of acquiring other people's things. I'd watch him, if I were you. He's untrustworthy and he has a volatile streak,' he says, frown deepening, words ejected like bullet casings from a smoking machine gun.

I shrug. 'He seems harmless enough to me.' For the second time today, I feel compelled to explain myself to someone I hardly know. 'Young men like Rory need purpose in their lives.'

'If you say so.'

'I do.'

'Just watch him,' Callum says, turning to Bella, hunkering down and tickling her behind the ears. Straightening, he returns his attention to me. 'OK?'

I shrug. *Do one fella. I can look after myself.*

Maybe it's his way of showing concern? Of looking out for a lone female neighbour? I dial down the indignation several notches to ambivalence. 'Thank you. I'll bear what you've said in mind.'

'You do that,' he says, stepping down from the veranda, setting off along the path, Bella falling in step behind him.

I tap my thigh. 'Come here, girl,' I call, irked. Whenever Christian was around, Bella always gravitated to him, too. She's a man's dog.

Reaching the end of the path, he stops, turns and settles a hand on the gate. 'I'll see you around, Mrs Moran.' He salutes and pulls the gate closed behind him.

Remembering the car, I call after him. 'Did you repair my car?' I yell, trying not to sound too desperate.

He slaps his forehead. 'Sorry, I forgot to mention... I went into Portree yesterday and ordered a replacement starter motor from the Land Rover dealership. They tested the motor. I'm afraid it's beyond economic repair.'

Damn thing's just three years old and cost me the thick end of eighty grand...

I swallow my frustration, yet a low growl escapes my lips. I don't know whether I'm more annoyed about the car needing a repair, or him forgetting to give me a progress update?

Am I invisible?

'Did they give you delivery date for the replacement motor?'

He nods. 'Two, maximum three days. Don't worry, when it's fixed it'll be as good as new.'

He appears confident. Since there's nothing I can do to speed things along, I elect calm. Me, getting angry, won't get it repaired any quicker.

'Don't worry, Mrs Moran. When it arrives, I'll get it done. Promise.'

'Erin. It's Erin,' I say, cringing at his use of the surname I've come to despise.

'That's right, Erin. Sorry.'

He's smiling like a lottery winner clutching the winning ticket. Bella pads up, tail swishing against the decking.

'Thanks. I appreciate your help. Before you go. Would you like a coffee? It's the least I can do,' I say. 'It won't take me a minute.'

'Thanks, but no thanks. I've got a lot on. Another time, perhaps?'

'OK,' I say, hiding my disappointment.

He smiles. 'See you, *Erin*. You too, Bella.' He turns, strides off and disappears along the path towards the causeway.

When he's out of earshot, I say, 'Men, Bella, are downright weird. At least, they are around here. What do you think, darling?' I say, ruffling her neck.

* * *

Needing coffee, I amble through to the kitchen where Bella joins me. Settling the coffeepot on the hob, I stare at my reflection returned on the inside face of the window and ponder Callum Cleland's words. I find myself dwelling on his accusations about Rory poaching and stealing. I recall how Alasdair Barr mentioned two 'young bucks' having had their disagreements. Perhaps the psychological scars of boyhood feuds still run deep? Why would Callum follow Rory on to Scalaig? It's not as if either of them have access rights to the island. Are there any access rights? I make a mental note to check with my solicitor.

I'm mulling over my encounter with Callum, when the coffeepot comes to the boil. With a dry tea towel, I snag the pot and place it on a trivet. Filling a mug, I remember the lemon drizzle cake.

I take my coffee and cake and retreat to the rocking chair. Relaxing against the wickerwork, picking on the cake, I realise how oppressive the air has become. I imagine a maelstrom of positive ions clashing against one another. There's a mysterious purple hue to the sky. I sense a storm brewing. I'll sit and enjoy my afternoon sojourn until it arrives. A thunderstorm will help clear the air.

Dorothy is a wonderful baker. Her cake is light and tasty. It reminds me of my mother's. Mother taught me how to bake as a child. In the school holidays, we'd batch bake cupcakes and pastries and make bottles of zesty, eye-squinting lemonade to sell to neighbours and unsuspecting passersby at a table on the pavement in front of our house. I was irresistible in pink gingham. Father would accuse mother of exploiting my Shirley Temple locks and dimples. She didn't care one iota. She wanted to bring her daughter out of her shell. 'We're making the most of your God-given talents, Erin,' she'd say, straightening my dress, fluffing my curls, winking. She coached me on how to perfect my sales pitch and how to upsell from lemonade for twenty pence, to cupcakes for fifty. It worked. By the end of the day, clutching a bulging purse, we'd sold out. The proceeds always donated to the local dog rescue centre. Happy days.

When I grew out of gingham and pigtails, and was far too self-conscious to sell cupcakes from the pavement, mother encouraged me to submit short stories to the local newspaper. My stories almost always had a serious theme. I'd write about teenage girls overcoming peer pressure, bullying or dumping show off boyfriends for affable geeks. They must've struck a chord with the editor, since he gave me a regular weekly column and a two-page monthly spread. For two years until university took me away, Erin Davis was hot property in rural Hampshire. At university, I wrote nothing of substance for three years. After a series of poor career choices, motivated to pick up where I'd left off, I slipped into writing romantic fiction.

A drop of rain lands on my ankle, releasing me from my reminiscences.

The sky is leaden. It's getting dark. The wind has strengthened and changed direction. I collect my laptop, go through to the kitchen and lay it down on the worktop. Bella follows in my footsteps. Scared of the thunder, she turns and skulks upstairs. I amble outside and settle into the rocking chair. I adore a storm. Bella is a scaredy-cat.

Charcoal clouds pregnant with rain scuttle overhead. Humidity claws at my skin. Everything stills. A deep bass rumble of thunder rolls over the treetops and vibrates through my chest. The wind holds its breath. I'm holding mine, too. A tangled arc of blistering silver splits the air, and the deluge begins. Raindrops the size of acorns pelt the dry earth. Within minutes, deep puddles form in hollows across the lawn and path.

Squealing in anticipation, I count the seconds between the spears of lightning and the claps of thunder. For ten minutes, I'm in the eye of the storm. I count the gap between the claps. First, five seconds, then ten, then twenty.

Having stolen the day, the storm drifts west along the coast.

Time for bed.

Bella joins me on the bed and I imagine a relieved expression across her chops.

I'm exhausted, but my mind is wide awake. I collect my paperback and start reading. At first, I'm carried along with the story; each word *means* something. After half a dozen pages, my eyelids weigh heavy, my concentration dulls, and fails me. My eyelids flutter closed, and the book falls to the floor.

I wake to a splintering crack. Somewhere beyond the door,

timbers creak. I bolt upright. Following my lead, Bella rises from the mattress and sullen doggy eyes turn towards the door. Cranking my head right, I listen. The silence is absolute, no rain or wind. A series of tortured creaks break the silence. They're coming from the staircase. I suck breath and hold it in. Bella nuzzles under the duvet.

We wait. Nothing stirs. All is quiet.

I decide the creaks are timbers settling after the storm. Needing to pee, I swing out of bed and tiptoe on to the landing. Wrapping my arms around me, I peer downstairs into the darkness. Everything seems to be as I left it. There's nothing untoward.

Who's the scaredy-cat now?

CHAPTER TWENTY-NINE

Bella mooches around the kitchen like a moody teenager denied spending money. She ambles to her bowl, turns her nose up at the kibbles and makes her way outside. From the door, I watch her slump into the dog bed.

Perhaps the storm has unsettled her?

I relegate the notion she's missing Christian to the darkest, most distant, recess of my mind. He never contested custody of Bella – even he wouldn't stoop so low.

Why is she still loyal to him? Why ask myself such a dumb question? She's a dog, she doesn't know any better...

Hungry, I rustle up an egg and mushroom omelette. Hunger satiated, I wash and put away the crockery and decide on salmon for dinner. There will be a fillet each. Bella will devour hers in less than a minute.

Since Bella's disinterested in exercise, I set about the house-work with gusto. I desperately need to use up some pent up energy. Last night's storm has cleared away the oppressive heat and humidity. Outside, everything gleams and sparkles. The least I can do is bring some order to the interior of Scalaig Lodge.

Changing the bed linen, the heady scent of lavender wafts

around the bedroom. I use lavender often. A drop or two helps me sleep. Lifting the lid of the linen basket, I realise to my horror I haven't done any laundry since arriving. I'm so used to taking it back to West Sussex for Rhoda to see to, that I haven't given it a second thought. I set about sorting the contents of the linen basket into two piles.

Downstairs, I load the washing machine and select, 'DELICATES'. Hovering over the sink, I fill a glass with crisp, cool water, and slug it down without coming up for air.

I spend the next hour reading over yesterday's work, with one ear listening for the washing cycle to end. When it does finally end, I make my way downstairs, drag the rotary dryer from the store and set it into the hole in the ground. I enjoy pegging out laundry. It never feels like a chore. A ridiculous sense of achievement swells through my chest as I peg out the last pair of knickers. I don't need a housekeeper, or a rich husband to keep me in the lifestyle I've become accustomed to. I need simplicity.

I'm an independent woman, Christian Moran, and don't you ever forget it.

CHAPTER THIRTY

With my fingers suspended over the keyboard, my mind goes blank. Words elude me. The nuances of my story dance around my head, but won't coalesce. This stop, start malaise, is annoying.

Maybe if I write freehand?

Actually, I much prefer to write in pencil. It allows me the freedom to erase errant words, sentences, sometimes whole paragraphs.

I check everywhere, but the pencil's disappeared. *Where is it?* I cast my mind back. *Did I last have it when I was working outside on the veranda? Did it slip from the table and blow through the gaps between the decking boards?*

Bolting up, I bounce downstairs, stride outside and fall onto my knees. Frantically, I search for it. Several fruitless minutes later, I remind myself that I've got heaps of pencils. But I love this one. Not the pencil part, but the heart-shaped eraser on the blunt end. Olivia gifted it to me. It's got sentimental value.

You must have taken it inside.

Turning the lodge upside down, I search everywhere and anywhere. Nothing.

'Where the hell are you? Elusive little bugger,' I say aloud.

Drawing up, I pinch my bottom lip between thumb and fore-finger in thought.

It was here... I'm not going mad. Did I put it somewhere so safe that it's impossible to remember where? And then I *do,* remember. I visualise a face angled to, and staring at the floor.

Rory Barr.

Yesterday, I'd noticed his gaze fixed on my desk. Watched him squeeze his hands together. I'd thought him anxious, agitated. He seems a sensitive, shy soul and a little odd. Perhaps his habit of squeezing his hands together is a prelude to stealing? It might be a behavioural tick? And he was here the day before I misplaced my hairgrip.

Did he take it? The pencil? The hairgrip? How could I have been so trusting?

Callum suggested Rory was a thief, and yet I didn't believe him. Didn't *want* to believe him. Now, I'm not so sure. It's only a pencil. If only he'd asked, I would have gifted him one. Acid bubbles in my gut. Rory is a stranger, yet I've invited him into my home.

A dark cloud of hurt billows inside my chest. People seem only to exist to let me down, or at least, that's how it seems. Hot, angry tears roll down my cheeks. The saltiness stings. I can't believe how stupid I've been. I wipe away the tears. Sniffle. Mascara covers the back of my hand. Massaging my neck, I draw a long breath. I'm doing it again.

Get a grip!

'This is madness. You're having a sodding breakdown over a hairgrip and pencil. You need to get your shit together, lady!'

I won't allow Christian to be right. I'm not going mad.

Rory is a child trapped inside a man's body. I ought not think of him as a common thief, on someone else's say so. So what if he's a magpie stealing trinkets? It's what children do, isn't it?

Leave it. I tell myself.

The day is ruined. I decide on a walk to clear my head. Bella stays put in her bed on the veranda.

Entering the woods, pine scent charges my nostrils. I stall beneath the sombre, cool embrace of tall pines and look up. High above me, the canopy conceals the sky. No daylight penetrates the thick thatch. I'm surprised how dry the ground is underfoot. A solitary raindrop lands on the back of my neck and courses down my spine. Shuddering, goosebumps bristle along my arms and legs.

Behind me I sense a presence, and experience a visceral feeling of being watched. Setting off along the path, I quicken my stride. A saunter becomes a march. At the edge of the wood, I halt and settle a flattened palm over my brow against the sun, since I've forgotten my sunglasses. I turn and look back along the path. I don't know what I'm expecting, but I don't see it.

Spooked, I bolt across open ground towards the clifftop without looking back.

Reaching the cliffs, I lower onto the grass and dangle my feet over the edge, scanning the ocean. Lines of yachts punctuate the ruffled blue-green ocean. White sails and primary-coloured spinnakers billow in the breeze. I wonder what day it is?

Is it the weekend? Am I watching a regatta?

With a start, I realise I've lost all track of time.

I'm bereft and alone on an isolated tidal island, without a phone or transport. I have human contact, yes, but can anyone consider Alasdair, Callum and Rory, company? They're acquaintances. Then there's Callum, and his promise to fix my car. That was almost a week ago, and it's still not repaired. These people are strangers, yet I'm treating them like I've known them my entire life. I'm trusting them with my possessions and inviting them into my home. I have a trust issue: I trust *too* much.

There's another reality, too. The reality that Alasdair is managing my diet. When did I become so pathetic that I can't even choose my own groceries? It's conceivable Rory is stealing from me, too. Is anything else missing? Potentially stolen items which, as yet, have gone unnoticed? Callum's making a dog's breakfast out of fixing the Range Rover. I'm bereft, upset.

I can't blame anyone for my breaking my phone – I had a fit of temper. If Christian had left me alone when I'd asked him, it would never have happened.

I'm struggling to sleep, too. I'm having nightmares in 4K HD. Nightmares so realistic, that when I wake up, I'm finding it difficult to distinguish between what's real and imagined. At night, the lodge creaks and groans like an arthritic giant, reminding me of the life I've lost.

What the hell is wrong with me?

Then there's the novel I'm writing: the reason I'm here. It's meant to be the salvation of my career; the kick start to my future as the 'ex' Mrs Christian Moran. At first the writing flowed, and I built up a head of steam. But I've lost direction. The sentences stumble onto the page, half-formed. And please don't mention the paragraphs. I've had days when I haven't written a single, solitary word.

Has my talent for storytelling gone south with the migrating swifts?

Is Christian right?

For most of my adult life, I haven't had to fend for myself. Am I deluded for thinking I have the strength of character to live alone on an island as isolated as Scalaig? Or for that matter, anywhere isolated? Look what happened when I shut myself away in a dingy flat in London. I wasted away, made myself ill with self-pity and depression, and spewed out a second-rate novel I didn't believe in. There's every chance that novel has cost me my career.

I'm not the independent woman I thought I was.

Am I pathetic, or being pathetic? It's a universe-sized question. And one I need to answer urgently.

The putt-putt of an outboard motor interrupts my thoughts. I close my eyes against the stinging sensation threatening to let loose a torrent of tears. The cobble looks familiar. Is it the one I saw moored from the jetty a couple of days ago? I'm not sure. Just like before, I watch a solitary figure in a hooded coat cast something overboard. Whatever it is, it splashes into the ocean and disappears under the surface within seconds. Was it a lobster pot? The figure rotates and looks in my direction. Is it a man or a woman? From this distance, it's impossible to tell, since the hood conceals the face. If whoever it is sees me, they don't react. The figure turns and heads to the wheelhouse. The engine note rises, and the bow lifts from the ocean as the cobble gathers momentum. Two minutes later, it disappears from view behind the headland.

Life goes on with no concern for me, or my troubles. I'm the interloper here – the alien invader in their world. The realisation is troubling.

I must try to improve my mood. I came to Scalaig of my own volition, to clear my head and write a novel. So far, all I've done is work myself into a lather. It's lunacy. I'm letting the hurt of the past, and the insecurity and paranoia of the present, get the better of me. It's a vicious circle.

I resolve to change. To put the past behind me. To relax.

Rising, I brush dirt from my bottom a little harder than absolutely necessary. I need a huge kick up the derriere. Moping about won't get me anywhere. I don't need Christian. Truth is, I never did. I don't need *anyone*.

I *will* have a great summer.

I *will* finish my novel.

I *will* get healthy in body and mind.

And above all else, I *will* relax.

* * *

Returning home, I give up trying to write and tidy away the chaos caused by the futile search for the pencil. I polish the furniture, vacuum, put a second load of clothes into the washing machine and bring the laundry in from the dryer. For a second, I lose my mind and consider ironing the contents of the basket. Electing not to, I chuckle and accept that I'll never be a domestic goddess.

When it's time for dinner, I poach salmon filets, steam rice and broccoli and congratulate myself on my healthy choices. Leaving Bella's portion to cool, I take a huge wine glass from the cupboard and brim it with ice-cold chardonnay – a third of the bottle dispensed in a single pour. I move to pour some back, but halt the glass at the neck.

'Why not? You deserve it!' I say, slaking my thirst with a huge mouthful, making my way outside. 'Healthy choices, one step at a time,' I chortle.

Bella joins me on the veranda. Head down, tail up, she wolfs down the salmon. It's her first proper meal in two days. My heart soars knowing she's always there for me. Christian would bounce off the ceiling if he knew I was feeding her 'human food.'

Sod him. Bloody control freak.

She's my dog. She enjoys it. I ought to buy different dog food, though. She doesn't like the brand Alasdair sends.

CHAPTER THIRTY-ONE

Day 24

It's a new day.

Our walk takes me to the north-east side of the island. It's nowhere near as dramatic as the south. It's a grass meadow with a gentle slope towards the ocean. Christian wanted to level the land, construct a swimming pool and install a tennis court, but the local Council wasn't having any of it. He gave up at the first bureaucratic hurdle – I'm glad he did. I don't come here as often as I should. This side possesses a natural pastoral beauty not found anywhere else on the island, or Skye.

I wonder how the grass stays so short. As far as I know, no one ever cuts it. Then I remember deer and wild pigs roam freely in the woods. At heart, I'm a city girl. I would be hopeless as a ranger, hiking guide, or god forbid, a farmer. The realisation makes me chuckle.

A cloudless azure sky elevates my mood and I reflect on the past few days.

It's been a week since the storm stole my confidence and I'm feeling much more optimistic. I've written over thirty-thousand words in record time. If I continue at the same pace, I will have a finished manuscript in three, maximum four weeks. My London editor is primed and ready to work her magic. I'm not sure she'll approve of the direction I'm taking with my heroine. Irrespective, my eleventh novel ought to be in bookshops soon.

Since there are no birds to chase, driftwood to drag from the ocean, or rabbits to bark at, Bella's bored. She scampers off towards the lodge to claim her favourite spot on the veranda. The weather is perfect for her. It's not too hot, nor too cold. She'll snooze to her heart's content, while I write.

CHAPTER THIRTY-TWO

Thirty minutes later, breathless, though feeling content and relaxed, I arrive at the lodge.

I'm about to clamber onto the veranda, when I notice an inch-wide gap between the door and frame. Startled, I halt with my hand on the handrail. Wisps of blue smoke roll out through the gap and blow away on the breeze. I feel the hand of panic tighten around my throat. I race across the veranda and spring the door.

An acrid fug of cigar smoke meets me. I waft it aside. The air clears and reveals Christian. He's on the sofa with Bella across his lap. A crystal tumbler – half full with whisky – balances on the sofa's arm. Languid coils of smoke eddy into the air from the cigar perched between the fingers of his left hand. He's wearing tan leather boat shoes, navy-blue tailored shorts, and a white polo shirt with a green alligator logo. I admire his golden tan. Checking myself, I notice his sickening grin.

'What are you doing here?'

'Darling, you banished me,' he says, pointing to the wall above the mantlepiece. 'I can't have that.'

He's taken it upon himself to turn the wedding portrait back over. Grinding my teeth, I fix him with an incandescent glare.

'I let myself in,' he says flatly, eyelids batting.

'How? Don't answer that. Just get out,' I bark, settling my weight against, and holding the door open. 'Like the song, you're not welcome here, anymore.'

'Eh, that's not very nice. This is my house, too.'

There he sits, Christian Moran, as bold as brass, stroking my dog without a care in the world.

'I said. Get out.'

My hands tremble with resolve.

'Don't be like that. Be reasonable. I only want to talk,' he says, silky voice hanging in the space between us.

Unable to look at him, I roll my eyes to the ceiling and exhale. 'I've nothing to say to you. I want you to go. Now!'

'Calm down, *dear*. Don't have a coronary,' he says, combing a hand though his hair, preening. 'Do you know something, you look great, much better than the last time I saw you. Scalaig is working its magic.'

Dear! Patronising git. He's turning on the charm. I won't fall for it.

'My well-being is none of your concern.' I roll my hand, point outside. 'Go!'

'Let me a stay a while. I'm worried about you. We all are,' he says, giving me doe eyes, searching, or so it would seem, for a glimmer of understanding to latch on to.

'You're not worried. You don't give a damn about me. I can see right through you. You're trying to manipulate me.' I look away. I won't allow myself to get caught in his hypnotic python's gaze.

'It's not what you think. Hear me out.' He's pleading, begging almost.

'I've heard it all before. Listened to your lies and lame excuses. You wouldn't know the truth if it jumped up and bit you on the arse.' He's not breaking through. I won't let him. I've erected a wall topped with barbed wire around me. Trump would be proud.

'I'm not begging.' His faux expression of concern evaporates. Darkness dawns in the set of his face. 'I'm a proud man.'

'Are you dense? I want you to go. Leave. Depart. Exit stage left. What part of leave don't you fucking understand?' I say glaring.

He looks to his lap and strokes the top of Bella's head. She angles her face towards him. 'Look, Bella wants me to stay. Don't you, girl?' The way he says it, it's not a question, but a statement. When I look closer, he's holding Bella by the scruff. She's looking up at him with wide eyes of confusion.

'Take your hands off of her. You're hurting her. Come here, Bella.'

His fingers tighten.

'You and I, we need to talk. You can't keep dodging me. Forget all this *speak to me via my solicitor* bullshit. You never return my calls. How am I supposed to communicate with you? Via a fucking medium?' He raises his left hand, fingers spread, wedding ring thrust forward. I consider it a symbol of ownership, not genuine love.

'It's a thought.'

'Ha, bloody, ha.'

'I'm not your wife, anymore. This is *my* house and *my* island. Go and never come back.' I press my back against the door. I'm just about holding it together.

I'm furious with myself for forgetting to lock the door. I won't let him see I'm ruffled. Tingles of fear circulate through my limbs.

Releasing Bella, he eases up from the sofa, steps over and halts in front of me. Leaning in, he stalls his face just inches from mine, whisky breath warm against my cheek. His face twists into a venomous sneer.

'This isn't over, it's only just beginning.' He draws breath. A silent moment passes. 'I've been thinking…'

'There's a first time for everything.' I can't help myself.

'Ugh, hilarious. I expect Michael McIntyre is quaking in his boots. No, I've been thinking about keeping this place. Keeping it and contesting your claim.'

He falls silent. I too elect silence.

He moves to stroke my face. I rear back.

'Darling, there's still time to change your mind,' he says. 'Things, *us*, we can be better than ever.'

I know he means it. That he's hoping I'll forgive and forget. He's deluded.

'I won't change my mind. We're history. You're an adulterous, conniving bastard. Goodbye,' I hiss, no longer intimidated by him.

His hopeful smile morphs into a wolfish grin. 'Listen to yourself, Erin. You won't last a year on your own. You need me. Without me, you'll shrivel up and die.'

He reaches out, hand poised to stroke my hair. I push his hand aside. Stepping right, I settle against the door, staring off into space.

'Get out!'

'No.'

Before I know it, I'm racing at him, screaming, fists balled. I can't take any more. Towering over me, he snags my raised fists just inches from his chest and twists my wrists, pushing down. Feeling my knees buckle, my resolve breaks. I growl a mongrel's growl: the bastard child of a scream and a hiss.

'Calm the fuck down. Look at you. What you've become…'

'Let go of me.'

'I'll let go when you calm down. OK?'

'I won't calm down until you've left this fucking island!'

'You're a mad woman. What the hell's got into you? I only came to talk. I didn't expect a screaming banshee, foaming at the mouth like a rabid dog. For fuck's sake, Erin, you need to get back to London and see a psychiatrist. This place, it's turning you feral.'

He's mocking me. Doing what he does best. Sowing the seeds of doubt in my mind. His twisting grip tightens on my wrists.

'You're hurting me! Let go and I'll talk to you.'

'So long as you promise not to hurt *me*.'

'Promise? You don't know the meaning of the word. Your promises never stopped *you* from hurting people. Hurting *me* with your infidelity.' I resist the urge to spit in his face. Doing that will only inflame him. I stop myself. I won't give him the satisfaction.

'What can I say? Guilty as charged,' he says. It's the closest he's ever come to an apology. The word *sorry* doesn't feature prominently in his vocabulary.

'Let go… Then…' I try hard to extract the hate from my voice. It's a tactic.

Releasing my wrists, he steps back and raises his hands, palms facing forward, in mock surrender.

'Friends?' he says.

'Not while I've got air in my lungs and bones in my body,' I hiss. 'You bastard.'

Where did that come from?

'I thought I was the one with the foul mouth. What would your readers think of your squeaky clean girl-next-door image now?'

He's goading me. I take the bait. Swallow it whole. Feel it settle in my gut.

'They'd tell me to get you out of my life. My house. And off of my island forever.'

'Touché. But not until we've discussed the future.'

'Future? We don't have a future. There's nothing to discuss. Let your solicitor speak to mine. You're paying him enough,' I say, nostrils flaring.

I'm getting good at this. I'm going to win this argument.

'It's not as if you haven't got enough money, is it?'

'Money isn't important. The future, that's what's important now. My future. *Our* future.'

'There you go again. Your future always comes first. It's always about you. It always was, and it always will be.'

'That's not what I meant, and you damn well know it isn't. It's your future, too. You're twisting my words, playing the victim. Stop it. It doesn't suit.'

'I'm doing no such thing. You need to accept we have no future together. Do whatever you want to do. Marry your slut of a mistress, or some other poor cow. I'll watch them bleed you dry, from afar. I've no desire for a front-row seat.'

He shakes his head. I sense resignation.

'Do you know something, you've turned into a bitch. I'm very impressed,' he says.

'I've had an excellent teacher. Now, if you've seen enough, I want you to go.'

'I'll go when I'm good and ready and not before.' He moves towards me. Too close for comfort, I slap his face. My fingers sting and burn. I stare him down. His hand shoots up to his reddened cheek, horrified surprise written on his face.

'You've changed.'

'You'd better believe it.'

I'm as surprised as he is. He nods. Shrugs. His expression suggests he's searching for the woman I was – the *owned* woman. She no longer exists.

A long moment passes between us. It's a stand off. The chasm between us has never been wider.

Picking up the crystal tumbler, he sinks the remaining whisky, weighs it in his hand, turns and hurls it against the stone fireplace. The tumbler shatters into a million pieces. Bella scrambles outside. I hear her whimpers. I stand my ground. Don't even flinch. Won't flinch. Defy him to speak. He cocks his chin. Looks down his nose at me. Sniffs.

'You haven't heard the last of me,' he says, stepping outside. 'It's not over until I say it is.'

I watch the ghost of the man I once knew, depart. In reality, he left years ago, after he did the dirty on me with another woman.

I will not allow myself to follow him.

CHAPTER THIRTY-THREE

It takes time to regain my composure. Since I burned his clothes on the pavement, today is the first time I've really stood up to Christian. I'm OK. The tingling fear has gone. He came close to intimidating me, but I held my ground. My resolve came out of this latest encounter, intact. It shows I'm getting over him.

I assume he returned to the cove and *The Storm Petrel*. I don't think I'll be seeing him anytime, soon. He's had his tantrum. Said his piece. And I sent him packing with a flea in his ear. If I know Christian Moran, he'll cut his losses and move on.

Do you ever truly know someone?

I go to close the door. Just as the latch is about to click into the frame, the daylight dims and I look up. Callum Cleland stands in the opening, staring at me. Startled, I step back.

Where did he appear from? I hadn't heard him approach.

'Hi. Is everything, OK?' he asks, glaring. 'Only, I heard voices raised voices.'

'Yes. Everything's fine.' Adrenaline scuttles through my veins. 'You startled me.'

'Sorry. I didn't mean to. Who was he?' he says, running a hand over his stubble covered chin, all wide-eyed.

'Excuse me?'

'The guy? The guy who just left. He had a face like thunder. He looked mightily pissed off.'

I shrug. 'Just someone I used to know. Can I help you, Mr Cleland?'

'I don't want to pry, Mrs Moran, sorry, *Erin*. Only, as I say, I heard raised voices. I've never heard a raised voice on Scalaig, before. I was worried about you.'

I realise I'm letting my argument with Christian blur my judgment. Men stir petulance in me. They like to pry. They're quick to assume single women are vulnerable.

I force a smile. 'It's OK. There's nothing to concern yourself with. It was just my soon-to-be ex-husband, Christian. We were ironing out the details of our divorce. We had a minor disagreement. It was a little stressful. Nothing I can't handle, though. With a fair wind, he won't come back.'

Why do I have to explain myself?

'Would you like me to hang around? It's no trouble. Make sure he slings his hook?'

'Good God, no. He won't return. I'm confident of that,' I say, selecting my words carefully, enunciating them with as much conviction as I'm able to muster. 'I appreciate the offer, though.'

'If you're absolutely sure, I'll leave you be. I'll see you later, *neighbour*.'

'Yeah. Bye. *Neighbour*,' I say.

Callum spins on a heel and ambles away, hands stuffed deep into pockets. Reaching the gate, he turns and waves. I wave back from the lounge window, but he doesn't appear to see me. He swings right towards the causeway with Bella at his heel.

Damn it, I forgot to ask him about the car!

Too late, he's gone. I don't have the energy to chase after him. Instead, I yearn for coffee.

Half an hour later, Bella pads in through the front door with seaweed wedged between her toes.

What is it with her and men?

She will have followed Callum. I imagine him sending her back from the steps leading down to the causeway. However, it's two o'clock and the causeway will be underwater. Won't it? *How will he cross to Skye? I suppose he must have a boat of some sort.*

I wonder whether the remaining slice of Mrs Barr's lemon drizzle cake is still edible. It is. Taking my coffee and cake, I step outside and lower into the rocking chair. Nibbling on the cake, I congratulate myself on my victory over Christian.

My heroine, Zoe, would be proud of me.

CHAPTER THIRTY-FOUR

Flipping the wedding portrait against the wall, I try hard to suppress the spinning top of nausea whirling inside my gut.

I spend the day staring at the same sentences. I'm wound up like a cornered rattlesnake. Concentration eludes me. My brain pulsates. An orb of white light moves across my peripheral vision and I beg it not to be another migraine flaring up. My earlier feelings of triumph have departed. By the time the sun disappears over the horizon, I feel sullen and ensnared by the chains of self-doubt. A thousand questions bounce around my head.

What would bring Christian here? From his perspective, it must have been something important. I never let him explain. Red mist blinded me. I sent him away with his tail between his legs. However much I try to deny it, I still find him attractive. And he beamed like a lottery winner. Deep down, was I happy to see him? It's obvious Bella misses him. Do I? Am I nothing without him? And he did seem worried about me. He mentioned, 'we all are.' What did he mean by that? Admonishing myself for letting him occupy my thoughts, I wonder how long he was having an affair? How many secrets did he have? Alasdair Barr witnessed his infidelity long before I did. Hinted he'd brought other women to Scalaig, often.

Once you remove the blinkers, like I did in February, it's funny what you learn about someone supposedly close. That day everything became clear. I hold on to that thought. The door to my heart for Christian Moran is closed and twice bolted. Now and forever. We have no future together. He can threaten me all he likes, but I won't, *can't,* let him into my heart ever again.

Exhausted, I crawl into bed and lay staring at the ceiling, listening to the lodge settling. I drift in and out of consciousness to the rhythm of creaking floorboards, rattling window blinds, and the shuffle of roof tiles.

Half awake, half asleep, I hear Bella's claws scrabbling over the top tread of the staircase onto the landing. The pad of her paws across the floorboards ceases at the bedroom door and she exhales a sigh. The staircase creaks as she slips downstairs. Sensing her confusion, I decide not to call after her. Poor dog. Her world was turned upside down, too.

Laying there, I realise I've never been alone on Scalaig for any length of time. I realise, too, that the phantom of lost love will always stalk this place. Scalaig Lodge is a cage built to house a canary and I was the canary. I was a rich man's trinket.

As the lodge wraps its possessive arms around me, my aching heart finds solace in sleep.

CHAPTER THIRTY-FIVE

Day 26

Refreshed, I wake ready for a new challenge. Low sun slips in through the gaps between the curtains, imbuing the room with a gentle pink hue. Rolling out of bed, I slip into a swimsuit, pull on shorts, a t-shirt and drag a towel from the rail.

The cove beckons. A swim will kick-start body and mind.

'Bella. Beach,' I instruct from the veranda. Bella rises from her bed into a near perfect arch. She yawns, yaps, cranks her head on one side and studies me with sullen eyes. 'Shake a leg, lazy head. I'll throw sticks. Promise,' I say, patting my thigh, making a clicking sound with my tongue on my teeth. Turning, she slumps into the bed facing away from me. 'Please yourself miserable so-and-so. You'll regret it.'

I leave the door ajar so Bella can join me at the cove when, and if, she so pleases. Sometimes, it slips my mind that she's ten-years-old. That's old for such a big dog. And she didn't get anywhere near this much exercise in London. I fear I'm wearing her out with my constant desire for exercise.

* * *

At the cove, the tide is out. Placing my towel on the boulder, I undress and look off into the distance towards the end of the jetty. I estimate it as a kilometre distant and I make it my goal to swim there and back five times. Given my current state of fitness, it will be enough of a challenge. If I've learned anything about fitness over the years, I've learnt to build it up slowly and methodically.

Rising from the sand, I step over to the water's edge and tip-toe into the ocean. Borne of habit, I spit and smear saliva over the lenses of my swimming goggles, flick the elastic over my head and adjust them until they fit snugly against on my face. The sunny morning becomes a blur of blue and green wavy lines. Hands out front – to help my balance – I creep into the surf towards the shelf. Moving into deeper water, the icy ocean closes around me and my breathing quickens. I can't help but gasp as the ocean reaches my belly button. I draw longer breaths and clench my teeth so hard my gums hurt. Pushing up on my toes, committing to the swim, I dive headlong into the ocean and take my first tentative strokes under-water. Bursting out through the surface, I swim freestyle. The rubber strap around my temples is too tight. Ignoring the discom-fort, I swim towards the jetty with long, easy strokes. I'm cutting through the water with aplomb. Every third stroke, I twist my mouth out of the water and suck a long breath. Paddling hard, I'm propelled forward at a rate of knots and my speed, and confidence, builds.

Arriving at the jetty, a vertical block of black fills my vision. Touching the rough timbers, I pull the stroke, flip and push off against the post with my toes. Swimming underwater, seaweed drags over my torso, legs and arms. The ocean fizzes and air bubbles cling to my goggles. Arriving at the surface, I resume long strokes. At the shelf – using the boulder as a marker – I flip and turn back towards the jetty.

I've never felt so alive.

Five strokes in, a stabbing pain knives into my right side just below the ribs. The jetty can be only twenty metres distant, but already I'm starting to lose momentum. The pain worsens and becomes more persistent. It feels like someone is twisting a molten blade deep into my diaphragm. Since the ocean is too deep to put my feet down, I turn to face the jetty, stop swimming and tread water.

Stay calm. It's stitch. It'll pass. I tell myself.

Bobbing on the swell, holding my head above water, the stabbing eases to a dull ache.

You're OK. It's going to be alright...

I tread water with a regular cadence. When I forget to tread, my chin dips beneath the surface and I swallow and spit seawater. Adjusting the goggles, I realise the current has spun me around and I'm facing open ocean. Losing sight of land and the jetty, with the pain reduced to a dull ache, I decide it's time to return to the beach. Five kilometres was too ambitious. I shouldn't overdo it. Gathering my strength, I paddle against the current, turn and strike out for the beach at the cove.

Just as I'm getting into a regular rhythm and the stitch is subsiding, something hard and unyielding smashes against my right elbow at the funny bone. The pain is incredible. I yell, gasp, and sink beneath the swell. Kicking for the surface, I feel fingers clawing at my neck and scratching my face. I'm being held under. Someone is near. Flailing, I break free and kick out. Breaking through the surface, I gasp for air. From nowhere, a hand settles on my right shoulder, pressing me down. Frigid darkness envelops me. There's no sound. Though my lungs scream for air, nothing will make me release my breath. I'm drowning, or being drowned, I can't decide which. Irrespective, if water enters my lungs, then it's game over.

Suddenly, the hand releases. I take two strokes and kick for the surface. Fingers envelop my right ankle, tighten, and catapult me upwards. Bursting up through the swell, I gasp for air. Before I know it, I'm on my back being pulled backwards through the ocean by a meaty forearm positioned under my chin. I'm reminded of life-saving classes at primary school.

Arriving in the shallows, I'm lifted clear of the surf by a huge arm across my chest. I'm dragged through the surf, waves crashing over me. I dig my nails into flesh, but to no avail. Whoever's doing this is persistent. Pebbles slip and slide under my bottom. Rocks tear at my calves. Salt stings my open wounds. I'm lifted clear of the ocean and dumped on my back on the sand. Ripping the goggles from my face, I see fluffy white clouds racing across a sapphire blue sky. I'm pushed onto my left side by an unseen hand. Water dribbles from my mouth and nose. Retching, I bring up seawater and bile. Something solid catches in my throat and I can't breathe. I cough, but nothing comes. I try again, but it's useless. The sky fades and everything goes black.

CHAPTER THIRTY-SIX

'Miss! Miss!' A panicked voice arrives through the ether. My eyelids quiver open and I see a mess of hair hovering over me.

Go away. I want to sleep.

'Miss Moran,' bellows a male voice, jagged nails digging into my arms, shaking me.

Leave me alone.

'Please, wake up… Please,' the same insistent voice. I'm being rocked.

Opening my eyes, I hear the low whoosh of the surf meeting the shore and remember where I am and what's happened.

'You alright, Miss?'

I'm being dragged into a sitting position by huge hands. Caught on a surge of adrenaline, I spin away, stagger across the sand and spin to face my attacker.

My vision clears and I see a familiar face.

'Rory!'

Wide, dark eyes bore into mine. *Rory.* Under my accusing glower, his chin lowers, and he diverts his gaze to the sand.

'What the hell's got into you?' I say, panting hard.

'Stopped. In the sea, Miss Moran,' he says, fists clenching and unclenching. 'Not swimming. Your head went underwater.'

I'm confused. 'Me?'

'Yup. You.'

I'm nonplussed. Then I realise. He thought I was drowning. 'I wasn't drowning, Rory, you came out of nowhere and dragged me under. What the hell did you think you were doing?'

A half-inch deep frown of concern sits between his eyes. I imagine the melee of disconnected thoughts rioting through his brain. I feel for him.

'Miss Moran, the ocean is bad,' he says, pointing over his shoulder. He's soaking wet; dark hair plastered against his forehead. Shirtsleeves cover his hands. Oxblood boots soaked dull brown.

Shaking my head, I expel an exasperated sigh. 'You stupid boy, I wasn't in any danger, you could have drowned me!' I blurt, not thinking. Rory's concerned frown becomes a hollow stare. I beg the sand to open up and swallow me whole. 'Sorry, I didn't mean that. I'm upset.'

'Drowning, miss. Like you said. Drowning…'

'Oh, Rory, I was having a stitch. It's a pain you get in your side. I was taking a breather. I didn't need rescuing. I suppose you weren't to know.'

His huge shoulders heave. I imagine the battle between his perception and actuality being waged inside his head. He's a toddler who's had his sweets taken away from him for kicking the cat. Several silent minutes pass. I reach out to him, but he rears away. The next I know he's rushing towards me, ferocious anger burning behind his eyes. Dodging his advance, I trip him and lands flat on his face in the sand.

'No! Bad boy!' I yell.

Boy? God, what am I saying?

He blubbers. His huge shoulders shake.

How did it get to this?

I stand over him. 'Rory, please stop. Look, I'm sorry. I didn't mean it. You weren't to know. You're a good … *boy*,' I stutter.

The blubbering ceases. Rory staggers up. Steps towards me. 'Friends?'

'Friends,' I say, throwing my arms around him. We hug for an entire minute. We must look ridiculous.

I pull away. Scan the rock. The beach. 'Where's my towel?'

Electing silence, Rory's gaze retreats once more to the sand. He turns and lopes away without looking back.

Remembering where I left it, I lean over and spot the towel laid at the base of the boulder. I wrap myself in a towel, slip into flip-flops and set off for the lodge.

Clambering up the steps, I realise Rory must have been watching me from the clifftop. That he must have seen me treading water and assumed I was drowning. His clumsy attempt to 'save' me almost drowned us both. He must've thought he was helping me. *I assume…*

Realising he'd snuck up without me knowing, I shudder at the thought. It could have been anyone. I'd not noticed him. My myopic focus on pushing the boundaries put me in real and present danger.

Reaching the lodge, I resolve to speak to Alasdair. I need to discuss Rory. Him, or anyone, sneaking around Scalaig is unacceptable. I can't have him 'saving' me from imaginary dangers and putting mine, or anyone's, life at risk.

CHAPTER THIRTY-SEVEN

With anger powering my legs, I cycle across the causeway towards Barr's. Despite my near death experience earlier, there's plenty of day remaining. The low sun – covered by wispy cloud – is an ochre blur. With the coming of the cloud, the air has cooled and the hairs on my arms bristle over goosebumps. I'm trying hard not to shiver. I don't want to lose my balance and pitch over the handlebars into the ocean. It was a mistake to wear shorts and t-shirt.

With sweat rolling from every pore and the heat of exertion banishing goosebumps, I stumble up the last step and push the bike onto level ground. I stand there panting, gathering breath, and see the Range Rover. It sits forlornly on the gravel across the lane from the castle. A thin layer of dust dulls the silver paintwork. Fist-sized splatters of guano cover the bonnet, wings, and roof. It's yet to turn a wheel since I arrived.

I look to the castle. It's eerily quiet. Beyond the fence, I notice the weeds are much taller than when I arrived. Nature is trying its level best to reclaim Isla's garden. Dandelions and stinging nettles smother hardy perennials. Variegated ivy covers every wall and fence. Years ago, Isla's archetypal English cottage garden won awards and featured in gardening magazines. I remember reading the articles, marvelling at it, desiring it. Isla's pride and joy has gone to seed.

I'm heartbroken for her. It's enough to make me cry.

In no mood for compromise, I determine to find Callum and press him for an update on the car. Crossing the lane, I prop the bike against the fence and push on the rickety gate. It moves an inch, then grinds to a halt on ancient concrete bristling with weeds and nettles. Not wanting to get stung – since my legs are grazed and sore – I linger at the gate, willing Callum to appear.

Why is he never around?

I call his name without reply. I call again.

If he's home, he doesn't acknowledge my calls or presence. Nothing stirs in or around the castle: no twitching curtains, turning locks, flickering lights, or noises of any kind suggesting human occupation. Harrumphing with frustration, I collect the bike, swing onto the saddle and pedal away.

Passing the last of the ground-floor windows, I sense movement in my peripheral vision and drag hard on the brakes. Settling my feet on the ground, I spin to face the castle.

'Callum? You there?' I call.

All is still and silent.

Listening hard, the only sounds are the low rasp of the ocean, wind rustling the treetops and seagulls cawing high overhead.

I shake my head.

I'm losing the plot.

I'm seeing things.

CHAPTER THIRTY-EIGHT

Alasdair Barr sits by the door smoking a pipe. He acknowledges my arrival by dragging the pipe from his mouth and raising his lips into a thin smile. I bring the bike to a halt by the kerb. Alasdair studies me with indifference and his brow slowly creases into a circumspect frown.

'I thought you'd come,' he says without preliminary, emptying the pipe into a dish at his feet, settling it on the edge. His glasses are wonky on his nose, hair slicked back.

'Do you know why I'm here?' I say, trying hard to conceal my irritation. I've had my fill of men. I don't need Alasdair Barr pissing me off, too.

'I've an inkling, yes. Rory got home an hour ago, soaked to the skin and shaking like a leaf. He locked himself in the barn. He does that when he's upset. It's taken Dorothy half an hour and a Mars Bar, to coax him out.'

'Did he say what happened?'

Alasdair nods. 'After a fashion… He says he rescued you. Said you were angry with him. That you swore. Called him a stupid boy. Told him you didn't need rescuing. You've got to understand something, Mrs Moran. Rory is terrified of the ocean. Whenever possible, he steers clear of it. Wee lad must've got confused,' he says, wringing his hands. 'I can only apologise for any misunderstanding.'

Dismounting, I push the bike across the pavement and settle it against the wall.

'Why was he on Scalaig, anyway? If he hates the ocean so much, why was he watching me?' I say, casting my arms wide. 'Mr Barr. I, *we*, could have drowned. Rory is all muscle. I didn't know what was happening. I panicked. Swallowed a lot of water. It's not good enough, Mr Barr.'

'Mrs Moran ... sorry ... *Erin*. You're in shock. Why don't you come inside and get warmed up? A hot drink and a wee dram of whisky ought to do the trick.'

The sky has turned black; it's about to rain. And it's true, I am cold. Relenting, I force a thin smile. 'Coffee. Do you have coffee?'

He nods. 'Plenty. Come in. We don't bite.'

Alasdair gets up from the stool and holds the door open. The doorbell rings. I step past him.

'Follow me,' he says, stepping to the counter, raising and passing through the flap and pushing aside the strip curtain. Following behind, I enter a lounge furnished with threadbare rugs, a seventies vintage formica faced table, a tan leather sofa, a small coffee table and a high-back paisley print armchair. By the solitary window, a glass-topped TV stand supports an archaic VHS video recorder and an ancient silver Grundig TV, about the size of a small hatchback. On my left, I glimpse pine kitchen units through an archway. The air is redolent with fresh baked bread. Stepping forward, glancing left, I see a thickset woman standing over a pine table, forearms covered in flour.

The woman is rotund, with healthy pink cheeks and long grey hair heaped into a pinned bun on top of her head. Kneading a round of dough, her ample bosom rises and falls. She's wearing a belted check dress and a white apron tied into a double bow around her waist.

She looks up, smiles, and rubs her nose with her forearm.

'Take the weight off your feet,' Alasdair says, gesturing to the sofa.

'Thanks,' I say, lowering into the three seater.

The woman enters through the arched opening. Wiping her hands down her apron, she pads over and offers a hand. 'I'm Dorothy,' she says, taking my hand. Her podgy hand is soft, warm and comforting. Collecting a wool throw from the armchair, she drapes it over my shoulders and turns to Alasdair.

'Don't just stand there like a spare part, Alasdair. Make our guest a hot drink. What would you like, my darling?'

'Alasdair mentioned coffee.'

'Then coffee it is.'

Alasdair jumps to attention. 'Yes, dear. Your wish is my command.'

'It better had be,' Dorothy says, with a wry smile.

'How do you take it?' Alasdair asks .

'Black, please.'

'There's some in the pot,' Dorothy says.

Alasdair nods and disappears through the archway. Dorothy lowers into the armchair. The way she moves suggests she's suffering from advanced arthritis. A minute later, Alasdair returns carrying a mug of steaming black coffee and sets it down on the coffee table in front of me.

'There you go. I've put in two sugars. They'll help with the shock,' he says. 'Careful, it's boiling.'

'Thank you,' I say, just above a whisper.

I collect and nurse the mug. Enjoying the heat, I blow across the rim and take a first, tentative sip. The sweet burned caramel, tastes heavenly.

Alasdair hovers beside the strip curtain.

Dorothy glares at him. 'Haven't you got orders to pick?'

'Yes, my sweet, I have,' Alasdair says, harrumphing, disappearing through the curtain.

Dorothy fixes me with a sympathetic smile. 'What a morning you've had, child. Let's get you warmed up.' Leaning over, she fusses and adjusts the throw around my shoulders. She's the living embodiment of a mother hen.

'Thank you,' I say, 'I'm feeling much better now.' Dorothy's frown suggests she's not convinced.

'Breakfast?' Dorothy asks. 'Have you eaten today?'

It's a question, but her intonation has more than a hint of instruction.

'Not as yet, no. I'm fine. Honest, I am. You're too kind,' I say, cheeks flushing. These are sweet, kind people, and yet I've offended them with my combative attitude. 'I've taken up enough of your time, already. Sorry, I'll go. I'm sorry I came...'

I make to get up, Dorothy presses me into the sofa.

'You'll do nothing of the sort, young lady. I won't have you leaving until you've eaten something. You're in shock.'

She's insistent. I have no say in the matter.

'If you're sure.'

'Oh, I'm sure alright. Please, call me, Dorothy. The pleasure, dear, is all mine. Now, if you're up to it, come and join me in the kitchen. There's more coffee, fresh bread and cheese. Beautiful it is, the bread fair melts in the mouth.'

She beckons me to follow. Dragging up, I collect the throw and go through to the kitchen.

I see where Rory gets his build from. Dorothy Barr is as wide as Alasdair is skinny. She's a formidable woman.

Dorothy ushers me into a chair and I set the mug down on the table. She takes it upon herself to top it up. Fussing, she sets the table; speaks without coming up for air. She stomps around the kitchen like a dervish on speed. Hard vowels hint at an east European lineage.

Feeling a chill, I nuzzle into the throw. Only when Dorothy

stops moving, do her words coalesce into coherent sentences inside my head. She slows by the table, hands on hips.

'Alasdair tells me you're a writer?'

'An author, yes,' I say, nodding, 'for my sins.'

'How wonderful. I love to read. I'd love to write too, but there aren't enough hours in the day as it is. Some poor soul's got to keep this particular house in order,' she says, setting down a platter of bread, cheese and butter on the table. 'Sorry. I'm a chatterbox. I don't have much female company,' she says, pointing at the food. 'Don't stand there on ceremony, my dear, help yourself. There's plenty.' Beaming, she lowers into the chair opposite and cuts inch-thick slices of bread. The aroma is very different to the bakeries in London. It has a homely, richer, natural smell. It's divine. 'What type of books do you write?'

'Romance fiction. Happy ever afters. Mushy stuff.'

'That's lovely. Your books make people happy,' she says, tilting her head on one side, gazing wistfully into space.

'They used to,' I say. 'I seem to have lost my mojo.' I collect the plate of bread and cheese.

'I'm sure that's not true. Butter?' Dorothy says, sliding the butter dish across. We're doing a round-the-houses dance, making polite chitchat.

I make a sandwich, take a bite. The bread is soft and light. The cheese is creamy.

'Thank you. This is delicious,' I say.

She's fixes me with a matronly stare. 'Look… I know it's none of my business… Only… Your husband… Nobody much cares for him in Scaloon.'

How surprising. 'Why? Any particular reason?'

Dorothy shrugs. 'Many things.'

'Such as?'

'Felling trees. Building the lodge – by popular consensus, it's far too big. Lording over everyone. Bringing loud friends. *Women.* I'm afraid the list goes on.'

She's matter of fact. Brutal.

'Women?'

'Sorry. Ignore me. It was a slip of the tongue.'

I don't think so.

Speaking from the heart, I say, 'We bought Scalaig and built the lodge in good faith. We never intended to upset anyone. It was our holiday home. As far as I know, Christian's never been here without me.' Realising I'm jabbering, and embarrassed that I've been lied to, I fall silent.

'Forgive me. My mouth runs away with itself, sometimes. I'm German. I don't understand Scottish, sorry, *British* sensibilities. Alasdair worries that one day, my mouth will get me into trouble. He's forever telling me to think before I speak.'

I shrug, reach across the table and settle a hand on hers. 'There's nothing to forgive, Mrs Barr. Don't give it a second thought,' I say. It feels good to have a stranger reminding me what a total bastard Christian is.

Dorothy rises, collects the bread and returns it to the worktop. She spins to face me. 'Still, I shouldn't have said anything. It's absolutely none of my business. You're entitled to your privacy. I ought to keep my big mouth shut,' she says. 'More coffee?'

'No, thanks. I feel I owe you an explanation about earlier; about what happened with Rory.'

I do. I feel compelled to discuss the incident with her. She's kind. And she's my first female contact – save for Bella – in weeks.

'Mrs Moran, child… You don't have to explain a thing.'

I make to speak, but Dorothy stalls me with a raised hand. 'Sorry dear, I forgot. Alasdair mentioned you don't like people calling you by your married name. Is that right?' she says, mischief dancing in her eyes.

I like her. 'That's right. I don't,' I say. 'Only, you and Alasdair, you've been so kind to me since I arrived. You don't know me, yet already you've welcomed me into your home, fed me, offered words of comfort and been sensitive to my marital problems. I turn up like a whirlwind and leave all kinds of destruction in my wake. No doubt you're wondering what's going on?'

I give her my biggest smile. Reciprocating, she lowers into the chair opposite and straightens her apron. 'We did wonder, yes,' Dorothy says, with a sympathetic smile.

Ordering my thoughts, I say, 'We're divorcing. My husband had an affair. I found out. He's a serial adulterer, I think. I'm mature enough to understand that I'll probably never know the full extent of his infidelity. To be honest, Mrs Barr, I'd rather not know. I believed we had the perfect marriage. Thought I was happy. I feel such an idiot for being so naïve. Christian is an adulterous manipulative monster. My world has fallen apart. These past few months, I've been in a dark place. For the first time in my life, I've experienced depression.' Dorothy squeezes my hand. My pained expression reflects in her glasses. 'It's been awful.'

Finding comfort in Dorothy's understanding and sympathy, I continue, 'Ever since we separated, Christian's been feeding family and friends lies and half truths. He's telling everyone and anyone our marriage is on the rocks, because I'm obsessive about my writing. Saying I've been shutting him out. Peddled the lie that nobody should disturb me until my novel's written. Nothing, I repeat *nothing*, could be further from the truth. I've worked him, and his dark agenda, out. He's been isolating me. Blaming the marital break up on me. Making out I'm a selfish, obsessive, narcissist. That I lack empathy for others. It's perverse. The funny thing is, he's describing himself to a tee. He shifts the blame to me. I believe psychiatrists call it, projection. It's worked. I'm persona non grata in our social circle. For all they care, I might as well be dead.' Sighing, I fall silent.

'That can't possibly be true,' Dorothy says.

'It is. I've had to isolate myself, because I've a contractual commitment to deliver against. The novel I wrote during my isolation didn't pass muster. In fact, my publisher rejected it. My agent agreed a working sabbatical on Scalaig was a great idea. She wanted me to get away from Christian's malign influence, in the hope I'd start seeing things in a new light and get back to being my usual, amiable self. For the sake of my well-being, I knew I had to shake off the depression. So I plucked up the courage and told Christian I planned on spending the summer on Scalaig. He promised to leave me alone. And like a fool, I believed him. Truth is, he'll never leave me alone. He keeps phoning, texting. I got so distressed after one of his texts, that I dropped my phone and smashed it to smithereens. And now he's stalking me. He keeps coming to the island bothering me and asking for a reconciliation. I can see through him. He's got an ulterior motive. I know he has.'

Looking past Dorothy, I notice my reflection in the oven door glass. I pinch my cupid's bow and stare into space. Huff. 'Now I'm here, weird things keep happening. Is there any wonder I'm becoming a nervous wreck? Some days it borders on hysteria. Perhaps, I'm blowing things out of proportion. All I know is, I'm mentally exhausted. I'm trying my best not to let things get on top of me. I know I need a fresh start. It's imperative I write a great novel and prove to everyone that I *can* cope on my own.'

Dorothy listens without interrupting. Talking to her is cathartic. I haven't talked to anyone like this – other than Olivia – for months.

'Tell me about today. What happened with Rory?'

'I was swimming. Rory must've thought I was in trouble. He appeared from nowhere. Surprised me. I panicked and there was a scuffle. I went under. I thought I was going to die. He frightened the life out of me.' I study her reaction. It's the first time since I've started talking that we've maintained eye contact for any length of time.

'Please, Erin, don't blame my Rory. He's a good boy with learning difficulties. He doesn't understand the world, or the people in it. The doctors say he has the mental age of a nine-year-old.'

I shrug. 'That's as may be, Mrs Barr, but he can't go around frightening people. It's no exaggeration to say I could have drowned.' Dorothy will always side with her son, I recognise that, but she's also responsible for him.

'I agree he's let us down. We've always told him to stay out of the water. He's a poor swimmer. He's never taken to it. Oh, how we tried. We put it down to what happened to him,' she says.

I discern some deeper pain.

'What happened?' I ask, sipping coffee, interest aroused.

'It was fifteen years ago. Rory was eight. He was a happy, healthy boy. Four of them were playing on Scalaig by the cliffs on the south side. Rory was there with two older boys, and Callum Cleland. The tide was turning. They were daring one another to jump from the clifftop into the ocean on the incoming tide. You've seen how steep the cliffs are. It's a very dangerous place.'

'Did he fall over the cliff?'

Dorothy's gaze fixes on the clock behind me. Ticks echo around the kitchen.

'After a fashion, yes, he did. They were playing chicken, taking it in turns to run up to the edge of the cliff and pretend to jump over. They knew full well how dangerous it was. I suppose they must've got bored. Someone grabbed Rory and threw him over the cliff.'

Tears stream down her cheeks.

'That's awful. I ought not to have asked. It's none of my business. It was crass of me.'

'No. I need to tell you. You need to understand.' She reclaims a hankie from an apron pocket, clears her throat. 'Rory landed on the foreshore at the precise moment the tide rolled back. He broke both legs. His left leg was in a terrible state. That's why he limps. His head burst open like a watermelon smashed by a hammer. He rolled across the foreshore and ended up in the surf. Caught on the tide, he was smashed against the rocks. As fortune would have it, a lobsterman was passing in his boat. He'd seen something fall over the cliff, so he went to investigate. When he dragged Rory out of the sea, he was almost dead. The lobsterman recognised Rory and brought him straight here. We called the air ambulance. With the Lord's help, they got him to the hospital in time. My Rory was in a coma for three weeks. I thought we'd lost him. When he finally regained consciousness, he was like he is now. Rory has no recollection of what happened. His memory is a complete blank.'

Her eyelids batt closed. I wait. The tension is palpable. She blinks.

'The others... What did they do?'

'They ran away. They kept quiet about it for weeks until one of them – James McCloud – buckled under the pressure and told his parents what actually happened. He swore on the Holy Bible that Callum threw Rory over the cliff. The police got involved, but it was James's word against Callum's. Back then, the Clelands were a wealthy and influential family around these parts. The police took the Cleland's side over ours.'

As she speaks, her gaze remains fixed on the clock. She's remembering events she'd rather forget.

'I'm not saying Callum did what he did with malicious intent. I suppose it could have been a schoolboy prank gone wrong. Anyhow, when the dust settled, Isla and Hamish sent Callum away to boarding school in Aberdeen. The other two families moved away. We'll never know what made Callum do it.'

She straightens, fixes me with a tearful gaze. There's tremendous dignity in the face of tragedy.

'I'm so sorry. What an awful thing to have to live with,' I say, words of consolation momentarily eluding me.

How can anything I say, make things right?

'It happened. We adapted. We had to. Today, considering what he's been through, Rory is strong, a good boy, and a big help around the shop. Now that Alasdair's getting older, it's a blessing having him around to help with the heavy lifting. The Lord, he takes with one hand, and gives with the other,' she says, crossing herself.

'Is it why Alasdair doesn't like Callum? He told me about young bucks and fallings out, but this is on another level. It must be terribly hard for you both?'

'Yes, it's hard, alright. We try our best not to dwell on the past. Hamish Cleland offered Alasdair £10,000 in compensation. His pride stopped him from accepting it. Ask yourself: what does it say about Callum's guilt?'

'Everything.'

'Exactly. Rory's no angel, I know that. He's done some bad things in his time. He's just a boy who doesn't know his own strength and struggles to relate to people,' Dorothy says, drawing breath. 'When he was a teenager, he used to love playing on Scalaig. He'd fish from the jetty, catch rabbits, shoot deer in the woods and camp out there like kids do. When Callum came home from boarding school during the summer, he'd go out of his way to bully, threaten and frighten Rory away from the island. Back then, Callum thought of Scalaig as his own personal fiefdom. The Clelands allowed the children from the town to play there unsupervised. People thought of it as a children's playground, open to all.'

Wide eyes bore into mine.

I read her thoughts. 'Until we bought it and turned it into a rich man's playground, you mean?'

'I didn't mean it that way,' Dorothy says, twisting her wedding ring. 'It didn't help when that young girl, the backpacker, went missing around the time the Clelands went bankrupt. Things were never the same after that.'

'A missing girl?'

'Yes, a teenager from Yorkshire on a hiking holiday. Her name was Rebecca Barrowclough. The last anyone saw of her, she was setting off alone across the causeway. No one has seen or heard from her since. They never found a body. The police interviewed Rory and Callum about her disappearance. They interviewed the boyfriend, too. They'd been arguing. She'd stormed off. Anyway, back then, Isla and Hamish were close friends of the Chief Constable. I'm sure you're more than capable of drawing your own conclusions. Rory was their prime suspect. They took his clothes and sent them away for forensic examination. Of course, they didn't find anything to incriminate him. As far as I know, she's still a missing person. Of course, Rory's oblivious to it all. At least, I like to think he is…' Her voice trails off. The colour has drained from her face.

Dorothy's revelations are a shock.

'I understand Callum returned to the castle after his parents died in a skiing accident. Surely, he wouldn't have done that if he'd done terrible things here, or if he was involved in the girl's disappearance?' I ask.

Dorothy shrugs. 'Perhaps, you're right. All I know is, Callum Cleland regards Scalaig as his, and his alone. He always did, and he always will. I know he doesn't care to share Scalaig with anyone.'

'Even now?'

Dorothy shrugs, looks away, looks back. 'I've said too much. Take no notice of me. I'm just a silly old woman trying hard to make the best of my lot. Rory shouldn't have frightened you this morning. I'll have words with him. Make sure he understands he's not to bother you, again,' she says, rising, bringing our conversation to an abrupt end.

'Please, don't punish Rory on my account.'

'I won't punish my son for being who he is, my dear,' she says, jaw set firm.

Rising, I place the throw on the back of the chair.

'I'd better be getting back. I've taken up too much of your time, already.'

'Alasdair,' Dorothy shouts. 'Mrs Moran is leaving. Fetch her bicycle.'

I'm dismissed.

'I made some chocolate cakes earlier. Take one with you. You, my dear, need fattening up. I can't have my customers wasting away to skin and bone,' she says, handing me a pink and white striped box, smiling a tight smile. 'It wouldn't be good for business.'

'That's very kind of you. Thank you, Dorothy. I'll enjoy eating it. It'll be a lovely treat.'

'It's no trouble. You'd better get going before the tide turns. Promise me, you'll take care of yourself. Scalaig is a beautiful place, but if you don't respect it, it'll jump up and bite you on the bottom, when you least expect it.'

'I will, I promise,' I say, turning to leave.

CHAPTER THIRTY-NINE

Alasdair waits by the door supporting my bike. He takes the cake box and places it into the basket alongside a brown paper bag.

'Hope you don't mind, only I put some essentials together for you. There's eggs, coffee and fresh bread. I can't have you leaving empty-handed.' His warm smile is comforting.

I'll look like an egg soon.

'Thanks. You're an angel,' I say, swinging a leg over the frame, hitching onto the saddle. 'Would you mind adding it to my account? I'll settle up next week,' I say, with a smile.

'Not a problem. I'll send Rory over with your order,' he says, stalling, realising the insensitivity of his words, glancing away.

Good God. Please don't.

'Thank you.' I smile to conceal my horror.

'Take care,' Alasdair says, turning for the door.

Pushing off, passing the gable end, I freewheel across the road towards the path. In my peripheral vision, I glimpse Rory in the barn door opening. Spying me from under his mop of brown hair, he looks up, sees I'm watching him, turns and slips into the gloom of the barn.

A chill races down my spine and I take a firm grip of the handlebars.

* * *

I reach the causeway as the rising tide is about to consume it. I pedal hard and don't put my feet down until I reach the other side. Pushing the bike up the short flight of steps, it occurs to me I'm becoming a much more confident cyclist.

At the top of the steps, I stall and look back. The sun has chased away the threat of rain. The ocean has reclaimed the causeway. Stalling, I listen to the hypnotic lap of the ocean against the rocks and steps. My fingers loosen their grip on the handlebars. The tension in my shoulders releases.

From somewhere close by I hear the drip of water against a hard surface.

Is the ocean finding its way into a subterranean void?

Smiling, I see the ten-year-old me racing inside the house to tell my father I'd heard a river running under the pavement at the end of our drive. I see father sitting me down, smoothing my curls, describing the labyrinth of tunnels and pipes beneath our feet for sewage and water supply. When, a month later, a sinkhole appeared at the end of the road, I remember father saying, 'Erin, water will always find a way. A month ago when you heard that river, odds are it was a water leak. It will have caused the sinkhole.' I was as proud as punch. Went around boasting to anyone and everyone that I possessed superhuman hearing. As a child, I was always making up fantastical stories.

* * *

Passing through the treeline, I see Bella in her basket on the veranda. Poor thing is probably starving. I left at sunrise and it's now a little after noon. She lifts, stretches, stands with her tail sweeping the deck. She yaps and whimpers. Bounding onto the veranda, I hunker down, press my neck into hers and tickle behind her ears. After a minute, she pulls away, pads over to the empty bowl and addresses me with hollow eyes.

'Non too subtle are you, babe?'

Opening up, I go through to the kitchen, take Bella's dog food from under the sink, step outside and fill her bowl with kibbles. She sniffs at the offering and rolls the kibbles around the bowl. Her nose is dry. And she looks a little thin. I sit and nuzzle into her again.

'What's up, babe? Don't you like this brand? How about a treat? Why don't I cook you a chicken fillet?' I tell her, pushing up from the deck. I hope she's not sick or pining for her old life, or Christian?

Half an hour later, I watch Bella wolf down strips of tender chicken. She cleans her bowl in less than a minute. I sit, balancing the tray on my lap, studying the chicken salad I've made for myself. Brown edged lettuce, sodden tomatoes and flaccid white meat stare up at me from the plate. A plug of bile rises in my throat and I gag. Unable to dispel the nervous acidic feeling sizzling in my gut, I settle the tray on the deck.

Fact is, I could have died earlier. Writing will have to wait. Today is a write off.

A rerun of my conversation with Dorothy plays in my head.

Christian visited the island with other women. Callum threw Rory over the cliff, causing him life-changing injuries.

Rory has done bad things, too. What things?

Worst of all, Callum considers Scalaig his!

And then there's the missing backpacker – the girl from York-shire – last seen on the causeway heading towards the island. No body has ever been found. What happened to her? Rory, Callum, and Alasdair, were they involved in some way?

It's all too much to take in.

I've worn rose-tinted glasses for far too long. My current

marital and creative difficulties seem insignificant against a girl's disappearance. They seem like the briefest of rain showers on a blossoming spring day. Unable to write, I spend the afternoon killing time reading and dozing in the rocking chair on the veranda.

As the sun dips over the horizon, I give up on the day and head inside. I take a long, hot shower, shuffle into pyjamas and roll into bed. Exhausted, sleep consumes me within minutes.

I wake after an hour and lay staring at the ceiling. I try to get back to sleep, but it's impossible. Dorothy's revelations ping around my brain like pinballs. Sleep is impossible. The lodge creaks and groans. Bella pads up and down the stairs, and when moonlight illuminates the bedroom, it forces me awake. Frazzled, I swing out of bed, drag on a cardigan, go downstairs and make myself a steaming mug of hot chocolate. Needing an injection of fresh air, I step out onto the veranda.

Lowering into the rocking chair, my foot connects with something soft. Looking down, I see a child's cuddly toy. It's a well-loved, faded-to-grey puppy. One ear and a glass eye are missing. Threads of cotton hold four frayed limbs in place, but only just. The initials 'R.B.' are machine stitched across the belly in an italic font.

Under my fingers, the close-cropped fur feels damp to the touch. I press it against my chest.

Rory Barr?

I sit gazing at the shimmering silvery dance of moonlight on the surface of the Atlantic at the horizon. Somewhere deep in the pines, an owl hoots. The cogs inside the gearbox of my imagination, turn.

Has Rory been creeping around Scalaig while I've been trying to sleep? Is the puppy an offering? Is it Rory's way of making amends? Or is it intended as a warning? I should have insisted he be told to stay away from the island.

Despite its beauty, I'm starting to resent Scalaig.

Sipping hot chocolate, I rock gently. Slowly, the strings of sleep drag my eyelids down. With a start, I bolt up, go inside, shuffle upstairs and roll into bed.

Imagining the soporific burr of wood pigeons and a breeze shuffling through fields of wheat on a hot summer day, I force myself to sleep.

CHAPTER FORTY

Day 30 - July

I wake and it's mid-morning. Though a beautiful day, I refuse to let it become another groundhog day.

In the early hours, my mind performed mental gymnastics and some home truths became clear. I've been here too long. Scalaig, though stunning, is driving me insane. The isolation is mentally draining. I've set myself a goal of two weeks to finish my manuscript. It's ambitious, but I'm confident. I have to go back to London to formalise the divorce and find somewhere to call home. Somewhere, I'm inspired to write. A view over water would be nice.

I know what I have to do.

After breakfast, I go upstairs and settle at my desk. I won't allow myself a walk or swim, or anything, until I've finished this damn novel, this side of eternity!

Apart from forays to the kitchen for coffee and toilet breaks, I write. I write thousands of words. They're good words; scrub that, they're *great* words. I adore how a story appears on the page. Most writers agonise over daily word count, twists and clever foreshadowing. They fear rejection and scathing reviews. I trust in detailed planning and fully realised characters to do my bidding. It may sound arrogant, but until that day in the coffee shop when Olivia dropped the bombshell that shattered my confidence, I'd never doubted myself. I like to think I understand what my fans love and expect.

I've come to realise that until my own 'happy ever after' collapsed around my ears, I've never been truly psychologically tested. My life with Christian was one long romance novel, and I've been regurgitating my candy-coated life via my stories.

And now I'm here, alone on Scalaig. Isolated. Edgy. Afraid. Hiding behind the sofa from boogeymen of my own making, which, with each passing day, seem more real.

I resolve to throw those fears into the long grass. To see the future through a prism of renewed optimism. To stop procrastinating, create compelling stories and deliver meaningful novels. In the future, my protagonists will be ballsy, my antagonists not so clean cut. My fans will adore them. Or at least, I hope they will.

A loud rap-tap-tap on the front door downstairs breaks me from my reverie. Unable to see the front door from my desk, I race downstairs and inch the door open. I don't need, or want, return visits from Rory, Christian or Callum – the three, not so wise monkeys.

I do a double take.

Olivia, clutching a handbag and an expensive bottle of red, stands on the veranda. I fling open the door and stand in the opening, mouth agog.

'Since I was passing, I thought I'd drop in,' she says, with a liberal dose of sarcasm and a wry smile.

I feel myself filling up. Choked with happiness, I cry, 'Olivia!' Taking her in my arms, I hug her like a long-lost relative.

'What a welcome!' Olivia whispers in my ear. With her hands full, she can't hug me back.

I release her from my embrace. 'What the hell are you doing here? Oh my God, I'm so pleased to see you,' I babble. Stepping left, she reveals Callum Cleland weighed down with bags, what looks like a gourmet food hamper, and a box of wine balanced against his chest. Bella sits at his heel.

'Aren't you going to invite us in? As luck would have it, this handsome young man rescued me from your godforsaken moat. This place is a bloody fortress.'

In a haze of intoxicating jasmine and vanilla, Olivia steps over the threshold. Managing a thin smile, I hold the door open for Callum. We head for the kitchen.

'Put the hamper down in the kitchen, darling,' Olivia instructs Callum. Turning, handing me the bottle of red, she waves a hand theatrically. 'Put it somewhere safe, Erin, darling. It cost a small fortune.' I'm watching from the wings as Olivia – in full party planner mode – directs proceedings. Callum unburdens himself of the bags, the hamper and wine. Familiarising himself with the layout, he locates the wine cooler, breaks out the wine from the box and loads the bottles inside.

Olivia and I share conspiratorial smirks and step into the lounge.

The clatter of glass on metal ceases and Callum appears in the opening. 'Shall I unpack the hamper?' he asks Olivia.

'I'll do it, thanks,' I say. Callum nods, but not before raising a questioning eyebrow at Olivia. She has that effect on people.

'Thank you, Callum. You're an absolute angel. We'll see to the hamper,' Olivia says.

I stand, arms folded, watching the drama unfold. I hope to God she doesn't try to tip him. Instead, she says, 'Why don't you join us this evening? There's plenty enough to drink. It'll be fun having male company.' She turns to me. 'Won't it, darling?'

Stunned, I don't know what to say. Five minutes and already Olivia's made me feel insignificant in my own home.

'Erin?' she prompts, nudging me in the ribs. I return a 'WTF' look.

'Sure... Of course... Why not? How does eight o'clock sound?' *What else can I say?*

Callum smirks. 'Sounds great, yeah. I'd love to. I'll look forward to it.' A hint of surprise in his voice.

'Great. Then it's a date,' Olivia says. 'And don't you dare be late.'

'Thanks... Yeah... I won't. OK... Well... I'd better be off. I'll see you both later,' he says, stepping outside, walking away with a boyish spring in his step. Bella follows him. I call her back. She ignores me. Callum gives her an instruction, she turns and trots back towards the lodge.

Like I say, she's a mans' dog.

'He's so cute,' Olivia says, kicking off city heels. Goodness knows how she walked across the causeway in them. 'You never mentioned you had a *male* friend here?' Her eyes sparkle with mischief.

'He's not a male friend. He's not even a friend. Callum's single and lives alone in the castle at the end of the causeway. You had no right to invite him. You put me on the spot. What the hell were you thinking?' I say, frowning.

'Well, in that case he's fair game then, isn't he, sweetlips?' Olivia says, grinning flirtatiously.

'How can you say that? For one, he isn't even the correct gender. For another, he's much too young for you,' I say, laughing out loud.

Olivia's right shoulder raises into a shrug, her nose wrinkles. 'You know me, I like pretty things. And he sure is pretty,' she says.

God, I've missed her.

'Stop it. You're making me blush.'

'You're such a prude, darling. Look at you, all wound up like a spring. For goodness sake, go and get me a drink. The drive up was an absolute nightmare. Thank God I stopped off en route. I got a last-minute deal on a room at a spa hotel in Penrith. Very nice it was, too.'

'Is it wine o'clock, already?' I say, deflecting her bitching, checking the time. It's ten past five.

'You bet it is. By now, I ought to be on my second gin,' Olivia says, chuckling.

Although Olivia likes a drink, usually she's an after eight kind of girl.

'Sorry, no gin. As you know, there's plenty of wine.'

'Beggars can't be choosers. Wine will have to do. Don't dawdle. We'll sit outside. I want you to explain yourself, young lady,' she says, dumping her jacket on the sofa.

'One minute, I'll put the hamper away. I'll be right back.'

I'm thankful that there's no chai in the hamper. I take my time putting the food away.

A lecture is the last thing I need.

CHAPTER FORTY-ONE

Since Olivia has chosen the rocking chair, I drag the outdoor sofa over and join her on the veranda by the door. I brim crystal wine glasses with cool white wine, sit and curl my legs under my bottom. Chinking glasses, I take a sip of the cool chardonnay. Tiny bubbles fizz on my tongue.

I turn to Olivia. 'It's lovely to see you. Why didn't you call? I would have met you at the end of the causeway had I known. Helped to carry things.'

'Call! Is that supposed to be a lame attempt at humour? I've been trying to contact you for four weeks. Four bloody weeks and not a peep. It would have been easier raising the dead. What's going on, Erin?' she says, draining the wine, thrusting the empty wine glass at me. 'Top me up. That didn't touch the sides.'

I obey.

She's right. How could I forget my broken phone?

'Sorry. My phone's kaput. I dropped it. The starter motor on the car's packed up, too. Getting it repaired is turning out to be something of a nightmare. Truth is, I've been so wrapped up in my novel, that I haven't given anything, or anyone, much thought.'

The last part is a lie. I've no desire to divulge my dark psychological state to Olivia.

Four weeks? Has it been a month already?

Olivia's eyes narrow, then widen. The sternest of glares burns into me. 'I've been frantic with worry. Although loath to do it, I had no option but to call Christian,' she says. She's exaggerating. The 'frantic' part doesn't ring true. Panicking isn't part of Olivia's DNA.

'Did you have to call *him*?' I say.

Perturbed, I don't want to show it.

'Ask yourself … who else knows where you are? I didn't know the postcode. I had to ask *someone, dearest.*'

'What did he say?' What web of deceit has Christian spun this time?

'All I'll say is…'

'Go on.'

'I will if you'll stop butting in… All I'll say is… He was less than complimentary about you. He said you were the last person on earth he wanted to speak to. Idiot suggested I've filled your head with delusions of grandeur,' Olivia says, placing a flat palm across her breastbone, studying me above her glasses. She's indignant. Offended. 'He's pissed off with me, because he thinks I've encouraged you. Given you belief that you can succeed without him. He's been telling everyone you've got cabin fever. That you've let yourself go. Cheeky so-and-so mentioned your hair was a mess. Mind you, darling, he couldn't be more right.' Her cackle echoes from the pines opposite.

I sigh and slug wine.

'Did he mention coming here?'

'No, he did not. When?'

'He arrived unannounced about a week ago. He let himself in. We argued. He freaked out and told me Scalaig was his. Threatened to take it back. Of course, I sent him packing with a flea in his ear,' I say, putting a less than accurate spin on my latest encounter with Christian. I don't want Olivia to see I'm rattled, fearful even.

'Don't worry, darling. Christian's full of wind and piss. He isn't worth the time of day. I came here to see *you*. And that's all that matters. I knew there would be a logical explanation why you weren't answering your phone. I worry about you.'

'I'm sorry. I've been wrapped up in the re-write. In myself...'

They're white lies.

'And...'

'You want a progress update?'

'Well?'

'I'm a happy bunny. Progress has been excellent.'

'Percentage complete?'

'Ninety.'

'Wow! Impressive. How long till it's finished?'

'Two weeks and I'll be typing those two magical words, The End,' I say.

'That's absolutely fantastic. Can I read it?'

'No. Too early,' I blurt, realising I've answered too quickly. 'I want you to read it *fully formed*,' I say.

It seems to allay her fears.

'Two weeks, and not a day more,' Olivia says. In that moment, she's my agent, not my friend. She presses home her point. *'OK?'*

'OK. Two weeks, and not a day more. I promise.'

'Excellent.'

We finish our first bottle of wine. Emancipated by alcohol, I start to relax. It's wonderful to see Olivia. To be in her company. For once, to be able to let my hair down.

Olivia stands. 'I need to get freshened up. Is it alright if I take a shower?'

'Of course.'

'Thanks,' she says, gazing down at me. 'You need to spruce yourself up, too. And while you at it, do something with your hair. You look like a bunch of marauding crofters has dragged you through a hedge backwards. When you've done, we're going to stuff our faces with something delicious from the hamper, washed down, I hasten to add, with copious amounts of fine wine. We need to be in the right frame of mind when that handsome young man of yours, returns. Looks to me like you need a good meal and some R & R,' Olivia says, smirking.

I won't rise to the bait.

Everybody wants to fatten me up. And he's not my young man! I elect silence.

Carrying Olivia's overnight bag upstairs to the spare room, I fetch fresh towels from the airing cupboard. Olivia arrives with refilled glasses. We shower and gossip through open bedroom doors, like teenagers getting ready for a double date.

I laugh so much my face aches.

Have I forgotten how to smile?

CHAPTER FORTY-TWO

The sultry air is heady with pine and salt. Olivia appears on the landing in a full-length lilac Kaftan. Her ears and neck drip with antique gold. She's added thick black eyeliner and swapped the slash of red for the palest of pink lipgloss. She's Elizabeth Taylor stunning.

'Wow!' I say as she twirls. In contrast, I've chosen simple summer attire. I'm wearing white linen. Flares hide a pair of tall wedges.

'You look gorgeous, darling,' Olivia says, collecting my hand. God, she's beautiful and sexy.

We're not yet downstairs when Bella pushes through the door with Callum trailing behind. He's the antithesis of David Blaine. He appears out of thin air when you least expect him.

'You came. Your timing is impeccable,' Olivia says. He looks dashing in a pale blue chambray shirt and beige chinos. His cologne is musky and overpowering.

'Hi,' he says, stepping across the threshold carrying a cardboard box. Glass chinks against glass inside. Two posies of hand-cut flowers lay on top of the box. Flowers *must* grow amongst the weeds in his deceased mother's former cottage garden. He places the box on the worktop, presents the posies, pecks our cheeks. His breath is fresh and minty.

'You two look stunning,' he says, hazel eyes glistening with sparkles of topaz. Olivia makes a show of smelling the blooms. She flicks an imaginary ponytail and her huge earrings jingle. She's overdoing it.

What the hell's got into her?

'Thank you. They're beautiful. I'll fetch a vase. Olivia, be a gem and organise a drink for our guest,' I say, in the hope I might reunite Olivia with her senses.

Olivia turns to me, lips puckered into a pout. 'Of course... Since it's such a beautiful evening, why don't we sit on the veranda? Is that alright with you, Callum?' She's piling on the charm.

Callum shrugs. 'Fine, yeah. I'll go get myself a beer. I brought the wine for you two,' he says, shifting his attention from the praying mantis.

Callum and Olivia follow me into the kitchen. He lifts a bottle of white wine and a stubby beer from the box. Rifling through the cutlery drawer, eventually he finds a corkscrew. He collects two wine glasses from the wall cupboard. Arranging the bottles and glasses on the worktop, he lifts the remaining contents out of the box and fills the fridge and wine cooler. He flicks the cap off of the stubby with his thumb. Opens the wine. Brimming our glasses, he hands them out with a genial smile. We chink glasses and beer bottle. Olivia does that thing with her imaginary ponytail, again. Olivia and Callum are finding it difficult to break eye contact. Clutching the wine glass, I look away.

I'm a gooseberry in my own home.

Sensing my unease, Callum turns his attention to me. 'I'd just like to say how much I appreciate you asking me over tonight, Erin,' he says, beaming. He's charming, friendly and oozes confidence. He's made himself at home. It occurs to me that the cordiality of country folk must come as a surprise to urbanites. In the sticks, it's natural for neighbours to make themselves useful.

Sipping wine, I start to relax. 'I'm delighted you came. Let's go outside. It's too hot in here,' I say, winking at Olivia. My smile is so broad, I feel my eyelashes touch my cheeks.

Stepping outside, we're bathed in a warm orange glow. The low sun is half revealed above the tops of the pines opposite. In less than an hour, it will disappear over the horizon.

Olivia eases onto the outdoor sofa, pats the cushion, and beams. Callum lowers beside her. I choose the rocking chair. Bella flops onto the deck at Callum's feet. Chinking three ways, we're a picture of conviviality. We sit in silence taking long draws on our drinks enjoying the last of the sun. After a minute, the silence is deafening.

Olivia clears her throat, turns to Callum. 'Erin tells me she knows diddly squat about you, other than you're the mysterious man who lives alone in the castle. Since my darling friend is socially inept, why don't you tell us a little bit about yourself?' she says, casting a mischievous smirk in my direction.

'Olivia! Don't be so rude,' I say, hot fingers of embarrassment spreading from my cleavage, along my throat. I know Olivia inside out. She's an outrageous flirt. She didn't become the most successful literary agent in London by being a wallflower. I ought to take a leaf out of her book. But I'm too polite to ask awkward questions, and too shy to flirt.

Callum settles the bottle of beer on the arm of the sofa. 'Don't worry, Erin, it's fine. What would you like to know?' he asks, settling against the cushion, crossing his right leg over his left knee.

'*Everything.* How do you earn a living? How long have you lived here? Are you in a relationship? Usual dinner party icebreaker stuff,' Olivia says, cocking her head on one side. She's being a tease. Callum picks up on it.

'I'll tell, if you do,' he says, eyebrows arching, dabbing beer from pursed lips with his fingers. 'Fair's fair. What do you say?'

The temperature rises a few degrees and I sip cool wine. This could get messy.

'You go first. I never kiss and tell on a first date,' Olivia says, teeth clicking against glass as she toys with her wine and our guest. I'm a voyeur watching foreplay. As I clear my throat, a nervous laugh escapes my lips.

Olivia peers past Callum to me. 'What's a matter, darling? You seem a little, uptight. Lighten up. Callum's a big boy. I'm sure he can take care of himself. Isn't that right, darling?'

'You bet I can. It's nice to have someone intelligent to talk to. This place, while beautiful, is a cultural desert,' he says, grinning. 'I suppose I've become a little wary around people.'

His gaze meets mine. 'I'm sorry,' I say. 'I'm not the most sociable of neighbours, am I?'

Olivia rescues me. 'Well, there you go. You've both been missing out.' She knows me like a sister. 'Callum, you go first. Icebreaker number one: your work?'

She's like a terrier with a bone.

Callum draws a long breath and slugs beer. His Adam's apple dances as he swallows. 'I'm taking some time out. I'm a physiotherapist. In response to your next question, I've lived here all my life, except for boarding school and uni. And, before you ask, yes, at the moment, I'm single.' A wistful expression settles on his face. He's must sense Olivia finds him attractive. That she's there for the taking. He's reeling her in by drip feeding her curiosity. 'How about you? Do you share your life with someone special?'

Sipping wine Olivia's pink lips glisten. I'm watching the spectacle unfold.

'Lots of special people, yes. Most of them are authors. I'm a literary agent. Modesty prevents me from saying I'm the best damn literary agent in London. I was born in Oxford, but live in London. It's where the action is. I'm single.'

They're ordinary words, but when Olivia enunciates them, they ooze sex. Callum will be lucky to escape with his chinos intact. He doesn't appear to care. The air crackles with sexual tension until my voice cuts through the static.

I clear my throat. 'My turn. As you know I'm an author. Modesty prevents me from saying, that I'm the most successful author on Olivia's list.' I say, tongue in cheek.

'By a country mile, darling,' Olivia interjects. 'Though sometimes, it pains me to say it.' She wrinkles her nose at me. I stick my tongue out in mock petulance.

'I was born in Hampshire. The New Forest. For the time being, I regard Scalaig Lodge as home. I'm getting a divorce. Citing adultery on his part. My soon-to-be ex-husband, Christian, is a two-faced, duplicitous snake. The End.' My bluntness has the desired effect. I have my houseguests complete attention. 'Anyway, as entertaining as Olivia's icebreaker game is, I'm famished. I'll fetch some nibbles. We can get to know one another better, while we eat. There's ice cream for dessert, if anyone wants some? You two need cooling down,' I say.

Olivia and Callum see the funny side and laughter restores a relaxed atmosphere to our informal gathering.

Callum bolts up and stands over me. 'Please, let me. I expect you two need a catch-up. And it looks to me like you both need a top-up, too. Do you have an ice bucket?'

Callum disappears inside before I can reply, or object.

'Somewhere,' I call, cranking my neck towards the open door. 'Try the bottom cupboard next to the pedal bin.'

'OK. Will do,' Callum yells. 'Leave it to me.'

I imagine him stepping into the kitchen with Bella at his heel.

Olivia leans towards me. 'What in God's name is wrong with you, woman? I'd have been jumping his bones for weeks. He's gorgeous. There's something really mysterious about him. He's yummy. I could swallow him whole,' she whispers.

'It may have slipped your mind, but I'm in the middle of a

divorce. I've enough on my plate without starting an affair with a guy ten years younger than me.'

'All the more reason, sweetlips. No strings uncomplicated sex with a younger man, or woman, is the best kind. Try it. It'll do you the world of good. You girl, need to learn to let your hair down. A little free love will get your juices flowing. And I'm not just talking about creative juices.'

Olivia knows she's embarrassing me, yet she's savouring every excruciating moment.

'Lower your voice. He'll hear,' I say, glancing over my shoulder. 'Just so you know, I don't believe for one minute, that there's anything remotely uncomplicated about Callum Cleland,' I whisper. 'He's *unusual.*'

Olivia giggles. 'Don't be silly, he's a boy. Of course, he's uncomplicated. If you're not interested then…'

The light dims as Callum arrives in the opening. Our eyes meet. I notice his cheeks are flushed. I suspect he's overheard part of the conversation. Olivia seems unfazed.

Passing between us, carrying the wine bucket, he hums. Olivia makes a show of appraising his rear as he sets the ice bucket down on the low table. Two uncorked bottles of chardonnay float on a sea of ice. I'm convinced he's overheard our conversation and noticed Olivia admiring his bottom. His lips purse into a smug smile and I'm sure I see his chest puff.

He turns, disappears inside and reappears a moment later carrying a tray with cheeses, hams, olives, tapenade, plates and cutlery. It's beautifully presented. It's obvious he's found his way around my kitchen.

'Let's eat. Afterwards, I'll answer your questions. Actually, I'm not the least bit mysterious,' he says, fixing Olivia with a knowing smirk, winking. 'I'm just a simple wee man who happens to live in a castle.'

He did overhear our conversation!

Callum tops up our glasses, flicks the top off of another Bud, slumps onto the sofa and manspreads within striking distance of the cougar.

'Of course you are, darling,' Olivia says, tilting her pelvis towards his thigh, licking her lips and doing the invisible ponytail thing, again.

Callum collects olive bread and garnishes it liberally with tomato tapenade and offers it to Olivia. Dragging his hand away, he licks his fingers and thumb suggestively.

He's not such a simple boy, after all.

CHAPTER FORTY-THREE

Much to my relief, Olivia dials down the sexual overtones and injects polite chitchat. Judging by the intensity of their flirting, they would have been having sex within minutes, had I not been present.

Olivia settles a hand on his sculptured forearm. 'You're such an enigma. Tell me... Why do you live alone in a castle? A young man like you shouldn't be shutting himself away,' she says, rolling her hand. 'Ours is a world of horizons and opportunities.'

I ignore her geographical critique. At least food has calmed her ardour. For the first time, Olivia seems genuinely interested in our guest's intellect and not just his good looks, and what's inside his trousers. I'm desperate to dig deeper, too. Perhaps it wasn't such a bad idea to invite him after all? It's a chance to get to know him. So far, I've only had secondhand titbits and they haven't painted him in a good light.

Give the guy a chance. I tell myself.

Callum has the good grace to follow Olivia's lead and tones down the flirting. He seems pensive, engaged. Cupping his chin between his thumb and forefinger, he massages his stubble. A sound like sandpaper meeting metal fills the air.

'Come autumn,' he says, pausing, 'I'm leaving for pastures new.'

'You surprise me.' It's not what I expected him to say.

'I came back to settle my parent's affairs. Paperwork. Legals. All that guff. It's taking longer than I expected. It's an administrative minefield. You see, my parents died in a skiing accident. Father's will was straightforward. His instructions were explicit. He told me to sell the castle, settle every debt, take what's left, go back to Aberdeen, and never come back. Father was a stickler for organisation.'

Olivia stares at him with hungry eyes. 'Sounds so absolute … so final… Didn't you get on with your parents?' she asks, bringing her circulating index finger to a halt on the rim of the glass.

'That's very perceptive of you. Father and me, we never saw eye-to-eye. He was cold, calculating. We didn't speak much. He never cared for me. If you were to cut his chest open you'd find a block of ice. It's fair to say my father never got used to having a child around. He was too strict by half, and mother didn't care enough, either. Brow beaten, she went along with him,' he says. 'She was spineless.'

He's baring his soul, and it's painful to watch. Olivia has that effect on people. She compels you to open up, even if you've no intention of doing so. Our inhibitions dissolve as the alcohol flows.

'Why Aberdeen?'

'I went to boarding school there.'

'Did you grow up here? In the castle?' Olivia's talons dig deeper into his soul.

'Father worked in corporate finance. He was an equity partner in a company which specialised in multi-million pound takeovers. It suited his personality. He stayed away a lot. Split his time between here, and London,' Callum says, sipping beer. 'The lion's share, alone, in the company flat in Kensington.'

'That must've been hard,' I say. I want to get to know him. Olivia nailed it, *him*. Mystery surrounds him. Call it author's curiosity, but I'm compelled to find out more. One day, he'll feature in one of my books.

He shrugs and his eyebrows raise. 'No, it forced me to become self-sufficient. My father said I was feral. But what did he know?' There's bitterness in his voice. 'My mother tried her best. When he was away, she overcompensated and failed to instil any discipline in me. I ran wild. I had the run of this place.' He waves the bottle of Bud, chews his bottom lip. 'Father was never around to take me fishing or hunting. I can't recall a single occasion when we shared quality father and son time, together. I taught myself how to tie a hook on a line, how to set animal traps, skin rabbits, and survival skills.' Staring towards the pines, his grip tightens on the bottle and I notice his knuckles have turned white. I fear the bottle might explode. Olivia doesn't pick up on it. He falls silent.

'You're quite the Bear Grylls,' Olivia says, sipping wine, moving closer. 'You could make a fortune on TV.'

I study Olivia. Find myself wondering whether she's being sincere.

'It sounds like a wonderful childhood for a boy. That said, you must've been pretty pissed off with your parents when they sent you away to boarding school? Glasgow has some excellent schools. Aberdeen is a long way to send a child,' Olivia says.

Olivia's curiosity is aroused. It's obvious she finds him fascinating.

'When I was ten, my father sold his shares in the company and retired. He worked freelance, though on a much smaller scale. His London trips all but stopped. He could see what I was getting up to, and he didn't like what he saw. He expected me to follow him into the business. Since I love the great outdoors, I wanted to follow my heart. Staring at a computer screen all day, would drive me insane. As a boy, I'd read and watched TV programs about farming. I set my sights on a dairy farm in Cornwall. Father and I, we had fierce arguments about it. *It,* being my future. Mother tried to keep the peace. It was tough on her, I suppose. Pissed off with everyone and anyone, I'd take off alone. Spend days, nights, hiding out here in my shack, on Scalaig,' he says, twirling the beer bottle around with two fingers, directing a smile at me, then Olivia.

Is he referring to the shack we demolished to make way for the lodge?

A shudder runs down my spine as I remember the humongous spider's web above my head, the night Christian and I slept in the shack.

'Is that why he sent you away to boarding school?' I say. In my mind's eye, I'm replaying Dorothy Barr's account of Rory's accident – the day someone threw him over a cliff. Now that I've Callum Cleland on my veranda, it's a chance to hear his side of the story.

'When my teachers started moaning about poor grades and my attitude, father gave me an ultimatum. Either I had to sort my head out, or I'd face the consequences.'

As he recollects every painful nuance of the conversation, his unflinching gaze passes straight through me.

'I rebelled. Thought, sod that. I wasn't used to having anyone pushing me around. It must've been a nightmare for my mother. I pushed every boundary and button to rile him. The harder I pushed, the more stubborn my father became. Mother toed the line. It did nothing to improve matters. I became distant. It was never going to end well. My relationship with my parents was always tenuous.'

He slugs beer. We hang on to every word in silence. It's a darkly compelling narrative.

'So what caused the final schism? I'm assuming there was one.' Olivia won't release him from her mandibles until she's squeezed every last juicy ounce out of him, and his story.

'It was the summer Rory Barr jumped off the cliff. Idiot almost killed himself. He broke his legs. Cracked his skull open,' he says. 'What a prat.'

I gasp, lean in, head cranked on one side.

'Rory jumped?' I query. I can't help myself. This isn't the version Dorothy recited. I need to hear this first hand. A wide-eyed Olivia gawks at me.

'Yeah, the silly sod jumped, alright. We were messing about on the clifftop, throwing stones at gulls and cormorants. The cormorants take a lot of fish. Fishermen hate them. The tide was coming in. Rory got bored and dared us to jump in. I told him to do one. I wasn't that stupid. He was, *is,* a dork. He jumped over, hoping to land in the waves. The tide had just rolled out. He hit the rocks. We all thought he was dead, panicked and ran away. I hid out in the shack. I was ten. I knew they'd blame me. Everyone always did. But it was all Rory's fault. The other kids lied. By reputation, I was a bad apple. And, with Rory in a coma, not able to tell everyone what happened, fingers were pointed at me. Alasdair Barr wouldn't let it go. He drove the families of the other kids out of Scaloon. Of course my wimp of a father did his best to placate him. He tried to pay him off, by offering him a lump sum. Alasdair wouldn't take it. It was a stupid thing to do. It made me look guilty. Barr went around blackening my name. He had the ear of the police. Mother had a nervous breakdown. They sent me away to boarding school. That summer, I spent four weeks there alone. All the other boys had gone home to their families.' I notice his teeth are clenched and his breathing has quickened.

He's reliving every painful moment.

'After this happened, did you eventually return home?' Olivia asks.

Olivia! Let it go. Please…

'After that first year, I was allowed home during the summer holidays. Not that I spent much time with my parents. I'd live here, alone, in my shack. I loved that place. Still do. I kept my head down until it was time to go back to school. I'd return to the castle for meals. For a while, it worked out well. We rubbed along until my father lost his money and sold the island to you and your husband. Eventually, we would have killed one another had we spent any time together, my father and I,' he says, huffing. 'Of course, I'm exaggerating. When I was sixteen, after a massive argument, I ran away. I left home and started sofa-surfing with people I'd met working evenings and weekends, in bars and night-clubs in Aberdeen. My parents continued to pay the school fees. Somehow, I finished my education. Then the money, and any residual love my parents had for me, dried up. Aged eighteen, I was on my own. Then, my parents died in the skiing accident in Switzerland.'

I suck a long breath, hold it in. I feel like I'm in a vacuum.

This is *his* island. We're on the site of his shack. The shack he still loves.

No one speaks. Several silent minutes pass. Lost in thought, I hear a voice. It's miles away at the end of a tunnel. It's Callum's rich baritone.

The pressure normalises.

'Eh, you two, you've stopped drinking. I'll fetch another bottle of wine, if you like? Can I use the bathroom?' Callum asks.

I hear his question, though it doesn't register.

'Erin?'

'Sorry, yes, of course you can. It's upstairs, the second door on the left,' I say.

Callum disappears inside. Olivia beams playfully.

'Wow! Didn't I tell you he was mysterious,' Olivia says. 'Quite a story don't you think?'

'I suppose so… Are you warm enough?'

'Ugh? I am. What do you think? Don't you find him fascinating?'

I shrug. 'He's had an interesting childhood, that's for sure.' I shake off the uneasy feeling.

Am I overreacting again?

'And to think it all happened *here*,' I say, joining in Olivia's game. We're whispering conspiratorially like schoolgirls hiding a half litre bottle of gin behind the bike shed. Olivia's drunk on his story, and him.

'It's a tragic story. Makes him even more attractive, don't you think?' Olivia says.

'No, it doesn't. I agree it's tragic. To be honest, I find him a tad creepy. He's not my type. He shouldn't be yours, either. Need I remind you, I'm supposed to be the romantic one.' I say, stabbing her playfully in the ribs.

'Romance? Did I mention romance? Watch and learn, my little rug rat. Before the night's out, I'll have him eating out of my cleavage. Watch,' she says, miming a feline's paw. 'And learn.' She's the living embodiment of a cougar.

'Olivia, stop it,' I say, feigning disgust. It's a pitiful attempt. We giggle so much I worry I'm about to pee my knickers. I fail to notice Callum standing in the opening behind us.

'Eh, you two, what's so funny? Pray tell,' he says, with an inflection of paranoia, nostrils flaring.

I roll my gaze to him. 'Sorry, it's nothing. We've had too much wine. We're a wee bit squiffy,' I say, cheeks reddening.

Shrugging, he hands to each of us in turn a glass brimmed with ice-cold, white wine. Bubbles cling to the crystal. Drops of condensation land on my knee.

'Enjoy. Choosing wine isn't my thing,' he says.

I believe I see him grit his teeth.

'Don't mind us, Callum, darling. It's just silly girl talk,' Olivia says, sipping wine. 'By the way... This wine is simply *divine*.' Olivia purrs like a cat being stroked under the chin.

Here we go...

'Thank you, Callum. Olivia's right, it's lovely,' I say. 'Are you having one?' I raise my glass, take a sip.

'I'm good with beer, thanks. I don't *do* wine. It doesn't agree with me; gives me a stinking headache,' he says, settling on the sofa beside Olivia. She slides against him and chinks her glass against his beer bottle.

The cougar moves in for the kill.

'Impressive house you've got yourself here, Erin,' he says. 'Did your husband build it?'

I can't decide whether he's bored with Olivia's advances or making small talk. It seems to be a conscious attempt to keep me in the loop.

'Yes, insofar as he briefed the architect. Christian wouldn't know one end of a hammer from the other.'

Olivia is scowling. 'Hold it right there! We are not, repeat *not*, going to talk about him.' She waves her glass and spills a little wine on Callum's lap. 'Oops, sorry,' she says, brushing the wine off of his groin, stalling her hand there for several seconds.

'You're right. Let's change the subject,' I say. 'Let's drink to us and new found friendships. To new beginnings.' Thrusting my glass forward, we chink a three-way toast.

'To new beginnings,' Callum says.

'I'll second that,' Olivia purrs. 'New beginnings.'

Callum refills our glasses. Bella's doggy snores roll off into the night and echo through the pines.

Another hour passes, and the alcohol continues to flow.

For the first time in months, I feel mellow. I grin like I'm high on something white and powdery – not that I've any experience with anything white and powdery, I hasten to add. My breathing slows. High overhead, silver diamonds gyrate against a black canvas. I'm trying to remember when I last drank several glasses of wine in one evening, when I realise we've – Olivia and me – drunk at least two bottles each, probably more. I clutch the brimmed glass against my chest and stare a dreamlike stare into space.

It occurs to me that I'm watching Olivia and Callum swoon over one another. They're whispering. Their words wash over me like the tide across the shore. Through the blur, I watch their mouths connect. *Are they kissing?* Olivia's lilac kaftan rises on the breeze and I glimpse tiny, ivory breasts, supplanted by dark, bullet-like nipples. She doesn't seem to mind. Callum has his hand on her hips. She's floating. She's beautiful and angelic. I sip wine. Weightless, I'm enjoying the spectacle.

I want it to be me...

Olivia and Callum dissolve...

'We had better get you to bed.' Callum's voice comes at me through the ether and I feel his warm breath against my cheek. The heady, hoppy aroma of beer fills my nostrils. Strong arms slide under my thighs and I'm weightless. Floating, I nuzzle against his neck and inhale his musk. I levitate in his arms. Olivia's legs swing up and she drapes her right arm over the cushion. She's a figure in a pre-Raphaelite painting – supine, serene and naked. I've never seen her so content. Her face is like alabaster. Her eyes are closed. She's no longer wearing her glasses. Her beauty is framed by her perfect black hair. The image fades. I reach out to touch her, but she's untouchable and beyond my reach.

Callum takes my hand and wraps my left arm around his neck.

'Goodnight,' I whisper.

The next I know, the bed rises to meet me and I'm falling through the air and landing in its warm embrace. The instant my head hits the pillow, I sink into it. I feel fingers brushing strands of hair off of my cheek.

'Goodnight, Erin,' a male voice whispers.

The last thing I hear is the latch clicking into the frame.

CHAPTER FORTY-FOUR

Day 31

Jagged teeth chomp at my face through an intricate web of orange fishing net. Calloused hands caress my ankles, calves and thighs from under the sheets. Firm on my wrists, they drag me down. Menacing mandibles move in for the kill, and I whip my head around. Yellowing, bloodshot eyes wild with madness glare at me. A fish tail slaps against the pillow by my ear. At the foot of the bed, a skeletal stickman wags a gnarled finger. Beside him, a hook-nosed old woman with a pumpkin-coloured face, scolds me in a tongue I don't recognise...

Bolting up, breathless, I blink into the darkness and try hard to chase away the apparitions. An agonising scream and pulsating thuds reverberate around my skull. Coming to, I realise it's *my* scream and *my* heart punching against my ribs. I'm covered in a sheen of cold sweat. I feel like a cat has puked a hairball into my mouth while I slept.

Where am I?

As my heart rate steadies, and my thoughts coalesce, I recognise the familiar outlines of the bedroom: the pitched ceiling, and the sunlit outline of the window beyond the curtains.

As the nightmare recedes, I rub my eyes, and snapshot images unreel in my mind. I see milky-white breasts, searching hands, and Callum's malevolent grin. As darkness envelops me, I hear the slap of skin on skin and the ecstatic groan of male release.

Are these things real or imagined? Did I watch?

I feel dirty. Last night is an uncertain haze. I hate not knowing.

Damn...

Did I take part? Do anything I'm going to regret till my dying day?

Reaching under the sheet, I realise I'm dressed. I push my hand down the front of my knickers and run my fingers between my legs. There's nothing to worry about.

Thank God.

The mother and father of hangovers drums a steady beat behind my forehead. I need water, a shower and coffee, before I can face my houseguests. I reach for the bottle of water on the bedside cabinet. Despite the sour and earthy taste, I drain it and stagger into the bathroom. A hollow ache sits where my gut ought to be.

Was I punched?

Leaning on the sink, I stare at my reflection returned in the bathroom mirror.

I look like shit.

I scour the fur from my teeth. Alcohol seeps from every pore. Stepping into the shower, I spin the dial to maximum. Gritting my teeth, I step under the deluge and let it get to work. Drawing exasperated breaths, I overdo it with the shower gel and squeeze out too much. A palm-sized dollop splatters onto the tiles, infusing the steam with the sweet essence of lavender. It occurs to me I've spent hours in this shower since I arrived on Scalaig.

Can I wash away ten years of marriage? Is it even possible?

As the stream of water stalls and spits, I realise I've been standing under the shower so long, I've drained the tank.

Stepping out, shaking off my stupor, I wrap a fluffy white towel around me and return to the bedroom. Tucking the towel in, I notice several ribs. Olivia is right. I've got skinny. Padding over to the window, I drag the curtains open and recoil from daylight like a vampire. My head feels like a ripe watermelon that's fit to burst. At the dressing table, I apply moisturiser, mascara and lipgloss and pull anti-frizz oil through my hair. It takes an enormous effort. Fearing the light, fumbling in the semi-darkness, I drag on a pair of cropped jeans and an oversized t-shirt. I can't bear the prospect of Olivia's wrath, if she were to see me in such a mess.

Creeping along the landing, I peek into the spare room, half expecting to see Olivia laid next to Callum. But the bed is empty, sheets dishevelled. A duvet lies crumpled on the floor beside the bed. It's obvious the bed has seen some action. I creep to the guest bathroom and press my ear against the door. Hearing nothing, I sneak downstairs avoiding loose treads to save my aching head. Unused to houseguests getting it on, I don't know the correct protocol. Have Olivia and Callum deserted me? Have they gone for a walk to blow away the cobwebs? Bella is absent, too. My addled brain demands coffee.

In the kitchen, wine-stained glasses, empty beer bottles, and plates of half-eaten food lay scattered across the worktop. It was a party of three, yet it looks like thirty-three. I pile the plates on top of one another and sweep the empties into a bin bag. Razor-sharp knives drive into my swollen brain as each bottle hits the floor. Filling the dishwasher is pure torture.

I feel nauseous, dizzy. The room starts to spin gathering momentum. To my relief, I make it to the sink in time. Retching, salty tears smudge my makeup. I'm having a *never again* moment.

Clutching a mug of coffee, I pad into the lounge and cross to the window. I stand gazing out across the garden, blowing across the top of the mug, taking tentative sips, until caffeine infuses the places only caffeine can. Glasses, bottles and party leftovers lie scattered around the veranda. It's years since I've had a night like last night, and it's blindingly obvious I'm not the twenty-some-thing party animal, I used to be. It will take me days to recover.

With a resigned huff, I turn from the window, pad over and collapse into the armchair by the fireplace. My gaze settles on a slip of notepaper wedged under the Caithness glass paperweight in the centre of the coffee table. Frowning, unsure of what it is, I reach forward and collect it.

> **sorry had to dash, sweetlips… tried but couldn't wake you…**
> **Fabulous night and sex! I'll see you soon in the big smoke…**
> **O xxx**

Sitting back, I re-read the note, not once, but twice. Fact is, Olivia has left without saying goodbye.

How insensitive!

Holding my head in my hands, I massage my temples. A plug of something nasty catches in the back of my throat and I swallow hard. Hurt morphs into anger. I'm alone, a sad and lonely character.

Selfish bi…

I stop myself. *What good will cursing Olivia do?*

I haven't got a clue what she sees in him. Yes, I have… Olivia isn't the slightest bit interested in him as a person. She's curious and bi-sexual. And he's a hunk. A conquest. One more notch on her headboard. Olivia collects notches like some people collect stamps. I rationalise she was asserting some kind of perverse, gynocentric dominance.

More fool him.

He could have ignored her overtures, acted like he didn't notice, or wasn't interested, but, no, not him, because he enjoyed it too. He got off on her attention. Older women must be his thing.

'Gigolo,' I snort.

I could cry, but I'm too hungover and I don't have the energy.

I shouldn't blame Olivia – she is who she is – revels in being unorthodox. Validates her lifestyle by taking what she wants, when she wants.

Last night is a blur. The fog of excessive alcohol obscures my memory. I recollect Callum refilling our glasses so many times that I lost count. In my mind's eye, I watch him lift, carry and lay me down in bed. After that, my memory is non-existent. I'll quiz him, later.

Heaving my exhausted body back to the bedroom, I swallow three paracetamol, close the curtains, roll into bed, drag the sheet over me and close my eyes.

It's kill or cure.

CHAPTER FORTY-FIVE

Day 32

I'm woken by a blinding flash of silver and the grumble of thunder. Bolting up, I see only darkness. I've lost the entire day to my hangover. The heat and humidity of the past week has worked itself into a frenzy. Everything quietens as the storm draws breath, before unleashing its violent wrath. A low rumble builds to a melancholic growl overhead. Rain pelts against the window in long diagonal spears. Slates rattle. Lightning strobes the sky in long meandering arcs of silver. The casements shake in the frame. Scalaig Lodge hunkers down against the assault.

Dragging the sheet over me, I hide like a frightened child from the raging tempest swirling outside. The storm rages for an hour until the comforting arms of sleep take me in their embrace. I sleep in intermittent bursts punctuated by dream-like periods of wakefulness. Sunrise brings the onslaught to an end. Drenching mizzle displaces the rain; not untypical for the West Coast of Scotland.

The thunderstorm has sucked the summer heat out of the air. Feeling the chill, shivering, I dress quickly, go downstairs and make coffee. Standing at the worktop, I gaze towards the causeway shrouded in a grey cloak of mist, and plead for the kettle to hurry up and boil.

I realise with a start: *Where's Bella? Where has she got to now?*

Glancing over my shoulder, I call her name. I realise with horror that I haven't seen or heard from her for hours. I've been so ill and hungover – not to mention angry with Olivia – that I haven't given her a second thought. Bella hates storms, yet I've left her to her own devices when she needed me most. An acid knot of anxiety tightens in my gut. My shame is palpable and acute.

Poor Bella.

Foregoing coffee, I step outside. An oily sheen covers the deck, dirty wine glasses, empties and plates of sodden food. Rain – driven on by the wind – has drenched the furniture and Bella's outdoor bed. Bella is notable only by her absence. I call her name. My calls – dampened by the mizzle – dissolve to silence. I call again without reply. No bark, yap, growl or whimper, responds to my increasingly frantic calls. I have to find her. Cold and afraid, she'll be sheltering somewhere.

I pull on my Helly Hansen sailing jacket, slip on a pair of striped boating shoes, and button up against the weather. Dragging the door closed behind me, I set out into the murk. Striding along the path, I drag the hood up. I pass through the garden gate and turn right along the waterlogged dirt path. Ten metres along, and the bottom of my jeans are sodden. I'll search Bella's favourite haunts: the causeway, cove and woods. I discount the cliffs, since she knows better than to go anywhere near them.

Reaching the steps down to the causeway, I call her name. If she's down there somewhere, she'll hear me. I imagine her bounding up the steps with a contrite look in her eyes, fluffy tail pressed high between her legs. Nothing moves. No yap or bark. Can she hear me against the mizzle, which seems to absorb every sound? I elect to search the area around the causeway.

I place my right foot on the top edge of the slimy timber riser, and, as I transfer my weight, my foot slips from under me and I dig my heel in. But it's already too late. Soaring through the air, I land on my bottom in the mud. In an instant, the impact drives the air from my lungs and a bolt of searing pain fires along my spine and reaches my brain.

'Argh!'

Gasping for breath, I push up from the ground. Straightening, massaging my right side, I manipulate my lower back to ease out the tension. Nothing is broken. Only my pride is injured. Green slime coats my hands, jacket and jeans. A damp patch encircles my bottom. I descend the steps one tread at a time.

Slow down! Otherwise, you'll break your neck...

It's early morning, and the tide is at its lowest. I scan the conduit of battleship grey rock bereft of seawater and pockmarked by rock pools. I call Bella's name, but the mizzle swallows my voice. Just when I decide the weather can't get any worse, pellets of rain drum against my hood. She's not there. I pause to think. A minute later, I've convinced myself Bella would never leave the island without me.

Would she?

We instilled in Bella the boundaries when she was a puppy.

Didn't we?

At the Skye end of the causeway, I peer into the murk and discern the dark outline of Scalaig Castle. Mizzle licks my face, trickles down my neck and clings to my eyelashes. The wind rises and the outline of Scalaig Castle appears from the frigid blur. A diffused orange glow catches my eye in a second-floor window.

Callum *is* there. I know he is. For an instant, I consider asking him if he's seen Bella, then, hesitating, I decide against it. A cauldron of anger boils within me. I could curse and yell like some demented Shakespearean hag, but I don't want to go there. What chance then would I have of getting the car repaired? Callum would abandon me. Just like Olivia has.

Damp penetrates my bones. Cold creeps over my skin and I shudder.

My thoughts return to Callum's repulsive behaviour. How I'd woken with an uncertain feeling of being violated. A dirty feeling. Deep down, I know he took advantage of me, and Olivia too. But in what way?

Callum professes to be oh-so-helpful and accommodating, yet he delights in maintaining an air of mystery. Something tells me he's not all he professes to be.

Casting my mind back, I see him making himself at home in the kitchen and on the veranda.

'Smarmy bastard,' I grumble.

I'm furious. He's stolen my best friend when I needed her most. There's every chance he's taken advantage of her in the most carnal of ways.

But how will I ever know? Did I watch? Was my drink spiked?

Somehow, my conscious mind fell off a cliff. One minute I was there, the next, I wasn't.

Huffing, I turn and set off back along the causeway to Scalaig.

Seeing the orange glow in the castle window has set my imagination running. The possibility Callum is at home, angers me. My heart rate soars. The balloon of hurt in my chest inflates. Stepping along the path, I kick the dirt and stamp my feet like a petulant child.

'You could at least have helped me clean up the mess, you bastard! And you haven't fixed my damn car!' I scream, stamping my feet.

The rain becomes a deluge against my hood and drowns out my thoughts. My temples throb. My breathing quickens. I stuff wet hands deep into pockets and try hard to calm my angst.

I have to focus. Where to next?

It's conceivable Bella's at the cove. I visualise her hunkered down against the boulder, sheltering from the rain.

CHAPTER FORTY-SIX

A darkening sky looms above the murk. Pines shuffle in the rising wind. The storm is returning. Scalaig is about to receive a second helping. Atlantic summer storms are violent and unforgiving.

Reaching the clifftop, I scan the cove and yell Bella's name at the top of my voice. Cranking my head on one side, I wait for a reply. When none comes, my heart fractures a little more.

Launching onto the sand, I set off across the beach in long strides. Treacle thick sand rags at my feet. It's hard going.

Reaching the shore, a fine mist of briny seawater assails my face and exfoliates my skin. I turn and jog to the rock. Satisfied she's not there, I set off for the jetty. The wind has dropped, and the murk closes in again. Mizzle conceals the end of the jetty.

My expensive jacket has failed me and I'm cold and wet.

Arriving at the jetty, dragging the hood aside, I listen hard in the hope I might hear a yap, whimper or whine. Something solid and unyielding crashes against the timber piles to a regular beat.

Ummpphhh... Ummpphhh... Ummpphhh...

It's an eerie lament.

I clamber onto the exposed, open-sided jetty to investigate. Feeling vulnerable, I cower down against the elements and shuffle crab-like towards the end. As I move across the boards, ancient timbers creak and fountains of icy seawater spurt up through the gaps, drenching me. Reaching the end, I halt, turn away from the wind and hunker down. Go any further and I could ditch headlong into the ocean.

I notice a cobble tied to the jetty. The deck is empty, wheelhouse locked. Nobody will be onboard in this weather. The fisherman will be at home, waiting out the storm, while I'm out here, alone, cold and wet.

Bella isn't here.

I'm forced out in the foulest of foul weathers to search for Bella because I was stupid enough to let my guard down and get so drunk that I couldn't even care for myself, let alone my most treasured possession, Bella. A shiver creeps up my spine. My head throbs in time with the boat crashing against the timbers.

I ought to search the woods.

Ten minutes later, I slide to a halt on the carpet of pine needles.

'Bella!'

Nothing. No echo. Or reply. If she's here, she could be anywhere. A network of paths runs through the woods. They're good for hunters and inquisitive canines, but not a cold, wet and distraught me. Not knowing where Bella is, is freaking me out. I'm torn. Paralysed by doubt, I don't know which way to turn. Which direction to take? Which path to follow?

Where is she?

I decide on a south-westerly direction towards the ocean, west of the cove. At least it's dry underfoot and not so sludgy. Every few yards, I halt. Yell. Listen hard. Twigs snap. Leaves crunch. Deer? Rabbit? A fox? I pray it's Bella. Hot and sticky, t-shirt clinging to my skin, I grapple with the Helly's zip. I can't unzip it quickly enough. Adrenaline fizzes through me. My breathing quickens. I stall, breathe deep, try to calm quivering fingers and drag the zip half way down, wafting the heat away.

Losing sight of the path in the undergrowth, disoriented, I spin around and study the ground. The path has petered out to nothing. My gut churns. Fear squeezes my chest like a vice. I try to yell, but my voice comes out as a wheezy rasp. Bella won't hear or recognise my voice. It doesn't even sound like me.

After searching for an hour, dispirited, I lower onto a fallen log, settle my head in my hands and massage my temples.

I have to think… *Where can she be?*

Behind me, something snaps. A twig? Something else? I can't be sure. Silence envelops me. Half a minute passes. High overhead something unseen scuttles through the canopy. I sit still, listening hard. Another crack, more scuttling, followed by silence.

'Bella… Bella…' I call forlornly.

Another sharp crack.

'Who's there?' I ask, moderating my voice.

Silence.

I sense somebody, or *something*, close.

'I know you're there. Show yourself,' I call, bolting up, whirling around like a spinning top.

'Who is it?' I moan.

A lump catches in my throat and I swallow hard, listening for movement. The rain has stopped.

Or, is the canopy so dense, rain can't pass through?

'Bella. Come here. Stupid hound,' I yell. I'm becoming desperate. Interminable silence surrounds me. No wind. No trace of movement. My heart races.

Another crack. Hidden from sight, something ricochets around the canopy. The wall of eerie silence around me amplifies the sound. Lowering onto my haunches, I cower in the ferns by the log and cover my face with my hands. Something rustles through the undergrowth behind me. I take a long breath and hold it in. Hardly daring to look, I peek through the gaps between my fingers. A flash of white disappears into the undergrowth.

It's the tail of a deer.

'You're losing it, lady. Pull yourself together,' I hiss.

It appears I've been tracking a deer. *Or am I the one being tracked? Hunted?* The great outdoors is a mystery to this particular city girl.

It's time I removed my finger from the panic button. I need to calm down before I go to pieces. I'm no good to Bella, or anyone like this.

I calm my breathing and feel my heart rate subside. I scan the area. To my surprise, I locate the footpath two or so metres ahead, half concealed by ferns. Fear has blinded me. It was there all along. I feel my hysteria dissipating. I need to focus. Bella *has* to be on Scalaig somewhere, hasn't she?

Although unfamiliar, I follow the footpath. It's well worn. Boot-sized footprints indicate recent use. Chances are it's one of Rory Barr's hunting trails.

Overhead, the canopy thins, and the rain strengthens. I stumble along the footpath negotiating knee-high ferns and nettles and clawing branches. The only saving grace are the narrow shafts of light that aid my progress. Reaching the treeline, I see the ocean. Directly ahead, several car's length away is the clifftop. I hesitate, telling myself Bella can't possibly have come this far.

CHAPTER FORTY-SEVEN

Passing into open ground, rain peppers my face and the howling wind rips at my jacket. I shuffle over to the clifftop with my head down. Slipping to a halt in the mud, I gaze down over thirty feet of vertical rock. Below the cliff, the foreshore is a series of rocky fingers creating deep ravines at right angles to the cliff face running toward the ocean. I'm not familiar with this area. I study the jagged coastline. The mizzle has lifted. A diffused yellow hue conceals the meeting of ocean and sky at the horizon. I take it as a portent that another storm is brewing.

Behind my temple, my brain throbs. Deep inside my chest, my broken heart yearns to see Bella; to run my fingers through her fur; to tickle her ears. I call without reply. I've failed her. I've turned over every stone and come up with nothing. Drenched, tired and disconsolate, the time has come to call it a day, return to the lodge and warm up by the fire.

In my mind's eye, I imagine Bella hunkered down on the veranda, shivering and hungry. Elated, I bound up the steps. Rising, Bella yawns, lays her head on one side and settles innocent, questioning eyes on me. 'Where have you been?' she asks.

A theory pops into my head. When I was sleeping off my hangover, unable to rouse me, needing to relieve herself, she'll have ventured outside in the rain. Poor thing. It's all my fault. I'm to blame. Panicking, I've taken off on a wild goose chase, searching for a lost dog that was never lost. That will be it. She'll be at the lodge waiting for me on the veranda. Tutting, I look to the heavens and shove my hands a little deeper into the Helly's pockets.

Turning, I hear what I think is a faint whimper.

Did I?

I turn and take a step forward. Any more and I'd fall over the cliff.

I hear a weak whine above the din of the surf.

'Bella? Bella?' I cry, scanning the foreshore.

Another whimper!

I try to triangulate the noise.

A whine, perhaps?

The whines and whimpers seem to be coming from the east. I turn, scan the foreshore, spin my gaze along the fingers of rock and the ravines between them. Everything blurs. I smash my eyes closed.

Slow down, I tell myself. *She needs you…*

I hear another tortured whimper above the surf. It seems to last forever. Revolving right towards what I hope is Bella, I stall and open my eyes.

In a ravine between two fingers of rock, I spy a foot-square patch of golden fur.

It's Bella!

'Oh my God… Oh my *God!*' I cry. She's still, lifeless. I take three agitated, though careful strides right for a better perspective. I see a narrow, meandering vee-shaped ravine. Bella is wedged in the bottom five metres from the rock face, two metres from the incoming tide. Her nose faces the open ocean. Her right hind leg projects up and behind her at an unnatural angle.

'Hold on, darling. I'm coming…'

Sucking air, summoning the courage to tackle the cliff, I step to the edge. Peering over, I'm overcome by a rush of vertigo. The world spins. Behind glass, I'm fine. High-rise buildings aren't a problem. This is different. The ocean wobbles at the horizon. Fearful of pitching headlong over the cliff, I step back, turn and face the pines.

Someone help me.

'Help me!' I bellow.

Rallying, accepting my options are all but exhausted, I grit my teeth and spin around to face my fears. Glancing down, I find Bella again. A laughing seagull reels overhead. It must, in some perverse way, find my predicament amusing. My cries go unanswered.

Try! She'll die otherwise...

It's madness to think I can scale the cliff without equipment.

She's going to die if you don't... OK! OK!

Lowering onto the saturated ground, I flip over onto my belly, shuffle back and hang my feet over the edge. The ground is cold and wet. Sucking air, I gather my thoughts. Glancing over my shoulder, I spot a tree root projecting from the topsoil layer above the rock. I estimate it to be three feet long, and an inch in diameter. I grab it with both hands and lower myself gingerly over the edge. The root creaks under my weight. My feet scrabble across the rock as I search for a foothold. My swinging right foot finds and settles on a narrow ledge. I move my left foot beside it. Just as I'm feeling a little happier, the root I'm holding snaps with a twang. My upper body swings back and away from the rock face. Weightless, I grasp out frantically. My fingertips meet rock. I drag forward and settle my cheek against the saturated, icy cliff. Holding on for dear life, I suck long exasperated breaths. Scanning the rock, I locate a crevice. It's perfect as a handhold. I reach out and push my fingers into it.

Stalling, I need time to think.

I have no choice but to climb down and try to reach Bella, since I'm her only chance.

'C'mon,' I yell. 'You've got this.'

With a quick glance at the waves crashing over the foreshore below, I release the fingers of my right hand from the rock face. I move my hand down. The time has come to trust my instincts.

To my relief, the next ledge is closer than I thought. First, I need to focus, concentrate on the climb and block out the fear. It's easier said than done. Gusts of wind surge and eddy up the vertical wall of rock. I take a firm grip of the uneven surface. When the wind eventually subsides a little, I start the climb down. Progress is slow and tortuous. Five minutes later, reaching the foreshore, I inhale a long breath and hunker down against the wind.

Peering over my shoulder, I watch geysers of icy seawater spurt over Bella. I have to act with speed, otherwise the rising tide will sweep her away and she'll drown. As will I, if I don't get a move on.

Crouching, I scramble across seaweed-covered rocks. It's as slippery as hell. I spread myself like a spider and move down the incline. I slip and crash against the unforgiving surface. Sliding into the ravine, I snatch at seaweed and halt my slide. My face stings. Tasting blood, I realise I've bitten the inside of my cheek.

I'm too slow. The tide is rushing in to meet us. I'm going to be too late.

'Move, Bella, darling, move,' I cry.

Slithering into the ravine, my calves tremble under tension and lactic acid burns my muscles. The urge to give up is overwhelming.

But I'm close, now.

I can't give up. I've got to push through the pain barrier. Inch by excruciating inch, I move forward. The incoming tide is just inches from Bella's nose. There's no time to waste.

I rip off my jacket and throw it over Bella. Any fool can see her leg is broken. Craning over her, I see snots of bloody foam bubbling from her nose and mouth with each shallow breath. Her eyes are closed.

'Bella!' I scream above the roar of the wind and crash of the rising surf. Tears cascade down my cheeks. Shaking her, I apply pressure. She's unresponsive. I'm too late. She's dead.

Then, just as I'm about to give up on her, her right ear flicks.

Thank God.

I scan the area searching for a way out. I have to find a route to safety via the cove. The beach beyond beckons. Bella needs urgent veterinary attention.

High above, something moves in my peripheral vision and I look up. A man stands silhouetted against the sky on the clifftop. He steps to the edge, leans forward and peers down. He's seen us. Is watching the spectacle unfold. Has he come to help? Praising the Gods, I wave my right arm and cup my left hand around my mouth.

'Help! Help!' I shout. 'Please!' A gust of wind plasters hair across my face. For a second, I'm blinded. I push the hair aside, blink.

He's gone.

There was someone there, wasn't there? I saw him, didn't I?

'Help me,' I cry.

Snot balloons from my nostrils and blows off on the wind. My desperate cries go unanswered. I return my gaze to the clifftop. Only a blank canvas of grey exists where he stood.

I'm hallucinating...

CHAPTER FORTY-EIGHT

I'm bereft. Bella's survival is in my hands. With Bella in this condition, scaling the cliff is impossible. The cove is my only hope.

The tide is rising. Another fifteen minutes and the ocean will cover the foreshore, the ravine, and us.

Hunching forward, I whisper, 'Wait here, sweetheart, I won't be long. Promise.' I tell her, placing the jacket over her comatose body.

I head east, scramble over the treacherous rock until I reach a huge boulder. It looms over me and blocks my route. Pulling up, peering over, I see the cove. I'm closer to it than I first thought. Waves of hope flood my heart, spurring me on. Sea spray scours my skin, rekindles my fear, and douses the flames of my resolve.

Do I have enough strength to carry Bella around the boulder to safety, before we're cut off and drowned?

'Stop it!' I growl. If I fail, then we'll wash out to sea and our bodies will never be found. No one will ever know our destiny. It's as simple as that.

On hands and knees, I slip slide over the foreshore to Bella. Pushing my hands under her jowls, I lift her head. Her ears flick.

She's still with me, just. But there's no time to waste. If we don't escape the foreshore and the tide, then we'll die. I'm sure of it.

I won't, *can't,* allow that to happen.

Bella is saturated and clinging on to consciousness. Sniffling a river of snot back up my nose, I swallow hard. Bella is a dead-weight. I'm going to struggle to lift her, let alone carry her any distance. I need a stretcher. But what?

My jacket?

Removing my jacket from Bella, I lay it down next to her and smooth it flat. I ease her up and push the jacket under her limp body as far as I'm able to. Crouching, I scramble across the ravine and drag the jacket under my injured dog. It's a gargantuan effort. I've fashioned a sledge to break the friction. It's our only hope.

'I'm sorry. I'm trying to be careful,' I whisper into Bella's twitching right ear.

Rain whips against my face. Saturated clothing drags me down. Ripping off my cardigan, I throw it off. I'm going to need all of my strength to lift Bella out of the ravine, over the foreshore, and around the boulder to the safety of the cove.

I swing across the ravine using the hood as a pivot. Landing on the other side, I draw a lungful of moist air. It's a life or death situation.

Dragging on the hood, Bella slides out of the ravine and slumps onto the rock beside me like a huge, wet fish. Elated, I lay back on the bladderwrack.

I can't get overconfident. A lethal layer of slimy seaweed carpets the foreshore. One slip and I could fall and smash my head against the rocks. Injured, I'd succumb to hypothermia within the hour. The ocean would take me first, Bella soon after. It's a deadly environment.

My saturated boat shoes feel leaden. Searing pains stab through my feet, up through my ankles and along my calves.

Taking a firm grip on the hood, I heft Bella across the rocks. Progress is slow, tortuous, and painful. Cramping up, the pain in my thighs is unbearable. My tortured breaths blow away on the wind. Each laboured step drags more heat from my body. My teeth chatter like a pneumatic drill against concrete. Biting cold freezes my fingers to a clumsy numbness. Losing my grip on the hood, Bella slides away and crashes into a boulder perched above a deep ravine.

My heart misses several beats. Another life or death moment.

'No!'

Sliding over the bladderwrack, I seize the hood and with a mighty effort, heft Bella away from the ravine.

I estimate the boulder to be about five metres away. If I can make it to the cove, then there's hope.

At first progress is uneventful, but as we reach a layer of glistening rock strewn with seaweed, the icy jacket slips through my frozen fingers and Bella slides off down the slope towards the boulder, again. Scrambling up, I launch after her feet first down the slope. Bladderwrack cushions my landing. We arrive at the boulder together and I slam my right foot against it and tense my leg. Bella crashes against my calf. My leg buckles and an inferno of pain ignites within my knee. I won't succumb. Tensioning my leg, I take Bella's weight, collect her collar and drag her off the jacket. She's limp, cold and unresponsive. With a mighty effort, I drag her around the boulder and lower her onto the sand, tail first.

We've made it.

CHAPTER FORTY-NINE

I lie on my back staring at the sky. My chest heaves and my heart gallops. I'm spent and relieved. Dark clouds rush overhead and fill my field of vision. I imagine them as demons, feasting on my despair. Squeezing my eyes shut, I try hard to dispel the waking nightmare.

Breathe. Just breathe. I tell myself. *Let it pass...*

Seconds later, dragging up, I sit and take in the scene. I spy the wooden steps leading to the sanctuary of the lodge and allow myself a smile. My relief is short-lived. We're still in danger. The tide is coming in at an alarming rate. Caught on the wind, clumps of coffee-coloured froth land on the sand all around. Having come this far, I have to get Bella to safety.

I need help.

Settling an ear against Bella's ribs, I hear a low rasp where steady breaths ought to be. Reaching over her prone body, I lift her right eyelid open. A lifeless dark eye returns my gaze. Pressing my fingers deep into folds of fur at her neck, I find a pulse. Though faint, it's there. I'm more worried about her temperature. Never have I known her so cold. She won't survive if I leave to find help.

A darkening sky hints at more rain. I will not let her die out here, on the beach, alone.

Somehow, I have to transport her to the lodge where a warm fire awaits.

My jacket is shredded. The right sleeve hangs by a thread. It won't take any more punishment. I've no option but to carry Bella to the lodge. It's only a hundred yards, but it's a formidable prospect.

You can do this. I tell myself, only half believing it.

'C'mon girl, let's get you home and warmed up.'

Bella makes no sound and doesn't object to my arms passing underneath her. Surprised at my adrenalin-fuelled strength, I lift her easily. She's limp, thin and vulnerable in my arms. Her right hind leg sticks out like an afterthought. Her golden fur clings to her diminished body in sodden clumps. My big, beautiful retriever is like the newborn puppy she once was.

Rain cascades from a leaden sky.

Staggering across the beach, head down against the downpour, sand drags me down. It's tough going and progress is slow. I take two steps forward, and one step back. Reaching the steps, I lift Bella against my chest and climb them, one careful step at a time.

Half way up, I halt and lay Bella down on a step and gather my breath. Two minutes later, dragging up on the handrail, a pencil-sized splinter tears into the palm of my right hand. The pain is excruciating. Blood oozes from the gash. Wincing, I pull the splinter out and pitch it into the dunes. A bluish-purple bruise forms around it. I press my thumb against the centre of the cut. Swirls of colour gyrate across my vision. I bite my lip against the pain.

When will the ordeal end!

Five minutes later, I reach the lodge. Exhausted, I lower Bella onto the dog bed and sit down beside her. Breathlessly, I whisper, 'We've made it. You're going to be alright. I told you… I told you…'

I place a palm against Bella's side. Her breathing though shallow is present. Dragging up on the door handle, I step inside and recover a throw from the sofa. Doubling it up, I race outside and dry Bella off. As I rub, her ribs rise and fall. When I'm satisfied she's dry enough, I return inside and throw logs on the fire. Returning outside, I drag the dog bed and Bella in inside and position her by the fire.

Everything stills.

Realising I almost hypothermic, I bound upstairs and take a long, hot shower. The tension in my shoulders slowly dissolves under the deluge of hot water. Spinning the dial, the deluge ceases and I listen. From downstairs, I hear the crackle and spit of the fire and the rattle and scrape of Bella's claws on the floorboards. Slumping, I settle flattened palms on the tiled wall and a tsunami of tearful relief courses through me.

I dry off, pull on a dressing gown and race downstairs.

Bella stands weak-kneed and trembling on the hearth rug. Twisting her head on one side, roaring flames reflect in dark, glassy pupils.

Satisfied the danger has passed, that Bella's flame will burn brightly again, I push my face deep into the folds of her fur at the neck. My chin trembles like a small child who's found her favourite doll.

'Oh, Bella,' I sob. 'We've made it … we've made it... Everything is going to be alright.'

Bella nuzzles against me. Her tongue and nose are pale and dry. Easing her into the bed, I fetch a bottle of water from the kitchen. Tipping her head back, I place the bottle against her mouth. With each swallow, she rallies.

'Good girl,' I tell her, supporting her neck, making her comfortable. My hand pulses and throbs.

I must get it seen to.

I search for a first aid kit. I've no idea where it's kept, or if, in fact, there is one. Five minutes later, hot, clammy and frustrated, I realise there's no option but to seek help from the Barrs.

CHAPTER FIFTY

I've lost track of time.

Since the sun passed its zenith several hours ago, I realise it must be mid-afternoon. The storm has moved on. The tide is out. Making my way across the causeway, the ocean laps gently at the rocks in stark contrast to the raging tempest of earlier. I climb the steps. At the top, tyre tracks in the gravel beside the Range Rover brim with muddy water. They are proof Olivia *was* here. Our impromptu hedonistic party, seems like a lifetime ago.

Exhausted, I lean against the driver's door and draw breath. The world beyond the causeway spins and everything goes black.

Coming to, I realise I'm laid on the ground crumpled against the wheel. Dragging up on the handle, I try the driver's door. I'm dead on my feet and need to sit down, but the door is locked. Had Callum replaced the starter motor when he promised, then I would have chanced the drive to a vet, or attempted the journey to London.

Reprimanding myself, I cast the notion aside. If I were to throw in the towel, now, here on Scalaig, I'd be letting Christian win. He doesn't think I can survive, let alone thrive, alone on Scalaig.

Stop press. He's wrong…

Turning, I study the castle and wonder if Callum possesses a first aid kit. It will save me the walk into Scaloon and the visit to the Barrs.

Lightheaded, unsteady on my feet, I check the towel wrapped around my hand. One corner is white, the rest a deep, bloody crimson. Overcome by anger, remembering I'm furious with Callum for stealing my precious time with Olivia, I stall sucking sharp breaths. Seconds later, I resolve not to speak to Callum Cleland until I'm good and ready. I'll push on to Barr's. The Barrs are kind and practical people. Mother hen, Dorothy, will take care of me.

* * *

I halt on the pavement opposite Barr's. Rory crosses the road heading towards me. As he comes closer, he looks down. A brace of rabbits – eyes bulging, tiny pink tongues limp from bloodied mouths – hang from a timber stake perched over his right shoulder. Abruptly, he swings right and marches off towards the barn.

It's too late, I've already seen his gruesome catch. Gooseflesh prickles the back of my neck.

Checking both ways, I march across the road.

Alasdair sweeps the pavement in front of the shop with an ancient broom. He stops sweeping and rests his hands on the handle. Something about his posture, the way he looks me up and down, suggests he's expecting me.

Is he expecting me?

I realise he's cleaning up after the storm.

Noticing the state I'm in, my bloodied hand, he settles the broom against the wall, and strides over.

'What in God's name has happened to your hand? Here let me help you,' he says, collecting my elbow. My knees buckle, and I collapse into his arms.

'I… I…' I mumble to my reflection returned in his glasses.

'Let's get you inside,' he says, eyes wide with shock. I must look terrible.

'Where's Rory?' I ask.

Alasdair's concerned frown morphs into confusion. 'Come inside. Dorothy will take care of you.'

'I'm fine,' I whisper.

'You're not, *fine*. Just look at your face. Your hand. All that blood.' Cradling my bandaged hand, he turns it palm up.

'Water,' I croak. Having spent all my energy saving Bella, I'm dehydrated, weak and incoherent.

'Let's get you inside,' Alasdair whispers. He turns, yells, 'Dorothy! Dorothy! You're needed.'

CHAPTER FIFTY-ONE

Once again, I'm on the sofa in the Barr's lounge.

The plump lady with the practical dress and efficient manner fusses over me. I feel like I'm floating an inch below the ceiling. Dorothy Barr removes the towel and lowers my hand into a bowl of tepid water laced with Dettol. It stings like hell. The astringency runs to my nostrils and forces my eyes wide. I grit my teeth. The pain is excruciating. Consciousness regained, I gasp.

'Relax, child,' Dorothy says. I'm mesmerised by the gold crucifix swinging from her neck. It gleams and returns the sun.

'It's Bella,' I say. 'She almost died.'

Dorothy Barr straightens. Her eyes flare with concern. 'Shh, now,' she says, pressing a cold compress against my forehead, dabbing the grazes on my cheeks. 'Everything's going to be alright.'

'Bella almost died,' I repeat.

'You poor child. Be still. Let me see your hand.' I watch as she dabs the wound with cotton wool and wraps a fresh bandage around my hand. It's too long and seems to take forever to put on.

Dorothy presses a hand to my forehead. 'You're running a fever. Let's get you warmed up. We don't want you getting pneumonia. Were you out in the storm long?' she says, frowning, dabbing my forehead with a towel.

'Bella…'

'What about Bella?'

'She fell over the cliff. Got stuck in a ravine. I thought she was going to die. That I was about to lose her. I need to get her to a vet,' I say, a detached, woozy feeling returning.

'Here, take these. They'll help you rest. Just swallow.'

Why won't she listen? Nobody ever listens…

She presses two tablets into my mouth and I wash them down with water. She raises my legs onto a footstool, lays me horizontal, settles a blanket over me, and tucks it in along the edges.

'Try to get some sleep. It'll do you good. I'll tell Alasdair to keep the noise down. You're safe now, child. I won't let anyone hurt you.'

CHAPTER FIFTY-TWO

A snarling dog rags at the bandage looped around my hand. Covering my face with my left hand, I crash my right fist against its snout. It whimpers, and scurries away. Waves crash over me. Seawater fills my mouth, throat and lungs. I'm struggling to breathe. I'm laid at the bottom of a rocky ravine, half covered by frozen ocean. A hooded figure leers down from the clifftop. I hear a haunting cackle above the roar of the surf. The figure turns and dissolves into swirling, grey mist.

'How do you feel?' Alasdair Barr stands over me.

'Where am I?' I say, speaking without processing my surroundings, bolting up. Alasdair presses me down with a firm hand.

'You're safe. That's all you need to know. Dorothy's gone out for a wee while. She's things to see to. Things that cannae wait,' he says, taking a chair from under the table, placing it next to me. 'She asked me to keep an eye on you, when you woke up.'

'How long have I been asleep?' I feel woozy, confused and not a little suspicious.

'Two hours. You were in a terrible state when you arrived.'

Rising, I place my weight against the cushion propped against the arm of the sofa. 'I'm sorry to have bothered you both,' I say, swinging my legs to the floor. 'I ought to go.'

He stalls me with a hand. 'Stay right there, young lady. I'll go get you something to drink. How about some Adam's wine?'

I nod.

'And don't you dare move a muscle. OK?'

'OK.'

'Good. I'll be one minute.'

Gazing around the room, I feel my consciousness gradually return. The room is dingy. A slither of daylight enters through a gap in the curtains. The rich aromas of gamey meat and simmering onions are rampant in the air. My stomach performs somersaults. Fuzzy white light shimmers from the huge TV by the window. It emits a low hiss. A neat stack of video tapes sits on the floor beside it.

There's every chance I might vomit.

Alasdair returns. 'Here, drink this,' he says, thrusting a glass of water at me. I accept it with my bandaged hand. Wince as pain rockets to my elbow. 'That will be sore for a wee while, yet. The wound's quite deep,' he says, nodding at my hand. 'You say it was a splinter from the handrail down to the cove?'

'That's right. I'd better get it looked at.'

'You're right.'

Sinking half of the water, I feel it revive me and recollect where I am, what brought me here.

Alasdair lowers into the armchair opposite. We sit facing one another in an awkward silence. Two minutes pass. I have to say *something*. 'If I'd had transport, I would have gone straight to the hospital and not bothered you. Thanks for taking me in.'

Alasdair shrugs. 'Don't worry your head, it's no bother. You're no bother. Dorothy has fixed you up for the time being,' he says. 'She's had plenty enough practice with Rory. Wee fella's got a habit of doing himself mischief.'

'Still, I'm in your debt,' I say with a thin smile.

'Car not fixed, yet, I take it?'

'No. Callum's dragging his feet,' I say. Alasdair's tone sets my nerves jangling. 'I'm more than a little annoyed with him.'

'Look, I know it's none of my business,' Alasdair says, scratching the side of his nose, 'only…'

He falls silent, studies me with wide, unblinking eyes. Having dangled the bait, he's waiting for me to take it.

'Is there a problem, Alasdair?' I say, removing the blanket from my shoulders, experiencing a hot flush.

'No problem, no. Only… Only, I would have expected Callum to have had it repaired by now,' he says. 'Usually, Callum's doesn't hesitate to sorts things, *people,* out permanently...'

'Sorry, I'm not with you? What are you implying, Mr Barr?' I sense he's holding out on me. That he's desperate to take this opportunity to get something off his chest.

'As I say, it's none of my business. I'm not one to go around spreading idle gossip,' he says, worrying at an invisible scab on the end of his nose. 'Only…'

'Alasdair?' I ask, fixing him with a questioning glare. 'If there's something you want to say, then say it.'

He shrugs, hesitates, says, 'Callum came back here after his parents died. He went around telling anyone and everyone, about the accident. Went into great detail about it. Seemed to enjoy doing it. Explaining in infinite detail how the brakes had failed on the jobbie that killed them. How it was the only accident of its kind in living memory.' Alasdair falls silent, folds his arms across his chest and sits back. He draws breath, makes to speak, seems to change his mind.

'Are you insinuating Callum caused the accident?'

'Insinuating? Me? No! I wouldn't do that. All I'm doing is putting two and two together. All I'm saying is…' He pauses. 'All I'm saying is … when Callum Cleland's around, bad things tend to happen. First, there was Rory; then, the backpacker from Yorkshire – the girl; then, his parents. It doesn't take a genius.' Alasdair checks himself mid-sentence, falls silent, glances towards the kitchen.

Rory, head-to-toe in camouflage hunting gear, appears through the strip curtain clutching a blood-covered knife in his right hand. Blood falls from the tip and splatters on the floor. He lumbers over and stands by the seated Alasdair.

Alasdair looks to Rory.

'Dad?' he says. 'Is everything alright?'

Rory fixes his gaze on me through bushy eyebrows. I look away.

Alasdair shakes his head and makes to rise. 'Don't worry, son,' he says, settling a hand on Rory's forearm, 'there's nothing for you to worry about.'

Dorothy appears in the kitchen opening. Her brooding frown suggests she's overheard the conversation.

'Alasdair,' she barks. 'What on earth have you been saying?' she says, wiping bloodied hands on a black and white check tea towel hanging from her waist.

'Nothing that isn't already common knowledge,' Alasdair says, frowning.

Dorothy rolls her gaze to the TV. She glowers. 'Haven't I told you often enough about leaving those disgusting things lying about the house?' she barks, pointing to the stack of VHS tapes beside the TV. 'It's time you started taking notice. I'm sick and tired of being ignored. Do you hear me?'

Her anger is accentuated by her European consonants. Turning to me, she settles her hands on her hips and clutches the bloodied towel in a tight fist. She leers at me as if expecting a response.

My eyes flare with surprise. A lump catches in my throat.

I don't know what to say. Does she expect me to say something?

'There's no harm in watching,' Alasdair snaps. 'Getting involved, now that's a completely different thing.'

Rory stymies a chuckle. Alasdair casts a, *don't you start,* glare at Rory.

Dorothy's glower deepens. 'I'll deal with you later, Alasdair Barr,' she says, settling her gaze on me. 'You'd better get yourself home, my dear. Only if you're feeling up to it, mind. Are you?' She adds, seemingly as an afterthought.

I'm dismissed. Dorothy Barr has honed the ability to switch the kindness button on and off in seconds.

I nod. 'Yes, I am. You're right. I'd better be getting back. Bella will be missing me. I've taken up too much of your time, already. Thanks for everything,' I say, rising. Straightening, the world tilts on its axis and I cast a steadying hand onto the arm of the sofa. A shooting pain races along my right arm and reaches my shoulder.

No one moves.

They stare at me in silence.

'I'll show you out,' Alasdair says, his furtive glance flitting to the corner of the room, the TV and tapes. He places his body between the stash and me.

What did Christian say? Something about pornography? Was Alasdair watching porn while I slept on the sofa across from him?

Rory and Dorothy stay put. Alasdair ushers me outside and swings the door closed behind me, without saying so much as a goodbye.

Checking the road, I cross and turn for Scalaig.

CHAPTER FIFTY-THREE

I arrive at the castle as the last trace of sun slips over the western horizon. The Range Rover still hasn't turned a wheel. The castle remains in total darkness. It's eerily quiet. No indication at all that Callum's in residence.

Alasdair's insinuations about Callum bounce around my head. Surely, what he said about him is conjecture: small-town gossip liberally garnished with fiction? Irrespective, I wish Callum would get the car fixed. If I had my phone, I could have called the coast-guard to rescue Bella.

'Oh, Bella, I almost lost you… What would I do without you?' I say aloud, pangs of guilt pricking my conscience.

There could have been a paw-sized hole in my heart. I've never felt like this before. Fatigue washes through me. I need to get back to the lodge, cuddle Bella, eat comfort food, and get some sleep.

In the corner of my right eye, an orange light flickers to life in one of the castle's many upstairs windows. I can't bear to look. With no desire to involve myself with Callum anymore, I turn my gaze south towards the causeway, Scalaig and home.

'Sod you,' I mumble, descending the steps, leaving the Barrs –

their weird country ways – and Callum Cleland rattling around in Scalaig Castle, on the wave behind.

* * *

The storm has deposited all manner of detritus across the causeway: a half metre thick tree trunk; planks of wood; plastic bottles; fishing nets; the lid of a lobster pot, and what looks like a rusted-out rear wing from a vintage VW Beetle. I make a mental note to return and carry out a clean up operation when I'm feeling up to it.

Picking my way through the debris, I catch my shoe on the ground and a two-inch long section of sole detaches along the front edge. Cursing, I hobble across the causeway, dodging rock pools. Within seconds, my right sock is drenched. Reaching Scalaig and the area of level ground under the steps, the loose sole catches on something solid, forcing me to a halt. I try to raise my foot, but it won't budge. Exhaling an exasperated sigh, I look down. My shoe is caught on a rusty iron bar. I slip my foot out of the shoe, hunker down and tug at the bar. It won't budge an inch. Brushing away clumps of seaweed, sand and soil, I reveal what looks like a three feet square hinged timber hatch, held together with flat iron bars. Stymieing a gasp, I ease my fingertips into the channel around the edge of the hatch. My hand throbs to the increasing rhythm of my heart. A dot of blood appears in the centre of my injured palm. Hesitating, I wipe my sweated forehead with the bandage.

What on earth is this?

Tensing, I lift. With a tortured screech, and much to my amazement, the hatch rises and rests vertically on its own weight on sturdy hinges. I step forward and peer down into the gloom of a circular hole set into the ground. When my eyes have adjusted to the darkness, I realise I'm staring down a shaft of red brick with a steel ladder bolted vertically along one side. A delicate yellow glow illuminates the bottom of the shaft.

Is it a cavern of some sort?

I've owned the island for ten years, walked every square inch of it, yet I had no idea this shaft – and the cavern below it – existed.

'Scalaig, you've more secrets than M.I.5!' I whisper.

Nagging curiosity compels me to investigate.

CHAPTER FIFTY-FOUR

Lowering my left foot onto the ladder, I begin my descent. I slip with ease into the shaft. The brick walls are smooth and covered in salty excretions. A narrow vein of water cascades down the wall behind the ladder. I count twelve rungs before reaching the bottom. Stepping off the ladder, I keep a firm grip on the freezing cold steel.

I'm stood in a three metre square brick cavern facing a tunnel leading off underneath the causeway. Two lit candles sit in shoe-box-sized recesses hewn into the brickwork either side of the bottom rung. Shadow flames dance across the cavern's vaulted ceiling. I take the candles as evidence someone has been here recently.

Are they still here? Who are they?

I shouldn't stay. Hearing faint scratching behind me, I grip the ladder a little tighter. I turn towards the source of the noise and glimpse the leathery whip of a rat's tail scurrying into a hole in the base of the wall. Every fibre of my being shouts, 'GET THE HELL OUT OF HERE!' but I'm fascinated.

For years, I've heard tales of secret tunnels along this stretch of coast, and now I've one of my very own here on Scalaig, I feel compelled to investigate.

Releasing my grip on the ladder, I spin and step into the tunnel. Two metres in, I halt. There's plenty of headroom. I can stand with room to spare. Several metres further along the tunnel, another candle flickers. After scaling the cliff, this is a walk in the park. I move along the tunnel one cautious step at a time. The ground is firm underfoot with the feel of smooth stone. Candlelight illuminates my path. I follow the light until the tunnel splits two ways at a Y-shaped junction. The left spur is dark, unlit. The right spur is narrower and lit by the faintest of yellow glows.

With no torch to guide me, I decide to take the right spur. Four metres along, the tunnel opens out into a dome-roofed cavern, similar in size to the one at the base of the ladder. Recesses in the brickwork dot the perimeter at irregular vertical and horizontal intervals. They remind me of bookshelves. Each recess features a candle. As I pass, the flames waver and quicken their dance over the walls and vaulted ceiling. I imagine standing in an ancient Egyptian burial chamber. Mesmerised, I visualise mummies, elaborate sarcophagi and diamond studded gold artefacts. Awestruck, I spin through three hundred and sixty degrees, step forward and peer into the nearest recess.

It appears to be a trophy cabinet of animal bones. The tiny skull of a rodent sits atop a rib cage. Severed limbs are neatly arranged in a triangle. The second recess – twice as large as the first – contains a deer skull. Glancing right, I glimpse a silver object in the next recess along. As I come parallel with it, my heart bucks and a scream catches in my throat. Gasping for air, I grab the frame containing the photograph of my smiling parents – the one from my writing desk. I hadn't noticed it was missing. Moving closer, I study the recess. It's wider and deeper than the others. My enquiring expression reflects in the mirrored lenses of my misplaced sunglasses. There are more items. I see my hairgrip – the one I haven't seen since my first week at the lodge, and, at the very back of the hole, my pencil with the heart-shaped eraser. Two pairs of my white lace knickers hang from brass hooks in another recess.

Collecting my things, I realise I'm hyperventilating. A heavy acid feeling burns deep in my gut. Anxiety, fear and confusion slug out a battle Royale inside my head. These are the objects I suspected Rory Barr of stealing.

Is this place Rory's secret?

I've got to get out of here before he finds me.

Turning to leave, clutching my things against my chest, I notice another recess. It's larger than the others. Since my curiosity is greater than my fear, I succumb to the compulsion to take a look.

I step over, lean forward and peer inside. I'm staring at a faded denim rucksack with tan leather straps. It's old, frayed, and covered in dust. The edges of the straps sport rodent teeth marks. Tin badges cover the front flap: Green Day; Blink-182; Linkin Park; CND. Reaching in, I drag it out and spin it around. It brings with it a fug of dust and a whiff of rodent urine. I cough under a clenched fist. Embroidered across the front flap are the letters, 'R.B.'.

Rory Barr?

Then I remember…

Rebecca Barrowclough, the missing backpacker from Yorkshire…

Recoiling with horror, the rucksack slips from my fingers and lands on the stone slabbed floor with a dull thud. Its contents spill out.

A human skull settles against my ankles. Empty eye sockets stare up at me. The jaw flops open as if to speak. The mandible, dislocated from the maxilla, screams a silent scream.

My own scream is blood-curdling.

My belly cramps. Slumping over, I settle my hands on my knees and retch.

From nowhere, a blast of freezing air blows across the back of my legs. My bones turn to ice.

Who's there?

I bolt along the tunnel towards the safety of the ladder. Progress is slow and painful. It's as if I'm running through quicksand. My lungs burn.

Reaching the junction, I halt, gasping for breath and glance back along the tunnel.

Which way now?

I'm disorientated. Left? Or right? I place a hand on the wall to save me from collapsing. I touch something soft, realise it's cobwebs. As the word pops into my head, I see Harry Potter cornered by enormous spiders in a subterranean cavern. I jump with a start and drop the photo frame. The glass shatters into a million fragments against the unyielding stone. My hand slips into another recess. Cobwebs cling to the bandage. I frantically brush them off. I'm terrified of spiders. I have to get them off of me.

It isn't cobwebs – it's a pocket-sized fragment of lilac fabric. There's something wrapped inside. Unwrapping the fabric parcel, I reveal a pair of distinctive designer glasses.

Olivia's!

I scream, but no sound passes my lips. Fear engulfs my whole being. Knees buckling, I lean on the wall and slide to the floor. Despair claws at my soul and I draw my knees up to my chest, sit and stare at Olivia's glasses.

'Olivia,' I moan. Her name jolts my brain. The synapses inside my head crackle like fireworks exploding on Guy Fawkes Night.

Did Rory murder Rebecca Barrowclough?

How can he have Olivia's glasses?

Where is she?

Did he murder Olivia, too?

If he catches me, will I suffer the same fate?

I have to get out of here!

But which way?

The waking nightmare seems to last forever, but only a few seconds can have passed. Cold sweat traces a course down my back and pools in the dimples at the base of my spine. A blast of frigid air licks my left cheek. Adrenaline rushes to my legs and releases me from paralysis. I drag myself up on the wall. Straightening, I shudder.

Run!

I see a faint slither of moonlight on the left of the junction.

I bound towards it.

Behind me, a door slams and a blast of cold, dank air rushes past my cheek. The echo of the door slamming reverberates from the walls, excites the air, and my ears pop. The ringing does nothing to hide the pound of footsteps closing in on me.

Fleeing along the tunnel, my loose sole catches on a joint. A frustrated growl rumbles deep within my diaphragm and escapes through gritted teeth. I stumble, kick out, shake my legs to loosen my shoes, sending them flying into the air ahead. The advancing footsteps echo from the walls and ceiling.

Seeing moonlight at the bottom of the shaft, I run as fast as I can towards it. At the shaft, I throw myself onto the ladder and climb up. Blistering pains sears through the soles of my bare feet. Three rungs from the top, I lose my footing and my chin smashes against the unyielding steel. Biting my tongue, I taste blood.

'Come on,' I yell, spitting blood. 'You can do this!' Reaching the top of the ladder, I clamber out into fresh air. Stalling, I swivel around and glance down the shaft. The yellow light dims. A hand appears on the rung. Then another.

The hatch! Close the hatch!

There's no time to lose. If I don't close the hatch, I'm done for. Rory will catch me.

Then what?

The hatch lands in the frame with a dull thud. Straightening, I spin and glance back along the causeway towards the castle. I see the felled tree trunk. Collecting it, I drag it onto the hatch. It rolls and settles.

It ought to buy me some time.

CHAPTER FIFTY-FIVE

Inside my head, a voice rages.

Which route?

Make a decision...

Now or never...

Hide in the lodge?

No! He'll burn it to the ground with you inside...

Find a weapon... A knife?

No! He's too strong. He'll overpower you... Turn it on you...

Hide in the woods?

No! He knows the woods intimately...

Run to the lodge?

Do it.

Do it now...

Slip sliding over the mud, I scramble up the steps. The desire to escape, to find refuge, to *live*, is all-consuming. I force my legs to drive me forward. My body and mind enter survival mode as I fly across the veranda and snatch at the door handle. It's locked.

Think! Did I lock it? Leave it on the latch? Irrespective, it's locked.

Sanctuary eludes me. I smash my shoulder against the door, but it won't budge.

Key. Key. Key... Where's the damn key...

I pat my pockets. I've locked myself out – and Bella in – I'm such an idiot.

'Stupid. Stupid. Stupid,' I hiss through gritted teeth. Then I remember the spare key, hidden under the plant pot.

I spin, press my back against the door, scan the garden in the half-light, pray that nobody has followed me. Between the lodge and the pines, nothing stirs. I reach down, lift the pot.

There's no key!

An agitated blackbird scuttles into the undergrowth nearby, startling me.

Run!

At a break in the clouds, moonlight illuminates my escape. I stumble through the garden and bolt into the woods, limbs flailing like a wounded deer. I decide on the cove.

Reaching the steps, I halt to catch my breath and let my heart rate slow. My heightened senses search for the telltale signs that my hunter is gaining on me. Steering my gaze towards the pines, I crank my head on one side and flick my hair behind my ear. But for the surf, all is quiet. A dark cloud steals the moonlight. Blinking away my dread, I try hard to think clearly.

Head for the cobble? The jetty?

I ought to feel safe in the lodge, but all along Rory has had a key. He's invaded my sanctuary – my home – and stolen my things. Fear gnaws at my gut. A mischievous demon whispers in my ear.

Weirdo's been creeping around while you slept...

Those sounds were him...

He wants you...

Was I violated while I slept?

'Stop it,' I bellow, squeezing my eyes shut, pressing my thumb on the ragged, bloody bandage. It's all I can do to drive the beast away. I draw a long invigorating breath deep into my lungs. I need to focus. Focus and act.

I *can* make it to the jetty. I *can* escape in the cobble. It's my only chance. I'll motor around to the next bay and find help.

Close by, a twig snaps and a fox heckles me from the woods south of the lodge. A cloud shifts revealing the moon and I see the cobble tied to the end of the jetty.

Thank God.

I inhale with relief. A cackle escapes my throat. My hand shoots over my mouth. I shush myself. Check behind.

Be quiet!

Sprinting across the sand, I launch onto the jetty and race to the ladder. Climbing down, razor-sharp limpets rip at my knuckles and feet. Imprisoned by fear, I can't, *won't*, look back. Landing on deck, the cobble rocks and rolls. I struggle to get my balance. Icy seawater sloshes around my toes. The shock of it does nothing to quiet the rush of blood in my ears and the bass drum thumping deep inside my chest. The cobble is secured by a line tied to a rusty cleat at the bow – another at the stern. I need to start the motor and release the lines.

Is that the correct order? Or do I release the lines and then start the motor?

I shouldn't doubt myself. The cobble is the size of *The Storm Petrel's* motorised tender, I've performed this manoeuvre hundreds of times before.

I can do this. Stop panicking!

With my memory failing me, I'm lost in a fog of indecision.

Just untie the sodding lines!

I waste valuable time trying to untie the line at the stern. The saturated rope refuses to release from the rusty cleat. The bandage around my hand gets shredded. When the rope finally frees, I turn my attention to the bow. The swell frustrates my efforts. Silent, angry tears course down my cheeks.

The planets align, the rope frees and the cobble drifts away from the jetty. At last, I'm escaping Scalaig, but I'm not safe, yet. *Start the motor!*

With the cobble seesawing crazily on the swell, struggling to stay upright, I negotiate my way to the stern. Sucking air, I desperately try to calm my breathing and stop my teeth from chattering. It's not working. Cold shivers race along my arms and down my legs. Reaching the stern, I fall onto the motor and push it forward. The propeller splashes into the ocean. I snag the start cord toggle between my fingers. Excruciating pains shoot along my arm. My frantic heart pumps more blood into the deep crimson-stained bandage. My temples burn.

Mustering all my strength, I drag on the starter cord. A frantic whirling sound dies on the night air. I pull again. Same result. I try again. Almost drag my arm out of the socket. Nothing. The motor stubbornly refuses to start.

Growling, I close my eyes and tell myself to concentrate.

Am I missing something. Think!

I see then that I've drifted to the rocky foreshore where Bella fell over the cliff. I whimper. Exhale. My heart hurts. I need to get Bella to a vet. Something catches my eye. A man silhouetted by moonlight on the clifftop. It's a déjà vu moment. He's got lucky since I've drifted here on the swell. He's watching me struggle, enjoying the spectacle, waiting for me to fail.

Then what?

Demons chatter their grim dialogue inside my head.

What does Rory want?

Did he try to kill Bella?

Did he push her over? Is he enacting some kind of perverse retribution for what Callum did to him?

What did Bella ever do to you, Rory?

Does he have a morbid fascination with cliffs?

And this place in particular? With Scalaig?

I've got to stop overthinking and start focusing on the present. I need to get the damned motor started. Then I remember. The choke! The engine will be cold and damp. It needs more fuel and air. I yank out the choke lever, pull on the start cord. The motor stutters to life. Thanking the Gods, I increase the revs, push the tiller away from my body and set a course for open ocean.

As the bow rises from the swell, smoke spits from the exhaust and I'm surrounded by the acrid, overpowering stench of unburnt petrol. The engine coughs and dies. The bow sinks. I've applied too much power, too early. Pushing the choke lever in, I stall and draw breath. I must regain my composure. After a minute, I drag on the start cord and the engine splutters to life and settles to a steady beat. Increasing the throttle, the bow lifts from the ocean and I'm pressed into the seat by an invisible hand. Wiping spray from my face, I aim the bow into the wind.

A moment later, with the cove receding behind me, allowing a spark of hope to enter my heart, I smile. It's an alien feeling, but it's there. I *feel* it. Sanctuary is within touching distance just around the bay.

The cobble bounces across the ocean and I cling to the hull with my left hand and clutch the tiller with my right. At any moment, a wave could hurl me overboard. I revel in the vibrations from the tiller. An electric hum rushes through the ragged bandage around my right hand. The discomfort reminds me I'm alive.

Alive! And free! They're powerful, all-consuming, wonderful emotions.

A triangular tendril of moonlight reflects from the surface of the ocean ahead, and I see the dark outline of an unfamiliar headland two miles ahead. I set a course for it and pray for safety.

Gathering my thoughts, the buzzing in my head subsides and I hear the wind above the din of the motor. I feel the bow sink sedately into the ocean. The engine has died.

What now?

Snagging the start cord in my *good* hand, I give it a good yank. The motor whines, splutters and dies. I try again. Not even a splutter. *Fuel!* Twisting off the cap, I peer into the fuel tank. I see shiny metal. The tank is empty.

'Shit!' I spit, raise up and launch my right foot at the transom below the motor in frustration. The cobble rocks uncontrollably. I sit and regain my balance. Glancing around, I spot a jerry can under a tarpaulin pressed up against the spars below the bow. I shuffle forward, grab the can, lift it against my ear, and shake. Liquid sloshes around inside.

There is a God!

Opening the can, I sniff the contents. My joy is short-lived. It's water. There's no sign of an oar. Throwing the can aside, I turn to confirm my position. The cobble is drifting towards a rocky headland, twenty metres distant.

Please. No!

I hear what sounds like a fly trapped inside a jar. Its volume increases, becomes intense. Forced to steer my gaze from the headland, I spin to investigate the source. The buzz becomes a crescendo. Above the buzzing, I hear the bow of a boat splitting the surface of the ocean.

A second later, I hear a whooshing sound, feel the rush of air across my left cheek and everything goes black.

CHAPTER FIFTY-SIX

Day 33

A fire engine races along a city street. The siren starts low and builds to a deafening bellow. My breathing is shallow and laboured, yet my heart threatens to punch a hole through my ribs. A scab has formed on my swollen bottom lip. An icy sword rips through my tailbone, lancing my organs.

I open my eyes, or at least I try to, and feel my left cheek pulsate.

Pus glues my right eye into the narrowest of slits. My vision has gone from nothingness to a blur of indistinct, subdued hues. Straining to see through my 'good' left eye, I wish I hadn't bothered.

I'm in a basement fetid with mildew. The fusty odour catches at the back of my throat. I fight the urge to vomit. Cold seeps into my bones. A solitary, low wattage filament bulb hangs on a naked cord in the centre of the ceiling. Caught on the draught, the swinging bulb casts long, languid fingers of dullish yellow light spinning around the room. There's an ancient boiler. Metal shelves stacked high with used paint cans, line the walls.

It's a serial killer's wet dream.

I'm shackled to a low metal chair with chains around my ankles and wrists. Someone, I've no idea who, has welded angles to the chair legs and fastened them with anchors to the floor. Shifting my weight, the chains rattle and clang. My head spins. My teeth chatter uncontrollably.

How did I get here? How long have I been here?

I don't know. I draw breath, hoping to summon enough energy to call for help. A weak moan parts my swollen lips.

I'm a prisoner. My fate is in the hands of my gaoler.

I have to escape.

Concentrating hard on my eyelids, I force my sticky eye open a quarter of an inch. It doesn't make what I see any less scary. The room is a blank canvas, save for the shelving and boiler. There are no doors or windows; no obvious entry or exit points. The walls are rough, whitewashed plaster. A sharp-edged metal bracket digs into my right shoulder blade as I try to support my back. Rust-coloured stains meander down the walls at irregular intervals from the timber boarded ceiling. Cobwebs – grossly exaggerated by every swing of the bulb – span every nook and cranny.

A metre above my head, the ceiling vibrates to the symphony of quickening feet. A minute passes in silence, but for the buzz of tinnitus in my ears. The symphony reaches its finale. All is quiet. A ticking clock fills the white space between the silence. I'm just about to exhale when the clock chimes.

Bong. Bong. Bong. Bong. Four o'clock.

Morning or afternoon? I've no way of knowing. Nauseous, I feel the fluid in my ear canal shift. I'm going to pass out.

The basement dissolves into the ether as I lose consciousness.

CHAPTER FIFTY-SEVEN

Coming to, my neck aches, pincers of fear grip my chest and I'm finding it hard to breathe. While I was unconscious, my head must have slumped onto my breastbone. A patch of spittle covers my shirt at the neck. I must have been out cold.

I've no idea how long I've been here, but the basement is no longer freezing. There's a hint of warmth in the air. It underscores the musty stench. Beads of sweat trickle down my forehead and salt stings my ruptured eye. The ringing in my ears has returned. Somewhere past the ceiling, a clock ticks. Weird shadows and fingers of light dance over every surface. I desperately need to pee. My mouth is Sahara dry.

I tug at the chains. Soon realise it's futile. As my mind awakens, my imagination does its worst.

Where am I?

Who's doing this?

Rory?

Someone else?

Christian?

Callum?

The fisherman? Woman?

Why?

Please God, I'm not ready to die…

I smash my eyes closed in the desperate hope it might stop my mind from performing macabre mental gymnastics. Instead, it's as if flash cards are being held up in front of my face. Technicolor images whizz past.

Bella floppy in my arms. A bloodied Rory performing a pagan dance perilously close to a cliff face, huge antlers protruding from his skull. Callum stands over Olivia stroking her hair. I'm captured by his malevolent grin and hungry eyes. Christian rattling keys in my face. Diamond-patterned snakes slithering towards me from the empty eye sockets of a human skull. Dorothy Barr wrapping bandages around my face. A plank of wood crashing against the back of my skull. A faceless figure dragging my limp body across a beach and lowering me into a hole in the ground on a rope…

I hear the clock strike the hour. This time, I count six chimes. Jerking awake, my eyes fly open, releasing me from the nightmare.

Six o'clock.

I slow my breathing in time with the ticking. The pain is intolerable.

Will it always be like this?

The croak of dry hinges brings me back to the present. I bolt upright, but my wrists are securely tied and cold steel digs into my skin. The ambient light changes. Dust motes dance in the yellow light cast from the bulb. Glancing left, I watch a man-sized rectangle of wall swing open. Realising I'm holding my breath, I exhale. The light dims and I see a man silhouetted in the opening. He moves forward. Closing my eyes, I hear ragged footsteps coming towards me. The footsteps cease. Someone is close. Their presence palpable. Breath almost touchable.

'Look at me,' he says, dispassionately. I squeeze my eyes a little tighter. I can't look. Won't look.

'I said… *Look* at me,' he repeats. He's calm, not angry or agitated. I process what's being said. Endeavour to recognise his voice. Another voice, the one deep inside my head, instructs me to keep my eyes closed.

'Erin. Look. At. Me,' he says, spacing his words, injecting menace.

He knows who I am. This isn't some random abduction.

I mustn't look at him. If I open my eyes, there will be no way back. Grabbing my hair, he smashes my head against the wall.

'Please. Don't,' I beg.

'Look. At. Me! I'm done with your puerile games.'

My eyes won't obey. I've no desire to see the person in front of me.

Because I know who he is.

CHAPTER FIFTY-EIGHT

The bottom of a metal chair leg screeches across concrete and cuts through the ringing in my ears. My eyelids are welded together. I will not look at my gaoler. To open my eyes will make this nightmare real. It will empower him. Make me *his*.

Warm breath tickles my cheek. Musky cologne invades my nostrils.

He sniffs, sighs and snorts like an angry bull in a corral.

'Water,' I rasp.

'Look at me.'

'Only if you give me some water,' I say.

Silence fills the space between us.

'Tell me why you came?' he asks.

I don't understand the question.

'You brought me here,' I say flatly. 'Please ... *water*.'

'I'll ask again… Why did you come to Scalaig?'

What does he want from me? He knows why I came here. It's my home and island. I'm here to write. My right hand throbs. I purse my lips.

He growls like a man possessed by the spirit of a wolf. Metal scrapes on concrete. A chair – his chair – being pushed back.

I won't look.

'Answer me, bitch!' Spittle mists my face. His rampant breath is hot against my cheek. 'Well?'

I ball my hands, yank on the chains.

My terror turns to anger and I'm no longer afraid of him. Perhaps my resentment at his unwarranted hatred has pushed me beyond terror. Unless I summon up the courage to overcome my worst fears, my life is worthless. The realisation emancipates me. The paralysing dread evaporates like dew from grass on a sunny spring morning, and suddenly I feel unstoppable. The situation can't get any worse than it already is. It's time to see what tools this evil bastard has in his toolbox.

One question: why is he doing this?

Opening my eyes, I see him.

Callum Cleland.

I meet his evil stare with a glower of my own. Digging deep, I spit in his face. His recoil is a second too late. My saliva lands above his right eye and spills down his cheek. Wiping it off with his sleeve, he laughs a Joker's laugh and leans in. 'Do that again, and you'll be signing your death warrant. I'll string you up like one of Barr's rabbits. I'll gut you, slowly. When I've done, I'll feed your entrails to the lobsters.'

'Just like you did the others?' I spit.

'Ugh. What do you know? You're a nobody. No one will miss you. I've made sure of that,' he says, turning, pacing around the austere basement like a traumatised bear in a cage.

'How can you be sure I won't be missed?' I say, defiance bubbling in my gut.

He races at me with balled fists, face contorted into a wide-eyed, sneer. He stalls his face an inch from mine. 'Oh, I'm sure, alright. You don't *know* me,' he screams. 'You've no idea what I'm capable of. What I've done to protect what's rightfully mine. *Ours.*' His face turns crimson, eyes pop. He spits manic words like a cornered cobra spits venom.

'You're going to kill me, anyway,' I say, numb to the core. 'Before you do... Why don't you get whatever's bugging you, off your chest?' I extract the heat from my voice. Elect to meet fury with calm.

Stepping back, he collects the chair from the floor, spins it around and positions it in front of me. He lifts his right leg over. Manspreading, he settles his chest against the chair back, casts his head back, runs his fingers through his hair and studies my face as if we've never met.

'You want the truth?'

'Yes. Why do I have to die?' I say. It's the truth. *My truth.* The only truth I have left.

'Scalaig is *mine.* It always was, and always will be. You and your wanker of a husband stole it from me. It's that simple.'

'We didn't steal it. Your father sold it to us of his own free will. There was no collusion on our part. We helped him out of a financial hole. Us buying it, helped *you* out. We gave you a future.'

He snorts, looks to the ceiling.

A silent minute passes. His breathing calms, deepens. He lowers his head. He's calmer, the anger behind his eyes, slightly diminished.

'My father had no right to sell it in the first place. It wasn't his to sell. The island is *mine.* It's the only sanctuary I ever had from the selfish bastard. He never cared for me, or mother. His motive for selling was to keep me away from it. To stop me from doing, *wicked* things. His words, not mine. What did he know? My father only ever lived a charmed life.'

I shrug. 'Lots of parents don't understand their children. And vice versa. It's a generational thing. I'm sure he didn't mean to hurt you,' I say.

Can I pull him back from the brink?

'Ugh. You believe that? Bastard hated the bones of me. I was never good enough. Everything I did, everything I was, everything I would ever become, would never be enough. My old man gave that snivelling runt, Rory Barr, more attention than me. He took him under his wing. He'd spend hours fishing from the rocks overlooking the causeway, fluffing his bloody hair, making small talk. I watched them from my bedroom window, while I was stuck inside doing assignments. He'd lock me in my bedroom until I'd finished the extra homework he'd set me. He did it to wind me up. I showed him. Reacted in the only way I knew how. I'd sneak out and hide in the woods whenever I got the chance.'

He shakes his head, as if he can't fathom something. Huffing, he directs his gaze to the opening in the wall. 'Do you want to know something?'

'Do I have a say in the matter?'

'No, you don't. Three decades we lived here, and yet my parents had no idea this part of the basement, or the tunnels existed. They date from the fourteenth century. Were used by smugglers. I mean, how stupid can you be? They even pre-date the castle. They built the castle above it. There's a secret opening. I worked it out. Kids are much smarter than adults. It was my secret.'

He's in a world of his own. A world of memories.

'Anyway, the past, it doesn't matter anymore. What's done's, done. Everything – the castle, tunnels and Scalaig – will be *mine* soon. I'll be able to come and go as I please. When I was a child – long before you came – I used the tunnels to escape from *him* whenever I could. At high tide, the tunnels came into their own. They're waterproof. I could visit my shack without anyone knowing. Hide out. Set traps. Hunt. I'd leave skinned rabbits on the doorstep for mother to find and point the finger at Rory. It spooked her out,' he says, running a hand over his chin.

He's reliving the past.

'Rory was a snitch. At school he enjoyed getting me into trouble. He'd run to the teachers saying I'd bullied him, stole his lunch, or pocket money. I showed him. He didn't dare cross me after...'

He falls silent.

'You pushed him over the cliff?' I can't help myself.

'You've been talking to Dorothy, haven't you?'

I shrug.

'Old hag can't keep her bloody nose out. I warned her. Told her that if she ever told a living soul what actually happened, I'd do the job right. That I'd take great delight in finishing Rory off. It would be an act of mercy.' He raises a hand to the side of his head, makes a gun with his hand, and mimes pulling the trigger.

'Dorothy never said a word. At the lodge the other night, I thought your version of events was too neat,' I say. I don't want him going after Dorothy, after he's done with me.

'What does it matter? It's irrelevant. Rory won't tell. You won't be able to either, by the time I've finished with you.'

Leaning forward, he closes the space and our eyes meet. I try my damnedest to gaze deep into his soul. Let him sense I'm begging for mercy. The hazel flecks in his irises burn amber with hate. It's futile.

'My father tried to make amends by offering the Barrs money. It was a mistake. He might as well have pinned posters up around Scaloon informing everyone I'd pushed Rory over the cliff. I was at the end of my tether. I threatened to kill Rory if he didn't stop giving him all his attention. As usual, he ignored me. He treated Rory like a son. My father was a nasty piece of work. He had zero emotional intelligence.'

He clams up. His eyes narrows. He appears to be conjuring up the past, again.

'Before I pushed him over, Rory was plain stupid. All I did was help him along on his journey to the complete fuckwit you see today.' He rears back, grins.

'Is that why your father sent you away to boarding school? To stop you from killing Rory?'

I twist the chains securing my wrists and ankles. Consider asking for water, but think better of it and elect to keep him talking.

'No. My father sent me away after I tried to kill *him*. We argued. I wanted a shotgun for my fourteenth birthday. Of course, he said no. I had a knife at his throat. It was mother who talked me out of it. I would've gone through with it too, if she hadn't intervened,' he says, wiping spittle from the corner of his mouth with the back of his hand. His glower sears into me. He's waiting for a reaction. I turn away. A minute passes and I return his glower with a glare of my own.

Shaking his head, he draws breath and continues with his macabre life story. 'Afterwards, father was shit scared of me. He stopped associating with the Barrs and started keeping Rory at arm's length. Mind you, he couldn't keep me away from Scalaig for the entire summer. Bastard avoided me like the plague. Weekends, he'd stay in the company flat in London. I was only a kid, yet he was petrified of me. I didn't mind. It meant I could spend every day alone on Scalaig. Everyone thought of Scalaig as mine. It was an open secret. I loved the notoriety,' he says, with a grim smile.

'But your father didn't sell Scalaig until much later. I suppose he must've wanted to keep it to placate you?'

'You're so fucking naïve. I've already told you. You don't know me. Nobody does. Father underestimated me. He sent me away to boarding school, in the hope it would instil some discipline in me. He hoped I'd grow up to be a fully functioning, law-abiding citizen. Again, his words, not mine. It was never going happen. By then, I was irreparably damaged. I knew what I was. What I *am*. I *like* it. I get a hard on from hurting and killing things. I can't get enough of watching living things suffer. Rats. Rabbits. Deer. Fuckwits. You name it, I enjoy killing it. The more they bleed, the better I like it. I acknowledge I overstepped the mark when I killed the backpacker, though. It was such a shame. She was a stunner.'

There's longing in his eyes. I imagine the void inside him. An unfathomable strange and empty chasm, bereft of love and compassion. He's gauging my reaction. A lump rises in my throat, but I remain still. I can't let him see me react.

'She tried to make a fool of me. Ugh, it was never going to happen. She'd had a fight with her boyfriend. I'd been watching them from the shack. He took off. Left her alone on the beach. She was crying. When I approached her to ask if she was OK, we got talking. In the blink of an eye, she forgot all about him. Said he was an arsehole. Told me she'd wanted to split up with him for months. She laughed at my jokes. Anyone could see she was smitten. I suggested a walk in the woods to cool down. She agreed. It was scorching hot. Getting up from the sand, she undid two buttons on her blouse. She had tits to die for. She was older than me, so naturally I assumed she understood what a walk in the woods actually meant.' He licks his lips, adjusts his crotch, returns his gaze to me and continues his gruesome soliloquy. 'Once we entered the woods, I tried to kiss her. She called me a freak and ran away. I got scared. Thought she'd run to the police crying wolf, saying I raped her. I couldn't let that happen. After the incident with Rory, the police already had me in their sights. So, I ran after her, tackled her to the ground, dragged her into one of the tunnels and brought her here. I'm sure you can imagine the rest. Fuck's sake, you're an author,' he says, smirking. 'Am I scaring you?'

'You know you are. What happened afterwards?'

He huffs. Shrugs. 'There was a police investigation into her disappearance. They interviewed me. I sent them down a rabbit hole, not literally though, that would've been dumb. I'll never give up my secrets. The tunnels... This place... I told them I'd seen Rory talking to some girl. They swallowed it hook, line and sinker. It was fun to watch. My father knew I was involved, but without a body, nobody could prove anything. But he knew alright. That's when he decided to sell Scalaig, to stop me. Sell it and rob me of my reason to come back. I couldn't ruin his reputation any more than it already was. He need never see me again. So I bided my time. I always dreamed a day of reckoning like today would arrive, eventually.'

Raising joined fingers across his lips, he rocks back and forth in the chair. He's reliving another gruesome memory.

'What about your mother? She must've loved you once?'

I have to keep him talking. Make him understand I'm not a threat.

'Mother was spineless,' he says, nonchalantly.

I have to make him see that not everyone is out to get him. If I do, there's a slim chance I might get out of this alive.

'She never stood up for me. She could've stopped him anytime she wanted to. She could've made father realise he was being cruel, destroying me from the inside. The final straw came when he cut off my allowance. I was just a boy and I had to fend for myself in a city miles away from home. Not once did she intervene. The pair of them didn't give a flying fuck about me. They were too wrapped up in one another, and father's bloody career, to care. The things I did to survive, would make your pretty little head explode.'

He strains his neck, left, then right. Vertebrae creak and crack. He exhales a long sigh. 'Father dominated the poor cow. She allowed it. She epitomised weakness. I abhor weakness. I despised her as much as I did him.'

'But why did you come back after their skiing accident?'

'Oh, come on, Erin, please try to keep up. They're still here. They never went away.'

His voice trails off. I'm confused.

'Are they laid to rest, here?'

'Christ, you're more stupid than I thought. There was *no* skiing accident. I fabricated the whole thing. I killed her first and made him watch. He begged me to finish him, but I took my time and savoured every delicious moment. I faked the accident. It was a masterful piece of deception. Journalists are so gullible.'

My parched throat tightens. The valve in my bladder flexes. I concentrate hard since I don't want to pee. I'm talking to a psychopath, of that I have no doubt.

'I'd got used to not having the support of my parents; to being independent. I was doing just peachy in Aberdeen, working bar, hustling, getting by. Until one day, some fancy London solicitor turned up on my doorstep. My father had him track me down, just to inform me he had cut me out of his will in favour of – you're going to love this, I mean, really love it... None other than Rory fucking Barr! Did he think I'd just roll over and let that happen?' he says, fixing me with wild eyes.

I remain silent. I don't think he expects an answer.

'So, I played father at his own game. I called him and apologised for everything. Apologised for me being, well, *me*. Told him I wanted to meet up. That I wanted a reconciliation. I said I wanted to discuss the future, and put the past behind me, *us*. Silly old bastard took the bait. We reconciled. He changed the will. I killed her first, then him. Then, I faked the accident. You ought to kill your parents, Erin, there's no better high.'

He could be reading a shopping list for his weekly trip to Sainsburys. There's zero emotion. I suck a long breath of fetid air.

'Didn't anyone ever question your story?'

He shrugs, exhales an exasperated sigh, like he's bored with my questions.

'Everyone around here knew my parents loved to ski. It was easy. You're the only living soul I've ever admitted killing them to. You ought to consider it a privilege.' The menace has returned to his voice. I'm losing him.

'But why me? You have the castle and inheritance? Why me?' Obviously, I know the reason, but I need to hear him say it. He picks up on the tremble in my voice.

'C'mon, use that beautiful brain of yours. You must have worked it out by now?' he snorts.

Tilting my head, I close my eyes. Of course I have: Scalaig is *the* problem.

He speaks down his nose in a plummy accent. 'Mr and Mrs Moran, privileged sassenach owners of Scalaig, the most beautiful island on the whole of the West Coast of Scotland. Rich. Fucking. Cuckoos.' He bows his head, feigns reverence. When he speaks again, the menace has returned to his voice. 'You're all that stands between me and my island, and the way things used to be. It's simple. You have to go, *darling,*' he snarls, jabbing a pointed finger in my ribs. I recoil. The chains chafe my wrists. I shut him out.

'Not so tough now, are you, Erin?'

'People know I'm here. I'll be missed. The police will come looking for me,' I say, with as much confidence as I can muster.

'Stupid woman. You have no phone. Huh, unlike ET, you can't *phone home*. You, being so clumsy, saved me that little job. Thank you. I must say, I thought you would've cottoned to the Range Rover earlier, though. An engine won't run if spark plugs are missing and the starter motor is disconnected. That was an easy win.' He laughs a self-satisfied laugh. More jigsaw pieces fall into place. It must've been him I'd seen in the cobble, dumping spark plugs overboard.

I've been such an idiot.

'My husband and my solicitor know I'm here. I'm due to sign some papers, today,' I lie, jaw set firm.

'I don't give a damn. I overheard your husband threatening you the day you two had a fight in the lodge. I'll tell the police. The ex-husband is always their prime suspect. Let's think... Maybe, I ought to secure a little blood... Some hair... Fluids... That part might be fun... Forensic evidence is so absolute, isn't it? And so very easy to plant. Yeah, I like that. I like it because it's simple.'

'Christian is a very rich man. He'll commission the best private investigators money can buy. They'll find this place, the tunnels and the catacombs. They'll discover your secrets. You can't fight a man as powerful as Christian Moran,' I say, voice animated.

'Now, you're the only other living soul who knows about the

tunnels.' He hesitates, scratching his chin. 'Hmm. Do you know something, I like that. *Catacombs.* I've never thought of them in that way, before.' He muses on the inadvertent notoriety I've afforded his macabre tunnels. 'How will anyone find them when you're dead? They've been a secret for centuries. Just like the backpacker, you'll disappear, never to be seen again. I'll say you've been acting irrationally ever since you set foot on Scalaig. The Barrs will back me up. Don't you get it? None of this is random.'

'Olivia won't believe any of it. She knows me better than anyone. Even better than Christian,' I say, clutching at straws.

'I wondered how long it would be before you brought her up. She was an unexpected bonus, turning up like she did out of the blue, delighted to let the country boy massage her vacuous ego. The seduction of older women is a skill. A skill I perfected in the pubs and clubs of Aberdeen,' he says. 'I had such fun. So many others…'

He adjusts his crotch. I feel sick.

'She's waiting for my manuscript. If she doesn't hear from me soon, she'll come to investigate. Olivia's more than a match for you.'

He laughs so hard I think he might fall off the chair. His booming guffaws echo around the basement. Dread wells up inside of me and I yank on the chains. It's futile. My battered eyelid throbs. I taste salt from angry tears.

'C'mon, Erin, ask yourself, would I let her leave?'

He lets the question hang in the air like a helium balloon on a thread. Leaning in, he strokes my cheek. I bite my lip. I don't want to hear the next part. He smiles, presses a thumb against my swollen lip, wipes away a smear of blood, puts his thumb in his mouth and sucks hungrily.

'With a little chemical assistance, she was putty in my hands. She followed my every instruction to the letter. Of course, I told her what to write. My little charade had you fooled. When I strangled her, she succumbed without a fight. Actually, she was a little disappointing. I did it in your ever so precious Scalaig fucking Lodge. I'm going to get the biggest hard on I've ever had, when I demolish it. They'll never find her body. She was never here. No one saw her arrive, and they sure as hell never saw her leave,' he sings the words, his mood swings from dark to light.

'No...' I whimper. I'm dehydrated. Even my tears have evaporated. My aching heart resigns to my fate. The light at the end of the tunnel fades.

'Just so you know, I never meant to hurt your dog.'

'Bella? What did you do to my beautiful, Bella?' I drag myself up. Clench my fists against the chains.

He shrugs. 'The dog was your fault. If only you'd fed her the food from the tub under the sink, she'd have died peacefully in her sleep. But no, you had to interfere. What else could I do? Stupid mutt followed me to the cliffs. I threw her off. I'm getting good at that. There's a skill to it,' he says, cackling like the madman he so obviously is. He doesn't seem to know she's survived. I have to keep it that way.

'You bastard. You're the devil incarnate!'

Jumping up, he drags a hunting knife from the pouch around his waist. It's huge. The blade is at least nine inches long.

He studies the tip. Roaring flames of madness leap behind his eyes.

CHAPTER FIFTY-NINE

As he twists the blade, it gleams in the light from the opening. He strokes his thumb along the edge, drawing blood. His blood splatters onto the floor in marble-sized globules. Several drops. His face is a blank canvas.

'If only you'd scared more easily. Took off back to London when you first felt uncomfortable; listened to your instincts. Fuck's sake I gave you enough clues and warnings. You're pig-headed. In a strange way, you remind me of my father. I almost spared Olivia. She's dead because of you,' he hisses in my ear, presses a bloody thumb firm against my cheek, makes the shape of a cross. It feels like a kiss. Yanking my head back, I grit my teeth.

I won't let him in. He mustn't see or sense my fear.

'Now it's your turn. I'm going to enjoy every delicious moment. Punish you. *Him.* That wanker of a husband of yours. You two have put me through hell.' He sets the blades' tip against the corner of my glued up eye, runs it down my right cheek, under my chin, along my throat, stalling it on my sternum, applying just enough pressure to draw blood. Blood pools in my cleavage.

Panic rises within me. 'People will look for me. You won't get away with this,' I hiss.

He shrugs. 'Of course they'll come. And just like last time, their search will be cursory and fruitless. As I keep telling you, none of this is random. Everybody thinks you're a fruitcake. The crazy paranoid bitch from London who's bitten off more than she can chew. The Barrs have witnessed first-hand your hysteria. They'll think you've gone back to London. Decided country life wasn't for you. I'll spin the police a yarn. Tell them how you and Olivia kept banging on about doing a *Thelma and Louise*, together. That you were getting it on. Were pissed out of your heads and tried to coerce me into a threesome. I'll say I made my excuses and left you to it. Christian will regard your behaviour as an affront to his manhood. He'll want to distance himself from you, and since I was one of the last people to speak to you, he'll want to talk to me. I'll empathise; be a shoulder to cry on. I'll offer to take Scalaig off his hands. He'll jump at the chance to sell Scalaig to me at a rock-bottom price,' he says, nodding, as if his warped plan is a given.

'It won't be that easy. There's too much evidence. My car's here for a start. And my things, they're at the lodge.'

'I'll sort everything. Offer to buy the Range Rover. Don't you see, I *own* you. You're my chattel. I have the keys to your life, the car, lodge, and shed. I'll come and go as I please. I'll erase every last trace of your miserable existence from Scalaig, just like I did with the others,' he says, pausing. A minute passes. His face contorts into a satisfied sneer as he adds, 'With a little non too subtle persuasion, Christian will gift Scalaig to me. When I want to be, I can be very persuasive.'

'He'd never do that. Money means too much to him.'

'He will with a blade stuffed against his gut. Unlike you, I've been keeping abreast of the news. The last thing Christian Moran needs in his life is a bat-shit crazy ex-wife cramping his style,' he laughs.

'What do you mean?'

'Maybe later, when you can't bear the pain any longer. By then, you'll beg me to kill you. Rory will be next. Arsehole's forever putting his nose into other people's business. Lately, he's started following me around. He thinks I don't know he's there. I reckon he suspects something, but he's too stupid to work it out,' he says, snorting.

Nausea congeals in my gut. I draw breath and smash my eyelids closed. Perfect grey replaces the bloodshot kaleidoscope of colours. Terror replaces calm. I'm going to die: tortured, mutilated, murdered in cold blood, by the serial killer Callum Cleland, for the love of his precious island. He's going to kill again, and this time, the victim will be me.

In time, my readers will find books written by new, up-and-coming authors and I'll fade into obscurity. All books have a shelf life, and mine are no different. My life's work will end up in charity shops, bargain basements, and discount bins.

No living person will remember me. When mother and father died, I remember feeling broody. A baby would mean the family tree would continue. I never discussed my hopes with Christian. Even then, I knew he didn't want children. They were never high on his agenda.

Gossip columnists will delight in printing sordid stories about the author who ran away with her lesbian lover, never to be seen again. It will make great copy. I'll be remembered as the romantic novelist who lost her talent for storytelling when the love of her life abandoned her for a younger, racier, prettier model. Isn't it always the case? Sooner rather than later, readers will grow tired of the story – *my story* – and the spotlight will move on to someone else.

The light from the door dims. Grey dulls to black. Chilled, damp air wafts across my face.

I brace myself...

It's time to stare death in the face. His mouth twists into a sick smirk. Toying with the knife, he's enjoying my pain. He settles the tip against my right breast just above the nipple. Drags it away. The cruel bastard is savouring my imminent demise.

It's too much to bear. I close my eyes.

A sickening crack ricochets off the walls and I'm caught in a fine mist of hot, wet spray. Screwing my eyes tight, I suck a last breath.

Ten eternal seconds pass.

Why is there no pain?

Overloaded, my senses are failing me. It's a blessing.

This is it. I'm about to die...

The clock upstairs chimes. I count the chimes.

I can hear the chimes!

I fling my eyes open.

I face a still captured from a horror movie. An unmoving Callum Cleland sits slumped over the chair back, with a deep raggedy gash running diagonally across his skull. The open wound is a horrific melange of blood and brains. Triangular segments of bone are impaled deep into brain matter. Repulsed, I look away.

Rory stands over the lifeless body. His expression is an inscrutable, blank tableaux. A bloodied axe hangs from the fingers of his right hand. He raises the axe high above his head.

I glare at him. Words form in my throat. But it's already too late.

The air parts with a whoosh. Blue sparks shoot past my right eye. The sharp retort of metal meeting metal reverberates from concrete, plaster and timber. The chain around my right ankle releases. He steps left. Repeats the process. My left ankle frees. He rattles the chain joining my wrists together behind my back and taps his lips with his index finger.

I nod.

I have to trust him.

He raises the axe and brings it crashing down in the space between my shoulders and the wall. Sparks cascade across the floor. A cacophony of metal on metal displaces the ringing in my ears. My arms fall down by my sides. I lurch forward. Rory catches me in his huge clumsy arms and lifts me up to shoulder level.

I slump against his chest and he carries me through the opening and into the light.

CHAPTER SIXTY

Blue neon strobes gyrate intermittently across a white plaster ceiling. The warmth of a wool blanket has replaced the ice-cold frigidity of my subterranean execution chamber. I'm propped up on cushions. The sweet aroma of baking bread fills my nostrils.

I hear a man's voice.

'She's waking up. Go fetch mother, Rory.'

I recognise Alasdair Barr's gruff voice. Tips of leathery fingers run down my right cheek.

A bloodied axe races towards me...

Pulling my head aside, I bolt up. Alasdair presses me down with a firm hand.

'Settle down, child. He's gone. You're safe. The police are on their way. Dorothy's coming, too,' he says, with a thin smile.

I remember.

'Where is he?'

'Who?'

'Callum.'

'He's dead.'

Through the numbness, the comforting arms of relief embrace me.

A kneeling Alasdair rises and reveals the source of the blue neon. Huge black reptilian eyes stare out from a bulbous grey head against a blue background on the ancient TV in the corner of the room.

'Where am I?' I gasp.

Behind me, the light dims and Dorothy Barr appears in the opening.

'Alasdair Barr, you never listen. I'm sick to the back teeth of those damn tapes! I mean… Roswell aliens! 9/11 cover up! Bigfoot! Yeti! Reptilians! For the love of all that's holy, won't you ever grow up? Turn it off. Poor girl's traumatised enough. The last thing she needs to see, is such rubbish,' Dorothy scolds.

'Sorry, my love,' Alasdair says, pulling his bottom lip tight over missing teeth, giving me an 'I'm in trouble now' look, stabbing the remote.

The ancient TV flickers and dies.

I return a weak smile. Dorothy leans closer and collects my hands.

'Here, let me have another look at that wound,' she says, taking a bottle of antiseptic from her apron, twisting off the lid, vapour stinging my eyes. She soaks and dabs cotton wool balls over my face, ankles and wrists.

'Is it true?' I ask.

'Is what true?'

'Is Callum Cleland dead?'

'Yes, my child, he is.' She sounds relieved. 'And not before time.'

My memory is vague. I sigh.

Think. I tell myself.

Two long minutes pass.

Images settle in my mind. I see Rory standing behind Callum. He's holding something. I remember sensing the air parting, then hot, wet spray landing upon my face.

I see it all. Every detail. *Will I ever be able to unsee it?*

'What's going to happen to Rory?'

'The police will come. Rory will tell them what happened. We'll put our trust in God,' she says, tending my injuries. 'This time, with God's help, they'll believe him.'

I nod. Smile. Stroke the back of her hand. 'Don't worry, I'll tell them what happened. Tell them how Rory saved my life. I'll make them believe. Trust me. I'll make them believe.'

'Thank you,' Dorothy says. 'Just speak the truth and the good Lord will see to the rest.'

'How did Rory know where I was?' I say.

Evading the question, she looks away. Her lips purse. She frowns.

'How, Dorothy, how?' I implore, collecting her wrist. She removes my hand and places it delicately on the blanket. Sighs. Wipes her palms down the front of her apron.

'Tell me, please.'

Resignation arrives on her face. 'Alasdair was cross with me after I sent you away. I should have been more sympathetic. Your dog getting injured like that must have been very traumatic. I assumed you'd noticed Alasdair's collection of conspiracy tapes. They're an embarrassment to me. Anyhow, I ought to have made you a meal and made sure you were alright. I ought to have shown more care. When you'd gone, we argued. Rory hates arguments, so he stormed off to the barn, to be alone. We sulked and steered clear of one another for a couple of hours. Alasdair cleaned the shopfront. I baked bread. We do that after a fight. It's a ritual of sorts. A couple of hours later, we made up. Only, I couldn't forgive myself for the way I'd treated you. So I baked you a cake and told Rory to deliver it to you.'

'But I wasn't at the lodge.'

'No. I know that now. Rory was gone for hours. We didn't think to worry. He does that when he's sad. Sometimes, he stays out all night, or goes fishing when he's had a bad day. Yesterday, was a terrible day in Rory's world. Upset, he was. Unsettled. So we figured he needed some time alone – to get things straight in his head. As you know, Rory thinks differently.'

She manages a tight smile.

'Did Rory say how he found me? Is he able to say what happened?'

'Rory is slow. And shy. He doesn't like to speak to strangers. People think him odd. They don't know the real Rory. He's a gentle soul. He knows the difference between right and wrong,' she says, fixing me with a stern glare. 'I won't have a nasty word said about him.'

'I'm sorry, Dorothy, I didn't mean to imply…'

She interjects. 'I know. I apologise. I'm overprotective. People have always misunderstood my Rory. Callum Cleland made his life a misery. If the police get the wrong idea about him and he ends up in prison, it will destroy him. Poor boy won't be able to cope.'

Her pained expression suggests she's about to cry.

'Don't worry, that's not going to happen. My memory is still a little hazy. I can't remember the finer details of what happened, but I know if Rory hadn't intervened then I'd be dead. Of course, I need to fill in the blanks for my own sanity. Can you understand that? When the police get here, they'll stop me speaking to you, Rory and Alasdair. They won't let anyone speak to me until they've taken statements from everyone, including Rory. If I say the wrong thing, there could be repercussions.'

'Yes, I'm aware of that. I know how the system works. Thanks to Callum Cleland, we've had our fill of police investigations over the years,' Dorothy says.

I nod. Hesitate. Wait until she's no longer preoccupied with the past.

After a minute, she sighs, says, 'Rory left with the cake for Scalaig. When he arrived at the lodge, you weren't there. Your veranda was a mess, and he got worried. He pushed on the door with his shoulder and it gave way. He found Bella by the fire and fed her. He put logs on the fire and locked the door on the latch when he left,' she says. Seeing my relief, she smiles.

Swallowing a lump in her throat, Dorothy continues, 'I'd told Rory to hand the cake to you, personally. Made him understand how important it was. So he set about searching the island, hoping to find you. Eventually, he spotted you from the clifftop in the cobble, struggling to start the motor. He thought it was strange, since he's never seen you in a boat before. When he got to the beach, you'd already gone. He saw the boat rounding the headland. Rory is like a dog with a bone, when he has an errand to run. He won't rest until it's done,' Dorothy says, smiling. 'Twenty minutes later, he saw a tall man in a black coat carrying you towards the causeway. He watched the pair of you disappear into a hole in the ground. It scared the life out of him. He ran back to the woods – he loves those woods. Confused, he'd sat on his favourite log trying to make sense of what he'd seen. He knew it was bad. It worried him. After a couple of hours, he returned to where he'd last seen you.'

'Rory found the shaft? The tunnels?'

Dorothy nods. 'Yes, he did. He climbed down the ladder and followed the candlelit tunnel to the castle. He heard everything. Heard Callum say how he was going to kill you, and that Rory would be next. Then he…'

Dorothy stalls, sniffles, settles a calming hand on her chest and draws an anxious breath. The thought of Callum Cleland making good on his evil promise to kill Rory is almost too much for her to bear. I steal the words from her mouth. 'He brought an axe down on Callum's skull to stop him killing me,' I say.

'Yes, that's right. That's exactly what happened. Rory killed Callum. He confessed to it.' She sobs. Silent tears cascade over pale cheeks. 'He had to, to save you.'

I embrace her. Tears wet my shirt. I whisper, 'Shh, I know he did… I know he did…'

Several minutes pass. Dorothy's sobs finally abate and I take her face in my hands. 'Everything is going to be alright. I'll tell the police everything. Rory isn't going anywhere. If I have to, I'll instruct the best solicitor money can buy. Rory is innocent. I'll do whatever it takes to protect him. Promise.' I tell her. She squeezes my knee and mouths a thank you.

Alasdair enters. Our eyes meet across the room. He says, 'The police have arrived. They'd like a word with you, Erin.'

'Then let them in,' I say, swinging my legs to the floor. 'We've nothing to hide.'

CHAPTER SIXTY-ONE

THREE DAYS LATER

Despite my protestations, the paramedics insisted I go to the hospital in Portree. The police took Bella to a vet on the mainland. They set her leg, and took care of her for two nights. I was diagnosed with a mild concussion and the skin above my right eye needed three stitches. The bruise is a flattering shade of bluish-purple tinged with green. They kept me in hospital overnight under observation and said I was confused and, 'slow to react to stimuli.' *No shit, Sherlock.* I've had enough stimuli to last me a lifetime.

I regard it as a ploy to keep me away from the Barrs, so the police can do their job. I may have overreacted to the blunt and incessant line of questioning from one particular detective. He was the older of the dynamic duo. His habit of jumping to conclusions was annoying, to say the least.

I told them everything. It must have sounded far-fetched and not a little hysterical, but I don't care. There is only one truth.

The initial interview in the Barrs' living room was unpleasant. I described Callum's tunnels, the weird collection of objects, and his gruesome confession. The older guy seemed disinterested and preoccupied with Rory's involvement. 'How did Rory find you? When did he appear in the basement? Did he help Callum in any way? Did they argue? Did I know how Rory got the axe? Did I think Rory was going to kill me?' he'd quizzed.

'Listen. I'm going to say this *only* once. Write it down. It's complicated. *It. Wasn't. Rory. It. Was. Callum.* Have you got that?'

He sniggered, shrugged. 'Don't be facetious, Mrs Moran. I'm only doing my job. I've got to get the facts straight,' he said. The junior detective seemed confused by the senior detective's line of questioning. Dorothy was beside herself. She knew him from before – the incident involving Callum on the clifftop – whispered to me that it was turning out just like last time. I felt her pain.

'You lot always believe Callum over Rory. When will you believe us, and not the damned, Clelands?' Dorothy screamed.

She sobbed so hard that Alasdair had to manhandle her upstairs.

'Believe me,' I said. 'It was Callum. Rory's innocent. Why won't you believe me?'

'Jim, enough. Leave it,' said the junior detective.

'Huh, over to you then, *Columbo*. If you need me, I'll be outside. Take statements. Do it right,' Jim said, setting off for the door.

'Sorry about Jim, he's old school. Don't take it personally. I believe you,' said the junior detective, pausing, setting the tip of a pencil against a notepad. 'Take your time. Tell me everything… Warts and all. Details are important.'

So I did.

* * *

They let me return to Scalaig the following day.

I'm sitting here now on the veranda nursing a mug of coffee against my chest. Bella snores at my feet and blue and white

'POLICE LINE DO NOT CROSS' tape flaps against the fence in the breeze. It's everywhere. Halloween has come early. My head hurts. My vision is still a little blurred.

I make more coffee. Spend the afternoon in the rocking chair, enjoying the feeling of being alive.

What more does a person need?

From nowhere, I'm pinned down in the chair by the weight of remorse. Olivia is dead because of me. I'm alone, facing divorce, and an uncertain future.

Will I ever be able to forgive myself?

Only time will tell.

Christian will be here soon and I feel numb. It's a lot to take in. I need to process what's happened and decide what I'm going to do in that place they call 'the future.'

* * *

They found Callum's fingerprints all over Scalaig Lodge and the outbuildings. The evidence suggests he spent a lot of time in the bedroom, writing den and wardrobes. Seems he touched just about everything I own. The thought of him here, touching my possessions, sickens me. The reality is, Callum Cleland enjoyed unfettered access to the island via the tunnels. Believing I was alone on the island, I never fully closed the curtains. Is it any wonder I often felt like I was being watched?

They've taken his body to the morgue in Portree. He won't hurt anyone ever again. My heart freezes at the thought of him.

Things are moving swiftly for the Barrs. The police released Rory on bail. He had excellent legal representation – someone expensive from Edinburgh, apparently.

I wonder who paid for that?

The junior detective, David, has taken over as lead detective. They've reassigned Jim. His superiors accepted without question the Barrs' written complaint. They'd submitted a similar complaint years ago following the incident on the cliff with Callum. Somehow, the complaint got lost. I'm led to believe it was one of many.

The police have confirmed they've no intention of charging Rory with anything. They've taken into consideration his mental age and learning difficulties. And so they should. I'm delighted.

They've taken statements, dusted for fingerprints and swabbed every surface at Scalaig Lodge, Scalaig Castle, the Range Rover and Barrs. They've searched the tunnels and, according to the officer assigned to act as liaison, recovered a substantial amount of evidence.

Aberdeen CID is involved, too. Three cold cases have been reopened because of events here on Skye. Three shallow graves have given up their secrets. The modus operandi used to kill the three female victims was almost identical. Witnesses claim to have seen the women with a man fitting Callum Cleland's description in the hours prior to their disappearances. The police hope to secure DNA matches linking him to the crimes. Investigations, as they say, are ongoing.

The castle has given up its secrets, too. The tunnel entrance in the basement dates to the 1460s, when Scalaig Castle was first built. It runs from the house under the causeway. The brick access shaft is located just far enough away from the end of the causeway that it never floods. Archeologists will be all over it like a rash, once the police wind up their investigation. The newspapers are having a field day.

In the basement room nearest the tunnel entrance, the police discovered three chest freezers. In one, they found the decapitated body of a young female. Tests confirm it's the missing backpacker from Yorkshire, Rebecca Barrowclough. Her skull is the one I found in the tunnel. In another freezer, the police found the bodies of Isla and Hamish Cleland. They were mutilated post mortem. It explains why nobody can recall attending their funerals. The other freezer was empty. There, but for the grace of God, go I.

The liaison officer confirmed they discovered Olivia wrapped in plastic sheeting inside a wardrobe in a second-floor bedroom. I assume it's the room with the orange light. She was sexually assaulted and then strangled. Her body resides in the morgue in Portree. Her mother has been informed. She's travelling up from Oxford as I speak. She's old and frail. A family friend is accompanying her.

Silent tears run down my cheeks. I slurp coffee and glance along the path.

I know what I have to do for Olivia. I have to finish writing my best novel ever.

* * *

Movement beyond the fence catches my eye and shakes me from my reverie. Christian passes through the gate. He strides along the footpath with purpose. I must admit he looks good. Hugo Boss has usurped Ralph Lauren. His summer sailing tan is all but gone. His handsome face glows in the late afternoon sun. As usual, his timing is impeccable. He's waited until low tide. Chances are, he's flown and taken a taxi. He doesn't possess the dishevelled look of a man who's driven for hours.

'I heard what happened. I got here as quickly as I could. You look terrible,' he says, bounding up the steps onto the veranda.

'It's good to see you, too,' I say, injecting a liberal dose of sarcasm.

'Jesus Christ, look at you. If that bastard Cleland wasn't already dead, I'd go over there right now, drag him out of that castle, and strangle the bastard with my bare hands,' he says, looking down at me, glowering.

'You don't have to. Rory Barr got there first. If he hadn't found me when he did, I'd be pushing up daisies. He tried to kill Bella too, Christian.'

I'm trying to be flippant – put on a brave face – but the enormity of my ordeal wells up inside of me.

'I know. I'm sorry,' he says, settling his gaze on the sleeping Bella. 'She's alive. And that's all that matters.'

Christian moves in, hunkers down, embraces me. He settles my head against his chest. I hug him back. As the dam bursts, I sob. He rocks us both. Strokes my hair and lets me weep until I'm all cried out. When I'm done, he raises up and stands over me.

'Better?'

'Yes, lots. I'll be OK,' I say, pushing up from the rocking chair.

He places a hand on my forearm, pressing me down.

'Can I stay? I'd like to.'

My eyes betray me.

'No. I'm OK. I need a drink. Can I get you anything?' I say.

I make to rise again and he pushes me into the rocking chair. I stifle a growl.

'Please. Let me,' he says, shuffling inside. A minute later, he reappears carrying two glasses of water. I accept the glass, take a sip and settle the glass on the deck.

'It took you three days to come,' I say.

He frowns. 'I told you... I came as soon as I could. I've been rushed off my feet at work. The police were a tad vague when they spoke to my secretary. She took their message and left a voicemail on my phone. When I got around to checking my messages, I was already in Birmingham.'

'Birmingham?'

'That's what I've been trying to talk to you about. It's why I'm here. The reason I came before. I'm running for Mayor,' he says, running a hand through his hair, preening, smiling a self-satisfied smile. 'I couldn't resist.'

So that's what Callum knew.

'Congratulations,' I say. I'm pleased for him. He'll be a good, Mayor.

'I want you to come home and be by my side. Birmingham has a lot going for it. I've seen an amazing house in Warwick. Pool.

Jacuzzi. Leisure suite. Sauna. The whole nine yards,' he says, thrusting a hand forward, like he's about to propose all over again. 'It'll be the making of me, *us*.'

It's the easiest decision of my life.

'No, Christian, it's over. I wish you all the luck in the world, honest, I do, but you and me, we're history. I'm going to stay here and finish my novel. It's the least I can do for Olivia. After that, well, who knows...'

He stares at me as if I've lost my mind.

'But...'

His eyes flare. I bolt up, settle joined fingers vertically over his lips, silencing him. I hear a gasp.

He doesn't get it and he never will.

In that moment, everything becomes clear. I know what I have to do. For me. And Bella.

'Please,' he says.

'No, Christian. I won't be that person. I'm *not* that person. There is something you can do for me, though,' I say.

He's crestfallen.

'OK. Name it,' he concedes. He's a businessman, potentially a politician, he knows when to hold and when to fold.

'When my novel's finished and the police have wrapped up their investigation, I'm going to sell Scalaig. You and I don't belong here, anymore. Truth be told, we never did. This place holds too many memories. We'll share the proceeds. I'm going to buy a nice little cottage in Cornwall. No doubt you're going to need funds to mount your mayoral campaign. It'll be the best for both of us. How does that sound?'

He smiles a wry smile, leans in and pecks my cheek. His kiss stings my stitched eye, and I wince.

'Ouch. Save your kisses for that brunette tart, the one you mixed my birthday up with. I never did find out her name.'

'I'm sorry. If it's any consolation, that relationship is over with,' he says, sighing. 'It was Ailsa. Like the island. The Scottish island.'

An apology! That's a first... Ailsa. Scottish. Interesting. The name means supernatural victory. Don't ask me how I know that, I just do. The bitch.

We face one another across an awkward silence.

After a minute, he shrugs. 'I suppose I'd better be going.'

'Yes,' I say, 'I suppose you better had.'

Watching him leave, I smile.

When he's out of sight, I settle into the rocking chair and get comfortable. I sit and watch the seagulls soaring across a cloudless, azure sky. When I close my eyes, it accentuates the delicate whoosh of the ocean across the sand.

Without thinking, I lower my hand to the deck beside the rocking chair and look down. Bella stirs. Her left eyelid flutters open. My reflection returns in her dark pupil. I look tiny, insignificant.

Looking away, I glance to the pines.

The reflection is the person I became. I'm not that person anymore. That person – the small person – belongs to the past. Now and always. Fighting the tears, since I don't want to cry, I turn to Bella.

'Tomorrow, girl, I'm going to dig out the phone number for the dog rescue place in Portree. You and I, we're going to take a trip. It's time you had a companion. A little boy puppy to keep you company. How does that sound?'

If she understands, she doesn't show it. Her eyelids stutter closed.

In time, I'll need a companion, too. Someone to love and cherish me for who I am, not the bestselling novels I write and the circles I keep.

But not for now.

Now belongs to me.

CHAPTER SIXTY-TWO

EPILOGUE
August 8th

I took the phone call a month after I'd seen Callum with his head split open in the dingy basement. Though the number was unfamiliar, I recognised the Edinburgh code.

'Hello?'

'Is that Erin Moran?' said a soft male voice in a cultured Edinburgh accent.

'It is. Who's speaking please?'

'My name is Douglas Andrews, Mrs Moran. I'm a partner at a firm of Edinburgh solicitors: Andrews, Toft & Blair. We specialise in property conveyance.'

I suppose he must've heard on the grapevine about my intention to put Scalaig on the market. 'Is this a cold call, Mr Andrews? Because if it is, I'm sorry, I really don't have the time.'

In the background, I hear hinges squeak, a mumbled *thank you*, and a door slamming. 'I'm sorry about that, my secretary just came in,' he says. 'I assure you this isn't a cold call. As a practice, we don't condone or take part in cold calling. My call concerns something a little more, well, lucrative.'

'Lucrative? In what way?' I ask, lowering into a chair, with the phone pressed against my ear. In the background, I hear paper rustling.

'I won't beat about the bush, Mrs Moran. We have a client.'

I'm sure you do.

'I would imagine you have many, Mr Andrews,' I interject.

'That we do. My client, whom I hasten to add, wishes to remain anonymous, is interested in purchasing the freehold to Scalaig. Would I be correct in saying that you alone are the sole legal owner of the island of Scalaig? That the title deeds are solely in your name?'

'They are.' No doubt he's done his homework and checked the land registry.

'And would you be receptive to a sale by private treaty?'

'It's a possibility. Subject of course to contract, and price,' I say, with a chuckle.

'Of course, I, we, Andrews, Toft & Blair, and the purchaser, wouldn't expect anything else.'

I imagine him gazing across a busy Edinburgh road, picking his lunch from his teeth with a wooden toothpick, an attractive young thing in a short skirt, catching his wandering eye.

Dragging the phone from my ear, I select speakerphone. 'Mr Andrews, I don't want to seem blunt, so I'm going to cut to the chase. How much is your client offering? How quickly can the money be in my account? Is a contract drafted?'

'I appreciate your candour, Mrs Moran. I find it, refreshing. The consideration proposed is one million pounds sterling. And, yes, I have a draft contract in front of me, now. If you find my client's offer and proposed contract acceptable, I will arrange for a bank transfer within thirty minutes of you signing the contract of sale, in person, at our Edinburgh office. The provisional sale date I've tentatively agreed with my client is... Just bear with me a moment, please... Is Tuesday the 10th of September. How does that sound?'

My birthday.

I almost fall out of the chair. Rising, I cross to the window. A million is five times what Christian paid for Scalaig ten years ago. I must have misheard. Sounds too good to be true, therefore it must be. There must be a catch...

'Are you still there, Mrs Moran?'

'Sorry, yes, I am.' I can't help myself. 'Mr Andrews, I'm no expert, but that seems like an awful lot of money. Can you repeat the amount, please?'

'One million pounds sterling.'

'I thought that's what you said. And does your client have a special interest in Scalaig? A particular reason they'd pay so much?'

'I'm sorry, Mrs Moran, I'm afraid client confidentiality prevents me from divulging that. My client wishes to remain anonymous. The offer is bona fide and made in good faith. My client would like an answer within a week from today's date. Might I suggest that I have my secretary e-mail you a copy of the draft contract? You may wish to instruct solicitors. I assure you it's a standard form. You won't find any nasties. Should your legal advisors have any concerns, I would ask they direct any emails to me personally.'

What have I got to lose? I can almost reach out and touch the thatched cottage with the writing den overlooking the Cornish coast. Visualise watching stunning sunsets from the deck... Bella and Gus racing into the surf...

'Mr Andrews, do you have a pen to hand?'

'I do.'

'My new e-mail address is freewoman01@xtinternet.com.'

'Interesting.'

'Yes, isn't it?'

'I'll get on to it right away. You'll have the draft contract by close of business.'

'You do that, Mr Andrews. I'll look forward to reading it.'

* * *

September 10th

I amble along the pavement, counting house numbers. The address I'm looking for is 14 Sandstone Row, Edinburgh 1, slap bang in the middle of the professional services district. Exquisite Georgian terraces dominate the street. I'm five minutes early. Arriving at number 14, I climb the stone steps to the shiny black panelled door. Pressing the intercom, I lower my mouth against the grill.

'How may I help you?'

'My name's Erin Moran. I have a meeting with Mr Andrews and Mr Blair at one. I'm a little early.'

'When you hear the buzzer, push on the door.'

A second later, the buzzer sounds, the lock releases, and I step into a lobby facing a glazed door. The reception beyond the door is visible as a blur through coloured stained glass panels.

I stall on the mat, composing myself. In an hour, Scalaig, The Lodge and Skye, will be history.

I'm greeted by a warm smile and sky-blue eyes from behind the reception desk. 'Mrs Moran,' says the blonde, Ulrika Johnson look-alike, as she slides the visitors book towards me. 'If you wouldn't mind signing in. I'll let Mr Andrews and Mr Blair know you've arrived. Please, take a seat,' she says.

Signing my name – the name I'll change back to Davis in the none too distant future – I return the book.

'Thank you,' I say, moving away, negotiating a glass-topped coffee table piled high with glossy magazines and lowering into a burgundy leather Chesterfield sofa. Settling back, I breathe deep and press my handbag and the draft contract against my chest. The offices of Andrews, Toft & Blair possess a hushed, almost monastic air. If I were to cough, I'm sure it would be frowned upon.

Two minutes of staring into space passes. To the right of the reception desk, a door swings open and a dark-haired man in an elegant grey pinstripe suit, black brogues, plain white shirt and sombre tie, steps out. I'm reminded of the English politician and professional toff, Jacob Rees Mogg. He pushes his glasses up along his nose and fixes me with a disarming smile. He floats over, offering a hand. Rising, I accept his firm handshake.

'Mrs Moran, I'm Douglas Andrews. It's very nice to meet you. I'm delighted you came. Our client is looking forward to meeting you, too.'

'I hope so.'

'Yes, well… Let's get settled in the conference room. You'll be delighted to hear, the documents are ready. The video link to your bank is all set up. I don't expect any problems. Mr Blair will be along in a moment.'

I follow him into a rectangular room sparsely furnished with an oak conference table, sideboard and tea trolley. Though the slatted blinds are pulled, sunlight bathes the room. I count twenty chairs around the table. A TV monitor stares down from the far wall above the sideboard. Two quarter inch think bound documents sit in the middle of the table by the window. I can only assume they're duplicate copies of the sale contracts requiring my signature. Andrews strides opposite the documents, drags out a chair and invites me to sit. I slide into the chair and settle my handbag on the table.

'Can I get you something to drink? A tea? Coffee? Water?'

'A sparkling water would be great. Thanks.'

'Excellent choice. I'll treat myself to one, too.'

* * *

An hour later, with the contracts duly signed, and the money confirmed as credited to my account, I'm one million pounds wealthier, and Scalaig is history.

'That went well,' I say.

'It did,' Andrews says, collecting the client copy of the sale contract, slipping it into a box file. 'It's extraordinarily fulfilling when everything goes without a hitch. As you might imagine, sometimes, things can go pear-shaped at the very last minute. Despite appearances, transferring that kind of money is hazardous. Money laundering rules are extremely complex, nowadays.'

'I'm sure they are,' I say, collecting my handbag from the table. 'It would've been nice to have met the new owner. I'm sure they'll fall in love with Scalaig as I once did.'

The corners of Andrews's mouth lift into a thin smile. Straightening, he settles his right hand on the box file, eyes flaring. '*I know* they will. Would you mind waiting here a moment, Mrs Moran? There's someone I'd like you to meet.'

I know they will?

His confidence, something in his intonation, gets me wondering. His eyes sparkle with mischief.

'No, not at all. Would you care to tell me who?'

'The new owner of Scalaig. She would very much like to meet you.'

'And does *she* have a name?'

'She does. I'm sure she'll want to introduce herself.'

Andrews turns, drags the door open and exits. I hear voices in reception.

What now? Something doesn't feel right. Is this a set-up? Have I been duped?

I reach for my phone. Open the online banking app. Refresh the account. The balance is healthier to the tune of one million pounds.

The door swings opens. Andrew enters, turns, presses his back against the wall and holds the door open. He fixes a blank stare on the TV monitor on the far wall. Why, I'm not sure?

A tall brunette in a navy business suit enters, strides over to the window and looks out over the city. She's statuesque. Six foot tall, if she's an inch. Her shiny brunette mane extends to her waist. I glimpse her ivory complexion. Freckles pepper her nose.

This is surreal. Weird. What's going on?

'Mrs Moran, may I introduce you to Miss Ailsa...' He stalls mid-sentence. I'm hanging on to every word. 'Cleland.'

Ailsa! A supernatural victory... Cleland!

Andrews mumbles something about, 'I'll leave you two ladies to it,' and drags the door closed behind him.

She spins and I'm staring at a female version of Callum. She possesses the same nose, bone structure and eyes flecked with hazel. Only the malevolent burn is absent from her eyes.

Do I recognise warmth? Concern? Can I be sure?

I collect my handbag, push the chair back and make to rise.

'Stay. Please. We need to talk. I owe you an explanation. An apology,' she says, in an accent mid-way between Scottish and American.

A flame of recognition flickers in the darkest recess of my mind... I've seen her before... But where...

'In part I'm responsible for this mess.'

My mouth falls agog.

'Go on.'

The penny drops. I know who she is.

'I recognise you now. You're Christian's bit on the side, aren't you? You were kissing him in Hyde Park in the photograph Maisie sent me. You're the *birthday* girl!'

The irony of today's date – my birthday – isn't lost on me.

'Guilty as charged.'

'Are you Callum's sister? Alasdair mentioned a long-lost sister?'

She huffs, smirks. 'I am.'

The breath in my lungs evaporates. I struggle to breathe. This can't be happening.

I pause, taking in the enormity of it all. Scenarios race through my mind. I can't make sense of it. I need to hear what she's got to say.

'Sit down. Tell me everything,' I say.

She drags out a chair, opens a bottle of water and takes a swig. Spins the top back on. 'It's all about Scalaig.'

'No shit. Go on.'

'Did you study the legal documents? The annexes?'

'To an extent, yes, I did. I scan read them. To be honest, legal mumbo jumbo isn't my thing. I just wanted shut of the place. As you might imagine, I fixated on the money. I take it you know what happened to Callum? To my best friend, Olivia?'

'Of course I do. I feel terrible about it… *Them.* I'll get to that. Anyway, Scalaig, Annexe B in the deeds. It confirms Scalaig's red line boundary extends half a nautical mile out to sea. The island sits on a plateau of rock. It's a legal oddity. Quite unique. Or so I'm told.'

'And?'

'And because of the currents, the plateau is the richest lobster breeding ground on the West Coast of Scotland.'

'Really?' My heart sinks.

'Yes, really. Dad never knew. I did. I kept it a secret from Callum, too. I've always known he was a bale short of a haystack, but I had no idea he was a serial killer.'

'Stop right there. Rewind. Your involvement in all this, is?'

'OK. When I was eighteen, I left home and enrolled on Camp America. Life around Callum became too, *intense*. I had to get away. Anyway, I met and married an American from Maine. He fished lobster. A couple of years ago I found out he was having an affair. He was screwing his latest deckhand. Is it any wonder his catches had turned to shit? Since, I had my own boat, I sold up and returned to the UK. I settled in Cornwall, bought a boat and plied my trade there. It was haemorrhaging money. Too much overfishing. Anyway, to cut a long story short, after mother and father died – were murdered by Callum – I longed to come home to Scotland. Callum was living in the castle and getting pissed out of his brain every night. He, *me*, in time, would have lost everything. So I hatched a plan. A plan to recover Scalaig and the rights to fish lobster. Altruistically, I also wanted to return Scalaig to Callum, since I knew how much it meant to him. I thought it would help stop him drinking.'

'So you stalked Christian and threw yourself at him, hoping to break up our marriage and end up with Scalaig, not knowing he'd put the island in my name?'

'Correct. I would have married him. Got a quickie divorce after a year. Taken Scalaig off his hands in the settlement. I would have insisted on it. Chris, bless his cotton socks, didn't have a clue. Imagine how pissed off I was when I discovered the title deeds to Scalaig were in your name, and that you'd found out about our affair. Even more annoyed when you left London to live on Scalaig. I ended the relationship soon after. There was no point to the charade after that.'

Charade? Nice. And Chris! She calls him, Chris!

'So you enlisted Callum to scare me off?'

'I'm ashamed to admit it, but yes, that's exactly what I did. I had no idea the tunnels existed, and he was a serial killer. I was as surprised as anyone. I wanted to get my hands on Scalaig and the lobster rights. You may not know it, but I've been fishing the island for over a year.'

'The cobble?'

'That's right, mine. I always hid my face when you were around.'

'I suppose the million pounds is to assuage your guilt?'

'You could say that, yes. A million reflects the value of the island, *and* the lobster fishery. You've got a fair price. I had it valued. You can check if you like.'

'What price almost getting killed by a psychopath, though?'

'I know. I'm sorry. I never knew. I'm glad he's dead. Murderous scum.'

She falls silent, uncaps the water, takes a swig, twists the cap back on and settles the bottle on the coaster.

'So what now?'

'I go fishing, you buy yourself a view of the ocean and write great romance novels. By the way, I love your books.'

'You do?'

'Yes, I do. I've read them all. Your latest is your best, yet.'

A.J. pulled out all the stops to get my novel published, to capitalise on the publicity. 'I wrote it on Scalaig. Dedicated it to Olivia.'

'I saw that. She would be so proud of you.'

'I think she would be, yes.'

'I *know* she would be. You've a God given talent. Make the most of it.'

I shrug. 'Perhaps…'

After a minute of silence, she glances at her watch. 'I'd better be going. With a fair wind I should catch the ten-past-two to Glasgow.'

'How will you get to Scalaig?'

'Drive. I've left the car at the station. I've bought myself a Range Rover. You need a car like that living in that part of the world.'

I never want to see another sodding Range Rover as long as I live…

We rise from the table. She steps over, stalls beside me, and comes towards me with open arms. Stepping back, I look away to the floor.

There's more to life than money.

Reaching the door, she turns, says, 'Sorry.'

'Go. Don't look back, or you'll miss your train.'

THANK YOU!

We hope you enjoyed reading **NOT MINE TO TAKE** as much as we enjoyed writing it. If you did, we would be forever grateful if you could take a moment to leave a review on your preferred platform.

Reviews help other people find our books and help us keep writing. We love hearing from readers. You can contact us via our facebook page, K W Cosgrave Author, or via our website. Here's the link to our **WEBSITE**.

www.indiumbooks.com

As a **THANK YOU,** I would like to offer you a **FREE SHORT STORY - MURDER AT DEVIL'S BRIDGE** when you sign up to my **PRIVILEGE CLUB**. All you have to do is follow this link and instructions. It's **FREE** to join and you can leave at any time.

www.indiumbooks.com

HAPPY READING!

ABOUT THE AUTHORS

We are Christine & Keiron, partners in life and crime. We live in Barnsley, South Yorkshire, UK. Keiron is a former Chartered Surveyor who enjoys reading, historic scooters, cycling and fair weather fishing. Christine is a retired Business Development Manager for a major FMCG business. She enjoys keeping fit, reading, leather working and holidays in the sun. Between us, we have three grown up sons: Dominic, Oliver and Louis and four grandchildren: Oliver, Harry, and twins, Margot & Layla.

Together we write standalone psychological thrillers and crime fiction.

We are passionate about writing, life and love. Keiron authored the Wardell & Watts British Detective Series, which includes the novels:
Promises, Promises,
With Menaces,
Beyond Absolution,
and the novella, *Murder at Devil's Bridge.*

Beyond Absolution was an Amazon Best Seller.

Keiron also wrote *The Celtic Cross Killer:* a standalone private investigator thriller spanning three generations and crossing continents.

Not Mine To Take is our first co-authored novel. ***Not Hers To Take***, our second.

ALSO BY KEIRON COSGRAVE AND CHRISTINE HANCOCK

Not Hers To Take

All lives are precious. Are some lives more precious than others?

Ruby Harper is lost…

Betrayed by the man she loves, ostracised by her wealthy mother and high-flying sister, Ruby runs away to a world populated by drug users and abusive men.

When her mother dies prematurely, Ruby finds the strength to rebuild her shattered life and start anew.

But life is never that simple… Ruby has something precious... Something people want…

Who can she trust?

Her sister? Her best friend? Her lover?

Who stands to gain the most from Ruby's death?

For more information, visit our website:

www.indiumbooks.com

Or my Facebook author page - K W Cosgrave Author

NOVELS

Promises, Promises

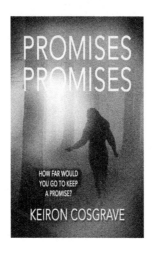

How far would you go to keep a promise?

After Kate and best friend Rose take revenge on their abuser at boarding school, their lives become macabrely connected forever.

Years later, Kate's father reveals decades old secrets. The veneer of middle-class respectability fractures. A childhood promise is stretched to breaking. A family implodes.

When Kate's father is found murdered, DI Alan Wardell unravels a complex web of desire, betrayal and greed. More family members are murdered…

Will Wardell catch the brutal serial killer before Kate becomes his next victim?

A roller coaster ride of raw emotion, which builds towards a breath-taking climax.

With Menaces

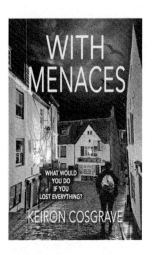

What would you do if you lost everything?

Cast on the scrapheap by his employers, pitied and despised by his soon-to-be ex-wife, Gavin Clark starts to lose his mind.

Homeless and hungry, Gavin gets caught up in the seedy underworld of a bleak seaside town at the end of the line.

As he descends in the abyss, Gavin hatches a sinister scheme to heap revenge on those he believes have wronged him.

He becomes a vigilante on the wrong side of the law.

Can Wardell untangle the dark psychology and motives of a vengeful and elusive serial killer, before more lives are destroyed?

A powerful story of hate, anger and revenge…

Beyond Absolution

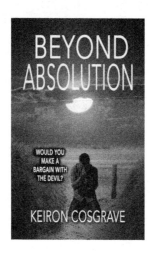

They thought the past was dead and buried...

A teenage affair in a church run boarding school attracts the wrath of priests and nuns... A pregnancy prematurely ended... A crime hushed up... A bargain made...

Years later, a suicide prompts disturbing allegations of historic sex abuse to surface...

A series of mysterious murders of boarding school friends...

Only one remains...

Wardell investigates the heinous decades old crimes and races to outwit a serial assassin before unholy secrets are taken to the grave...

A darkly compelling, yet ultimately heart-warming story of love, power and conspiracy, which will enthral and entertain the reader, to the final paragraph...

The Celtic Cross Killer

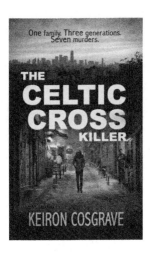

One family. Three generations.

Seven murders.

It is January 2005. New York is blanketed by snow. A killer driven by hatred roams the streets of Brooklyn.

Brooklyn pizzeria owner Ernest Costa leads a normal life. His business is thriving. He has a beautiful wife, and everything to live for. Returning home from work one freezing night, his life is snuffed out by a brutal and frenzied knife attack in a dark alley. His throat is slashed. A Celtic cross is slit deep across his back. Is the cross the signature of a psychopath? A recidivist who will strike again? Or is it an isolated attack? Someone knows the killer's identity…

Two years pass. The murder investigation stalls. Fingers are pointed at the senior detectives leading the manhunt. Removed from the case by his superiors, disgruntled NYPD Detective Antonio Pecarro decides to leave the force he once loved. He resigns and sets up as a private investigator.

Another body defiled with the same signature is discovered within sight of the victim's home. The victim's wife witnesses the killer leaving the scene. The killer's modus operandi is identical. Both victims are of Italian American heritage, of similar age and social standing. Is there a deranged serial killer driven by a compulsion to kill and bad blood walking the streets? Someone who will stop killing only when they are captured?

The investigation is re-launched. Criminal Psychologist Gerard Tooley is brought in. Progress is anaemic. Tensions bubble. Tooley is 'cut-free' from the team to pursue his own lines of investigation. Progress is made…

The heartbroken wife of the second victim decides to take matters into her own hands. She commissions P.I. Antonio Pecarro to identify and apprehend her husband's killer.

Another murder striking at the heart of the NYPD happens…

Will Pecarro solve the riddle before the NYPD and catch the serial killer before he strikes again?

The Celtic Cross Killer is a complex fast-paced historical crime thriller with a twist that will keep the reader guessing until its breath-taking climax.

NOVELLA

Murder At Devil's Bridge

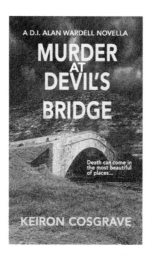

Death can come in the most beautiful of places…

When adulteress Claire Tomlinson is found murdered at a local beauty spot, suspicion falls upon her husband, Drew, and her lover, Owen.

But things aren't quite that simple.

Both men deny involvement in the killing and profess their innocence...

Can Detective Inspector Alan Wardell unravel this complex tale of lust, anger and revenge?

ACKNOWLEDGEMENTS

People think writing a novel is a solitary endeavour…

That's only half the truth.

There are special people who, without whose help, none of this would have been possible.

Jenny May, your eye for detail and nose for a great story helped to smooth out the rough edges. We are eternally grateful.

Lynn and Mick Clarke thank you for you 'very' early feedback and motivation. We took onboard every word.

We would also like to extend a warm thanks to our ADVANCE READER GROUP. Your input has been invaluable and we look forward to developing our relationship over the coming years.

THANKS EVERYONE.